ACCLAIM FOR BETH M

A Touch of Jen

"*A Touch of Jen* is bananas good. Funny and sharp and surprising and bittersweet. Just 🤌🤌🤌."

—Carmen Maria Machado, author of *Her Body and Other Parties*

"A twisted, brutal, and legitimately frightening tale of a parasocial relationship so toxic, it has interdimensional consequences."

—Layla Halabian, *Nylon*

"Morgan has created a fabulous monster here... a wicked, unflinching, dynamite novel out of razor-sharp dialogue, toxic social-media culture, and the nonsense notion that the self is just another brand to be plumbed for content. *A Touch of Jen* is truly a touch of genius. I loved every minute of it." —Kristen Arnett, author of *With Teeth* and *Mostly Dead Things*

"A bold, wild ride that takes our collective dependence on social media head on."

—Maggie Panos, *Popsugar* (Best Books of the Summer)

"The funniest (and most twisted) book of the year."

—Tony Tulathimutte, author of *Private Citizens*

"A satirical, ferocious, shape-shifting novel... What started as an acerbic millennial sex comedy grows the gnashing mandibles of supernatural horror with a spiritual self-help twist... The structure is unconventional and disorienting, but Morgan manages each breakneck turn without spinning out of control. There's an almost fanatically concrete simplicity to her prose that makes the storytelling absurd and unnerving and consistent in effect—like someone smiling at you without blinking, showing too much of the whites of her eyes... Chimeric and deliriously original, emitting an eerie power." —Steph Cha, *New York Times Book Review*

"The perfect novel to pick up the next time you feel vaguely ill after spending too long on Instagram."

—Kate Knibbs, *Wired* (Best Summer Reads)

"*A Touch of Jen* is hipster noir, acerbic social parable, and slasher gore-fest: as if Patricia Highsmith, Chris Kraus, and Ann Quin all crashed a Hamptons beach party, and John Carpenter dropped in with some weed."

—Tom McCarthy, author of *Remainder* and *Satin Island*

"An ambitious debut that captures the loneliness of the internet age in deft strokes." —*Kirkus Reviews*

"I quickly became addicted to this sharp, upsetting novel... *A Touch of Jen* explores the gulf between aspirational content and real life, with notes of both hyperrealism and psychological thriller."

—Jenny Singer, *Glamour* (Best Books of Summer)

"Darker and more ironic than other entries in the genre... Morgan suggests that authenticity can be just as hideous as its opposite... It succeeds where similar works have faltered by deflating the fantasy of the real. The fear of living dishonestly, it appears, has made it easier than ever to justify sacrificing others on the altar of our own self-actualization." —Jess Bergman, *New Republic*

"Morgan masterfully brings dark comedy and psychedelic horror together at a slow-burning pace. Her mundane but over-the-top characters and brilliant dialogue add to the surreal and fantastical tone of this spellbinding book." —*Booklist*

A Touch of Jen

Beth Morgan

BACK BAY BOOKS
Little, Brown and Company
New York Boston London

The characters and events in this book are fictitious. Any similarity to real persons, living or dead, is coincidental and not intended by the author.

Back Bay Books / Little, Brown and Company
Hachette Book Group
1290 Avenue of the Americas, New York, NY 10104
littlebrown.com

Originally published in hardcover by Little, Brown and Company, July 2021
First Back Bay paperback edition, February 2023

Back Bay Books is an imprint of Little, Brown and Company, a division of Hachette Book Group, Inc. The Back Bay Books name and logo are trademarks of Hachette Book Group, Inc.

ISBN 9780316704267 (hc) / 9780316704274 (pb)
LCCN 2020946141

Printing 4, 2023

LSC-C

Printed in the United States of America

"Les attractions sont proportionnelles aux destinées."

—Charles Fourier

A Touch of Jen

Part 1

This Could Be Us

Alicia says that maybe she should print out a photo of Jen's face and tape it over her own while they have sex. "I could cut little holes in the eyes."

Remy says that would be creepy. "But I love how your mind works."

She scrolls through photos that Jen recently posted.

"Definitely that one," says Remy.

"I'm just joking around. Unless *you* aren't."

Later, when they're sluggishly moving towards the bed, Remy takes Alicia's face in his hands. "Ah, Jen—how I've longed to hold you in my arms!"

"Remy, it's not right!" says Alicia, pretending to be Jen. "What if your girlfriend finds out?"

Their movements are theatrical and corny. They mash their faces together like soap opera stars. Remy shuts his eyes and plays a movie in which Alicia has been replaced by Jen, with her freckled boobs and baby hairs and adult braces.

He's talked to Alicia many times about these adult braces. They've discussed the spectacular, loopy temerity of a beautiful person like Jen taking such a risk with her appearance. She could have done Invisalign. But no. Now she looks like a hot shark.

Alicia imagines herself morphing into Jen's light-struck, perpetually tan body, and her body language is much more tender than it would be if she were just herself. She takes off her dress and tries to picture Jen's body naked, but can't imagine her without an outfit. When she's Jen, she's always wearing clothes.

Afterwards, they keep looking at Jen's photos from Cambodia, each of them on their own phone.

"I like this one," says Alicia.

"She looks great here," says Remy.

"The waves were amazing!" says Jen's caption.

The next day, Alicia showers with the door open. She shouts down the hall, "What would you do if Jen were in the shower right now?"

"What?" He stands in the doorway.

"Jen's in the shower. She has no idea you're here. Maybe you walk in by mistake."

"How would that happen?"

"You're in the wrong house. Or you're the gardener."

"Am I me, or am I the gardener?"

"My boobs are so freckly and slick!" says Alicia in a porny voice.

Remy says he feels like she's making fun of him. He was the one who told her that Jen had freckly boobs—not that he's ever seen them in their entirety. She says he should hurry. Jake will be home soon.

Jake is their perfectly nice roommate. They despise him passionately. His ringtone is the sound of a baby crying.

Remy and Alicia watch a television show about a spy with exceptional fighting-slash-torturing skills. Most of the plot involves the spy protecting either his family or the American way of life. They only watch it when Jake isn't home because Jake always wants to pause the episode until he figures out what else he's seen the actors in.

About once every episode, someone gets their kneecaps drilled, or is dissolved in a tub of acid, or stabbed with an unusual object like a wine opener or a soccer trophy.

They watch an episode in which the spy's dog is kidnapped and tortured by an evil scientist. The apartment is filled with the off-screen sound of the puppy—an intermittent cheeping, like sneakers on a basketball court.

"Bitch!" screams Alicia at the evil scientist. "Fucking cunt!"

"Why is it that the people are always tortured on screen but the puppy they torture off screen?" says Remy.

Alicia calls him a sicko. Does he *want* to see the dog tortured?

"It's just a question. It's not even clear what she's doing to this dog."

"Kick her in the stomach!"

"He can't—he's tied up."

"I hate this!"

"I think you love it," he says. He watches Alicia instead of the show. She's eating waffle fries from a takeout box slanted with age. Alicia's eyes don't move from the screen and her hand searches blindly for the fries. She's not as appealing as Jen and never will be. But in this moment, he feels a surge of affection for her that he doesn't think about too hard. He just likes her anger.

"Fuck her up!"

"Yeah!" says Remy, quieter than her.

He would like, in this moment, for Jake to come into the apartment. He would like for both of them to turn their eyes on *him*.

He has a sixth beer. "I'm so proud of you. You used to hide behind a pillow during the gory parts. Now look at you. Eating waffle fries."

Jen posts a picture of herself with fiberglass earrings she made. "Cuts all over my hands but it was worth it!" says the caption.

She posts an old photo of herself in Belize.

She posts a photo of herself on a mountain somewhere, holding a baby goat. "Say hello to my little friend!" says the caption.

Remy and Alicia look at these pictures amid the chaos of their separate jobs, and then again the next day when they sleep in together.

Remy says, "Normally, I hate pictures of mountains. But this is a great mountain. She did a good job capturing it."

"She's so beautiful. You can tell by the expression in her eyes that she has a good heart."

"I wonder who took this. It could be a self-timer, right?"

"I like how the sun catches on her braces," says Alicia. "There's such a sense of destiny about this photo."

"One thing I remember about her is that she really knew how to take up space."

Alicia points out a shadow that looks like it belongs to the person taking the picture. She wonders aloud who was there with her. He argues that the shadow could be a rock, or a tree, "or another one of those little mountain goats."

The idea of Jen surrounded by goats thrills Alicia. "I bet animals love her. I bet they aren't afraid of her at all."

"You never even met her," he says, but Alicia imagines songbirds making Jen's bed in the morning, and woodland creatures brushing her hair. She imagines Jen crushing a small animal beneath her foot, slowly. Maybe a bunny.

Alicia goes to her lunch shift. Remy keeps texting her every five minutes. He sends her a video of a toddler stuck in a claw machine, then a video of a guy shitting himself on a roller coaster, and then a screenshot of Jen's latest post—Jen in a car with some guy Remy doesn't recognize. He says:

That guy looks horny as hell. He isn't tagged.

The comedy of the caption is multilayered: "No sleep till Martha's Vineyard!"

Remy wouldn't put it past Jen to take a trip to Martha's Vineyard for purely ironic reasons. He feels annoyed at his inability to gauge if she belongs there or not. Just how fancy is she? Is she Martha's Vineyard fancy? Has he lost his sense of her? Is this something he would have known before?

Around three, Jake comes home lugging a frame so large that only his frat-boy calves are visible. It's a movie poster for *Seven Years in Tibet* that Jake is excited to put in the living room.

Remy tries to close the laptop but the movement is too furtive to go unnoticed. It makes him look guilty, and Jake is thrilled. Remy keeps the laptop open, to seem more casual, but this only allows Jake to get a better look at the picture.

"Wow!" says Jake. "Who is she? Circle of trust!"

Remy says it's just someone he used to work with. "I'm catching up. Seeing what's going on in her life."

"Did you, ah, *boink* her?"

Only Jake would say "boink." Remy has a vision of himself poking Jen in the forehead with his finger and shouting, "Boink!"

"It was complicated. We worked together. She was in a weird place...and I was recovering from all this dental work so I wasn't able to be *present,* you know?" Remy complains about the cost of the dental work, and how if it weren't for all the distracting molar pain, everything might have been different.

Jake leans the poster against the wall and sits at the kitchen table, stinking of his macho soap. He gives Remy a serious talk about how Alicia's *super cool.* "Take it from me and my personal experience. You don't want to give up a good thing when you've got it. And hey, man, there's a lot of temptation out there."

Remy can't imagine what personal experience Jake could be referencing. Jake rarely goes out, except on Thursday nights. "I really don't think that's going to be an issue," says Remy. He looks at his hand, resting on his cup of coffee, and then observes the distance between his hand and Jake's helpful face. It's amazing how people live day to day without hurting each other.

"The other day she was telling me all of these interesting facts about tropical parrots," says Jake. "I didn't even know Alicia was interested in birds."

"She wants to go on a tropical vacation. I don't think it's going to happen soon."

"It gave me a great idea for her birthday. That maybe you should, like, bring the tropical vacation to her. You should get her a parrot! I wouldn't mind at all. And I'd take care of it if you guys went away for a few days."

"It sounds like maybe *you* want a parrot," says Remy. Then he says, "For the record, it's not that this girl wasn't interested."

"For sure, man."

"Have you ever reached a state of equilibrium with a person and not wanted to disrupt that?"

Jake says something inane about "the friend zone," and Remy says that no, it wasn't that at all and then tries to explain the holy, delicate suspense of nothing happening with Jen, and the beauty of their perfectly calibrated distance from each other. "We used to play this game where I'd see how many pens I could stick in her bun without her noticing, and in a way *that was erotic,* even though it wasn't technically sexual."

Jake nods and nods. "I'm trying to follow, dude, but I don't always get that"—and here Jake makes a motion above his head as if screwing in a light bulb—"that intellectual level you're working on. Don't get me wrong—it's very cool, dude. Very cool."

After a few moments of silence, he says, "The only problem with the parrot is that you have to put newspaper in the cage…for the poop. And I don't even know the last time I saw a newspaper."

Alicia has a terrible day at work, since Cassie didn't show up and she has to handle dispatch as well as sandwich orders at the counter. During her single bathroom break, she notices that her hairline looks as if it's thinning, although only from certain angles.

When she comes home, she and Remy argue about whether or not Jen is rich.

"She has to be," says Alicia. "She's not like other people in service. She travels all the time."

"She's not rich." He says it like he knows for a fact, even though he doesn't. "She still picks up shifts at that tapas place. So she must need the money. And she didn't go to private schools or anything crazy like that."

"A public school in Vermont is more luxe than most private schools."

"You're talking out of your ass. You've never even been to Vermont."

"We should take a vacation sometime. There's no reason we can't." Alicia says it would be nice to have something to post other than funny content from other accounts. "Wouldn't it be great to post about our *lives* for once?"

They have a repetitive conversation about money that doesn't deviate meaningfully from any of their previous conversations about money. Remy tries to convince Alicia and himself that by not posting about their lives, they're actually superior. "It shows we're not self-absorbed."

He goes to the bathroom and when he comes back, Alicia's swiping through Jen's pictures on different social media accounts, her lips parted.

Remy and Alicia decide to see an afternoon movie on a day when neither of them has a shift. They pick something with zombies. Before they leave, Alicia spends an hour in front of a palette of eye shadow that seems as complex and intimidating as a pipe organ. She asks Remy over and over if it's "too much."

"I'm putting on my shoes," he says, meaning that they should leave.

Remy looks at Alicia, dabbing at her face in the mirror. Her wrist is held at an awkward angle, and her attitude towards the mirror isn't at all performative, the way it is when she's pretending to be Jen. Her hands are too large and taper weirdly at the fingertips, as if she were wearing another pair of hands as gloves. Her mouth is ovoid and horrible.

"I don't know why I'm doing this," says Alicia. "It's not like we're going to see anyone."

"We'll be sitting in the dark."

"I actually look *frightening*. *I* would get scared if I saw me walking down the street."

For the next few minutes, she paces from bedroom mirror to bathroom mirror, working herself up into a state of self-conscious mania about her eye makeup. She gets something from the closet and hits her head on the frame. She holds her forehead and cries in a silent, annoying way.

"This is just going to make things worse," she says. She says this because she believes that she suffered brain damage as a teenager and that every time she bumps her head, it speeds up an ongoing process of deterioration. She believes in this more than she believes in the moon landing.

"I'm putting on my shoes," Remy says. He doesn't want to hear her paranoid little speech about brain damage again.

There's an issue with the trains, and it takes twice as long as usual to transfer to the right uptown platform. The next train doesn't come either.

Alicia's eyes are scrubbed raw and swollen from removing all her eye makeup. She says, "I'm really sorry. Who did I think was going to see me?"

"We might still make the movie," says Remy. Then, when she doesn't respond: "I should have put on a jacket. I thought it was finally summer."

He looks at the people around them on the platform. He'd be ruder to Alicia, but he doesn't want them to think he's a bad boyfriend.

The train still doesn't come and they shiver and don't touch each other. They both try not to breathe in the cold, fruit-punch smell of the transit deodorizer.

Remy feels that Alicia's silent misery must be disrupted, but the idea of talking about the weather anymore depresses him. He complains about one of his coworkers. Alicia doesn't say anything. He complains that his manager, Rocco, is always coming into work drunk.

A woman waiting next to them is eating a banana and Remy says, "I read that bananas are going extinct. Like honeybees."

Alicia's eyes fill with tears.

"Jesus Christ," he says.

"I'm sorry!"

"It's going to be fine. They can put robots into people's bloodstreams now. I'm sure they can figure out the banana situation."

Alicia excuses her tears by boring him with a complicated explanation about when her menstrual hormones kick in. Even a cursory analysis would reveal that the timing doesn't make mathematical sense.

The movie start time comes and passes while they're still waiting for the train, and Remy has to pretend he's not irritated. Alicia continues to apologize abjectly, her face slimy with tears.

Eventually they stop waiting for the train and go aboveground, trying to figure out what to do now that they've missed the movie. They go into a thrift store, both agreeing not to spend any money unless they find a shirt for Remy, which he needs. The store is small and no music plays. The clothing-insulated quality of the silence makes it more bearable not to talk for a while.

Eventually, Alicia holds up a crocheted halter-top. "Doesn't this top look like the one Jen was wearing?"

Remy knows which top she's talking about. He's actually seen it in person. He remembers Jen working the patio and then coming back inside with sweat in her cleavage, asking the barback can she *please* eat another cocktail garnish because she's absolutely *starving*. He tells Alicia this.

"It's strange how much I've forgotten her." He's transfixed by the halter-top. It's not exactly the same, but close enough. He can almost visualize Jen in front of him—*almost*. Alicia pets the top while she listens to him, as if trying to wake it up. "There's a difference between being reminded of someone from their pictures and viscerally remembering them," he says. "One thing I forget is how her face moves. Now when I picture her face moving, it's just a blank space attached to a ponytail."

"I can put it on," says Alicia. She goes to the fitting room and puts on the top. She moves around for his benefit and for the mirrors. She tells him to bring her something else.

Remy looks around the store, picking out items that Jen might wear. Some sort of shiny tunic. A weird Dust Bowl–era dress. Something eighties. Alicia reads aloud the brand names on the tags, which mean nothing to Remy. The project makes him feel stupid, but it's better than not connecting to Jen at all.

"I'm Jen and I'm headed to a yoga retreat," says Alicia, stepping in front of the dressing room curtain and turning in front of the mirror. "I'm Jen and I'm allergic to synthetic fabrics." This makes Remy laugh.

The other customers stare intensely into the clothing racks or their phones. Alicia puts on a dress and does a wholesome milk-maid spin. Remy squints his eyes and looks at the outfit. To the best of his ability, he erases Alicia. Perhaps it's the close, woolen atmosphere of the shop that makes him so suggestible.

"Ah!" he says, batting his hand in front of his eyes. "That was so weird. It's like she's close or something."

"Sometimes you talk like she's dead."

"I remembered the specific intervals of the rings on her fingers. Not the rings themselves, but the spacing. I don't know why, but it sort of *did it* for me. Like, brought her to life." It's been two years and seven months since he's seen her.

"Do you want me to wear rings?" says Alicia.

He analyzes the mechanics of this. Alicia's hands aren't like Jen's and the rings wouldn't look right. Jen has stopped even wearing rings, at least as far as he can tell from her recent posts.

He buys the top for Alicia to wear, on the condition that she only wear it at home.

"It wasn't so much that you reminded me of Jen," he says as they walk back to the train, "as that I was able to superimpose my memory of her on you." He holds her shoulders. He asks if that makes sense.

Alicia says, "The things I do for love!" Then, to push this charged word out of the air, she says, "It's been a long time since you've seen her. Maybe we could invite her over." They both walk down the street with the overwhelming sense that they could bump into her at any second.

"No," he says, smiling in a way that implies he could be persuaded. "No, no."

They watch an episode of the spy show and then lie awake in the dark, predicting what the evil scientist's punishment will be. The show's punishments reveal a creative, often biblical sensibility not evident in any other aspects of the show's writing.

Alicia says that since the evil scientist has so much plastic surgery, she should be subjected to a nose job without anesthetic. "You know," she says, her voice eerie and sourceless in the dark, "that with a nose job, the doctor has to pull the skin up over your eyeballs. So maybe she could just be, you know, peeled apart and then left like that."

"You know so much about nose jobs."

"I'd do it if I had the money. But I don't really need it. Honestly, all I want is eight thousand dollars." Alicia's always talking about eight thousand dollars. "Eight thousand dollars would really set me up. I could quit the Hungry Goat. I could just chill for a while."

The room is filled with cold light. They sit up. They've each received a notification that Jen posted a new photo. They laugh at the simultaneity of their movements.

"God," he says, "you know we have a mystical connection."

Alicia laughs, and the pleasure on her face is so naked that he's embarrassed for her.

"I mean…me and Jen. Not you and me."

"What?"

"Just kidding," he says. "Kidding!"

"Ah," says Alicia.

"Still thinking about the coffee in Reykjavík!" says Jen's caption.

Remy gets up for work before Alicia and sees the halter-top slung over the side of the bed. He feels quieter. He notices this quiet feeling, but doesn't interrogate it for fear of disturbing it.

He works at a health food restaurant with a casual atmosphere but high-maintenance clientele. Jessica Alba came in once. Everyone on staff made a big show to each other about how they didn't care (except for Inez, who kept fanning herself with her hands).

During brunch, he's surprised to find that he isn't bothered by the low buzz of anxiety he normally experiences at work. A woman comes in, alone, undulating her arms like Isadora Duncan. He doesn't think he's seen her before, but Inez tells him that she's a regular and that she always does that—never stops moving.

"Don't be alarmed," says the woman when she sees how he looks at her, holding his notepad. "Movement keeps you young. I'm a holistic doctor. I know what I'm talking about."

"...Okay," says Remy.

"Movement is the essence of life. No one tells you that. Right now I'm adding *years* to my life."

He recites the specials to her. She raises her arms above her head and asks if the rice in the vegan pilaf contains arsenic. He informs her, with a phrasing that has become more practiced and scientific over time, "All rice contains arsenic on a molecular level. But it's not present in harmful quantities."

"That's incorrect. There's a difference between organic and inorganic arsenic levels, and it varies by region. Do you know whence the rice is derived?"

Remy watches her movements for his opening, like the spy from the TV show, who times his jump off a road bridge so impeccably that he lands in the villain's convertible. When rhythmically permissible, Remy suggests the tartine.

Normally this interaction would make him cranky, but as he leaves her table to input the order, he enjoys the sensation that he's pulled something off and that if he were being filmed, he would appear confident. There are times—when he's not too hungover—when the monotonous rhythm of food service gives Remy a druggy sense of satisfaction, as if he's slipped into some preordained stream of motion in which his decisions aren't made but assigned to him.

As he navigates each wave of diners, keeping track of the tables in his section and vaguely enjoying his own long-developed intuition about how and when to give each of them his attention, and as he weaves through the tables, balancing plates, sensitive to every aspect of his surroundings (the different quality of chatter as he moves from the kitchen to the dining area, the water droplets trembling on plates fresh from the dishwasher), he feels so capable that he forgets that this repetitive churning goes nowhere, except towards the end of the day.

The holistic doctor waltzes to the bathroom, lightly touching bars and booths as she passes. He punches her order into a POS system petaled with fingerprints and he can almost hallucinate Jen right next to him, a few inches lower, tying the tacky apron that was part of the Belasco's uniform—one day around two years and seven months ago, before Belasco's closed.

He gets the chance to check his phone and sees that Alicia has sent him a long string of superstitious texts. She says, not for the first time, that she's getting "vibes" from the apartment. That the TV remote started working again, although she thought the batteries were dead. That the showerhead isn't making its usual gothic moans, and that she fried an egg for dinner and it had two yolks.

Alicia: I have the best feeling. Like something momentous is about to happen.

In a slow moment, Remy complains to Inez about Alicia's superstitions. He tells her that none of Alicia's predictions ever come true, and when they don't, she finds a way to blame it on her period, "which half the time is imaginary, and never comes when she says it will."

Inez says that he needs to stop being "so negative." Remy can't help looking at Inez's boobs as she lectures him.

"What's your necklace for?" he says. Inez's necklaces always mean something.

The stone bobs in the marsupial indent of her cleavage while Inez tells him that *moss agate* promises abundance in love and money. She gives him a technical explanation that makes the stone move around a lot.

"Well, I have abundant love for you," says Remy.

Inez makes an *aww* sound identical to the one she directs at children small enough to require booster seats.

After the brunch shift is over, Remy overhears several of the wait-staff talking about getting a drink and choreographs a movement close by, plausibly as part of a work-related task. He approaches and then retreats, but never elicits an invitation.

"Remy, why do you keep grabbing napkins?" says Rocco on the third attempt.

Remy stares at the napkins in his hand and then says that he's afraid he has a nosebleed.

"Look at me," says Inez.

Remy looks at her.

"You don't have a nosebleed."

"Sometimes I can feel them coming."

"You were just complaining that Alicia had imaginary periods. And now *you're* complaining about imaginary bleeding."

The fact that Rocco turns his head to laugh informs Remy that this joke doesn't include him. Maybe it's part of an ongoing narrative between Inez and Rocco *about* him. He still doesn't get an invitation, and they leave. He could be remembering things wrong, but he's sure he wasn't this awkward before he started dating Alicia.

Remy is invited to the house party of a friend from school with whom he's not particularly close. Neither of them wants to go, but Alicia keeps saying that something momentous is about to occur.

Remy treats this as a joke but has started to get the same feeling, no matter how irrational it is. Yes, something momentous might occur. Maybe he'll see someone he hasn't seen in a long time.

The party is in an expensively renovated brownstone, the front door bracketed with security cameras that don't attempt to blend into the prewar moldings.

"Isn't it crazy? I'm house-sitting!" says the friend. He gestures at the chandelier, the artwork, and a shaggy little dog. The dog flips down the staircase towards them like a hairdo. The friend scoops up the dog and aims it at them in a way that demands compliments. They compliment the dog.

"I love showering here," says the friend. "I had to look up some of the shampoos online. Each bottle is like sixty dollars." He tells them about other expensive items in the house. He gives them an update on how his career is doing and then disappears for the rest of the evening.

Remy and Alicia wander around with plastic cups. They don't know anyone except an old coworker that Remy doesn't feel like talking to.

Alicia says, "We should just be friendly! We never go out."

"I'm sure we'll know some other people here."

Remy walks systematically through each room, onto the patio, then back into the house. He doesn't look back to check that Alicia's following him, since he knows she will.

They wander into the kitchen, near the alcohol, and examine the greeting cards on the refrigerator. One of them has a picture of a donut on the front and says, *I donut know how to thank you enough!* Another one says, *Out of all the faces in the world, yours is my absolute favorite!*

"What a weird card," says Remy.

"Yeah. It sounds like this person wants to peel off your face and wear it."

"Haha!" says a strange girl, trying to participate in the conversation. "Yeah, that's exactly what it sounds like! Weird!"

Alicia looks at the stranger with frightened eyes. The girl's face is made up into try-hard brilliance. Remy and Alicia adjust their bodies to shut her out.

"I thought," he says to Alicia, "when I was walking through the rooms just now... I thought for one second that maybe there was a chance, you know..."

"She might come later."

"She's been posting pictures of jewelry, so I don't think she's traveling."

They refill their cups. Out of boredom, they do shots of vodka.

"Woo!" says Alicia, after her second shot. The strange girl claps confusedly.

They stay for an hour, but don't see anyone else they know.

The next day, Remy finally has the time to deal with the broken fan in his laptop, and he and Alicia go to the Apple Store. There, they run into Jen.

Remy, shell-shocked, introduces Alicia and then monitors Jen's face for a reaction when he refers to her as "my girlfriend." Alicia monitors Jen's face too.

"Jen was another server at Belasco's before it closed," he says.

"Oh *really?*" says Alicia. He and Alicia both use exaggerated gestures of goodwill and surprise in order to appear casual, as if meeting her there affects them in no way and is just the sort of unremarkable accident one can expect in day-to-day urban life. It makes them both look very wild, they realize afterwards.

Jen smells strongly of body odor. She shakes Alicia's hand and hugs Remy with a total lack of self-consciousness about how she smells. Remy finds this terrifying. "Remy, I wish you would come out with us sometime," says Jen. "You know, everyone else has really stayed connected."

"I'm sure you're not *really* connected," he says. He hears his own laugh as if from a distance. It's deranged.

He turns to Alicia and explains, pretending that he's never told her this before: "Jen and I hated those people. We really bonded because Belasco's was such a freakshow."

Jen says, "I don't remember us hating them. I thought it was a great crew."

"Allie and her phobia about chewing gum!" says Remy. "And what's-his-name, the oyster-shucking guy. That you were always avoiding! And"—Remy looks heavenward before naming the greatest hit—"*Harry the Homophobe.* What did he always used to say? 'Don't be so open-minded that your brain falls out'?"

"Aw, those were such fun times," says Jen. She doesn't take up the old, mean line of conversation. "I've really missed you!"

Alicia notices how Jen's boobs are large enough to make her stomach—as round and well-hydrated as a yoga instructor's—seem smaller by comparison. She glows with health and well-being. Her upper lip catches on her adult braces. She's real. She's right there. "Actually, I think you'll know some of the people I'm going to surf with in July. We're going to this amazing place in the Hamptons. You should come. You should *both* come."

They say that they don't know how to surf, and Jen says that beginners are perfectly fine—that several other people coming don't have much experience at all.

Their close, attentive grouping around her suggests that Jen is an Apple Store employee, and several customers approach and then back away once they realize that she doesn't wear a lanyard. Other customers linger nearby, sensing a dramatically charged quality to the atmosphere.

Jen tells them about her latest trip, in Indonesia, and Remy tells her about his computer fan. Jen's body language remains attentive while he talks, but he can sense that he's boring her. In order to appear unaffected, Remy doesn't stop talking about his computer fan. Then he overcorrects and becomes hostile. "I cannot fucking *believe* how these companies train you to be dependent on their unethically assembled products, and then when they break, the world stops, and they get to squeeze a few more dollars out of you."

"Yeah," says Alicia. She's trying to help. She's sweating.

"Yeah," says Jen. "Totally."

After Jen leaves, they give her a fifteen-minute head start, even though they have no reason to stay. They watch the demo animation on the iPads—a multicolored line twisting on a black background. They can't see Jen anymore, but they know that right now, she's making a similarly bright path through space, somewhere. Always, in fact.

His hostility about the computer fan was completely manufactured, but Remy still feels hostile an hour later. He doesn't talk about what happened. Alicia doesn't say anything until he does.

"How did you like those earrings?" he says, finally.

"I wanted to yank on them. I wanted to unzip her from top to bottom."

After they leave the store and go out into the heat, Alicia says, "Can you imagine us surfing?" She laughs.

That night, Alicia wears the halter-top while she boils water for pasta, swearing it's the last time she'll eat pasta this month. "And no more cheese, after this."

Remy sits at the kitchen table, watching her cook too slowly. "You should just eat what you want. Pasta's cheap."

Alicia tells him her shift meal always has to be dabbed with a napkin in order to remove the grease. She smiles as she wears the halter-top and complains. "Can you believe this? Some guy yelled at me yesterday that I needed to oil my bike chain. Like, he rolled down his window to tell me this. He said it could snap."

"So oil it."

Alicia goes into greater detail, outlining how she'd have to spend money, how the chain is already ruined, and Remy is more bored than he's been in months. He knows that, eventually, concrete changes will take place in his life, but he can't conceive of any meaningful change that he's capable of bringing about. Something will have to happen *to* him.

After his shift, Remy looks at his phone and sees that Alicia has sent him several pictures. Two are of beaches in Montauk. One is of a dog on a surfboard.

Alicia: This could be you!!!!

The other picture is of Jen at a movie theater, with her arms around two cardboard cutouts of movie stars.

This could be us!!!!!

The picture is from when Jen was younger and cheesier. Remy recognizes that Jen's current presentation is more stylish, but without Alicia's help—her nuanced analyses of clothing and feminine beauty—he's unable to identify the components creating this effect. All he can see is that her face was rounder then, her joy more obvious.

Remy texts her back and says that if she's that far back in Jen's posts, she needs to be careful not to like anything.

Alicia: I know jesus

He doesn't reference going to Montauk, since Alicia's exclamation marks grant both of them plausible deniability. It's just a joke.

* * *

Jen uploads a picture of some polymer earrings on a fabric background and announces that she's finally put up a website where you can buy her "creations." Alicia scrolls through the selection, a series of geometric shapes in primary colors. Despite their baby-mobile simplicity, most of the earrings are genuinely attractive, and Alicia is annoyed by her desire to possess them. The website says, *Please allow two to four weeks for assembly and shipping.*

She says, "What if I bought a pair and then wore them in front of her on the surf trip?"

"We're not going to Montauk."

"And then if she asked me where I got them, I'd pretend I didn't even know it was her website."

Remy says that this isn't funny. He's returned from a late dinner shift, unhappy because he bought a new pair of shoes that rubbed a blister on his foot (Rocco referred to Remy as "Tiny Tim" for most of the night).

Remy rebandages his foot. He says that Jen was different than he remembers. "It brought back all these memories. I forgot how she can kind of be a bitch."

"I thought she was being really nice."

"She didn't have to pretend to be interested in my computer fan. Before, she would have been like, 'Remy, you're boring me. Talk about something else.'"

"That sounds bitchier to me."

"She's only nice to people she isn't close with."

Alicia doesn't say anything, and Remy continues complaining about his foot. He says that he read about a man in Florida who got gangrene from a paper cut after not taking it seriously.

"It doesn't sound like you're in danger of not taking it seriously."

Remy looks up from his foot.

Alicia says, "I'm just being a bitch. Like Jen."

Alicia buys the earrings, using a pseudonym in the mailing address. She turns to reveal this to Remy as soon as she presses Buy, but he's madly searching for the article about the man with gangrene, even though she didn't accuse him of making it up.

"So are we over Jen now?" she says.

"I'm the one who knows her. You've only met her once."

A few minutes pass, and Alicia doesn't tell him about the earrings. Keeping this a secret triggers a minor psychic implosion. It isn't completely unpleasant. Blood goes into her face and then her earlobes, where the earrings will be in two to four weeks.

When he gets home from a dinner shift, Remy brushes his teeth while Alicia's in the shower. He can tell she's been in the shower for a long time, because the toilet paper has rippled while still on the roll.

She's in a bad mood because of some minor fall from her bike, especially since one of her many narratives about herself is that she's a good driver and a better bike rider.

He tries to initiate sex when she gets out, but she freezes after she drops her towel.

"Listen!" she says. She holds up her hand, and her wicked expression dissipates. Her normal, fragile expression returns. Her wet hair shines uncannily from the red twinkle lights she put around the mirror "because red light makes you look younger."

Remy has lost the sexual interest that he felt only seconds ago. He finds himself wishing she had more of a chin and opens his mouth to say so, but stops just in time. "I don't hear anything," he says.

"We're haunted, I swear. I saw the lid of the trash can moving last night."

"There are squirrels in the walls. Or maybe we have a rat."

"It happens after you're asleep, too. It's not just that I hear things—I *feel* them."

For several minutes, they're still. Then they hear the sound of

Jake's key turning in the lock. Alicia shuts and locks the bedroom door. Neither of them feels horny with Jake in the apartment.

Jake knocks on the door and asks them, in his booming, friendly-uncle voice, if they would like smoothies too while he's making one for himself.

"Gee that's so nice, Jake!" says Remy. "I think we're good though."

They watch *Zodiac* and Remy gets bored. "We already know they don't find out who did it," he says. "It's just a bunch of people running around following meaningless clues that don't ever go anywhere. Any dumbass could tell that it's not one guy—it's probably a bunch of different killers." Alicia tells him to be quiet, because "Jake Gyllenhaal's performance is supposed to be phenomenal."

"I thought this would have more serial killing. This shit sucks."

Jake knocks on the door again, and when they don't respond, he speaks through it. "You guys, you gotta see this video. This dude is popping his tonsil stone. It's wild. I wouldn't disturb you if it weren't really worth it."

Alicia makes a gun with her fingers and pretends to shoot Jake through the door.

In the middle of the night, Remy is awakened by an awareness that Alicia isn't in bed. He calls her name. It takes a full minute before she appears in the doorway. "Are you sleepwalking?" he says.

"I thought I felt something."

"Did you hear a squirrel?"

He tells her to come to bed, and Alicia says something that might be taken from a caption on one of Jen's pictures: "It's important to pay attention to what my body's telling me. Sometimes a person is sensitive to larger forces without realizing it."

Her voice is sexy and different from normal. It's also unlike the voice she uses when she's pretending to be Jen.

Remy tells her to come to bed again, and she says, "Now I'm hungry." She disappears back into the dark. A few seconds later, he hears the wet, suckling sounds of Alicia eating. He tries to guess what it is. It sounds like turkey, although he doesn't think they have any.

He goes into the kitchen and takes a flash picture of her, because otherwise she might not believe she was sleepwalking. Alicia reacts to the flash with a sludgy movement of one arm.

He forgets to show her the picture before she leaves the next day for work, but looks at it later on his own. The gloss of food matter on her cheek might look glamorous on any other girl with a similarly vacant expression. He's noticed, lately, that most girls in ads have wet faces.

Cassie is late to work again, and hungover, but looks more put together than Alicia. Alicia forgives Cassie when she shows her a video of something cute her sugar glider did that morning. Cassie often makes the mistake of assuming everything about her pet is fascinating, and Alicia is the only person at work who reliably reacts with enthusiasm.

"I would love an interesting pet," says Alicia. "Do you think I should get a parrot? I feel like I'm a really anxious person. I think an animal would be therapeutic."

"Barry isn't relaxing at all. He's always doing retarded shit that stresses me out." Like Alicia, Cassie is from one of those states where everyone calls everything "retarded." She gives Alicia advice in a cursory way that makes it clear she'd like to get back to her phone. She tells her to meditate or to read *The Apple Bush,* a self-help book that everyone has been into lately.

Alicia gets a notification that Jen's posted a new photo. Jen is in a bubble bath, reading the very book that Cassie just mentioned—*The Apple Bush.*

"Trying to find out if I can be my best self and still be a huge bitch:)"

Alicia shows Cassie the picture. "Isn't that a crazy coincidence? We were just talking about that book!"

Cassie puts down her phone. "Fuck I just remembered. You can drive, right? What would you charge to help me move?"

Alicia has to concentrate in order to prevent her voice from wandering into a register that will reveal her investment. "When are you looking for? I'm going on a surf trip in a couple of weeks."

"August first. How much do you charge?"

"It's fine, I'll do it for free. It'll be fun." Alicia adjusts the bandana she's required to wear over her hair. "Maybe we can get a drink afterwards."

"It won't be fun," says Cassie. "I'm serious. You wouldn't like me when I sweat. I'm even crankier."

"Ah. Like the Hulk!"

"Excuse me?"

"You know how he's like, *You wouldn't like me when I'm angry*?"

Cassie is confused and says that she *didn't* say she'd be angry. She talks about her Irish heritage and explains how her complexion is completely unsuited for temperatures above sixty-eight degrees. Cassie isn't pretty, but aspires to perfect skin as if it's the same thing.

Cassie offers her a hundred dollars and Alicia says, "No really. I wouldn't charge a friend."

The word *friend* hangs in the air between them, menacingly.

"We'll see," says Cassie.

Before getting on her bike, Alicia looks at the photo more attentively. She would expect Jen's bathtub only to have expensive shampoos, so it surprises her to see the mix of special and unspecial brands on the rim of the tub. At the outer edge of the photo, Alicia recognizes the trademark bottle shape of a specific skincare line. The advertising campaign for this brand makes use of tropical landscapes and refers to a "skincare journey." Alicia has always been susceptible to advertising that references a journey.

Riding her bike home, Alicia occupies a mental state between pleasure and boredom, akin to her state of mind while showering. She catches herself repeating Jen's caption under her breath: *trying to be my best self and still be a huge bitch.*

When she gets home, Remy calls to her from behind the bathroom door and asks if she'll hand him a new roll of toilet paper. "We're all out in here."

Alicia gets a new roll from the closet, and Remy stops the door with his foot when she opens it too far.

"Here you go." She holds it just out of his reach.

"C'mon, Alicia."

"What's wrong? Take it." Alicia keeps yanking it away from his hand, as if it's too hot for him.

"You're acting like Greta," he says.

"Excuse me! Greta wouldn't even get the toilet paper from the closet for you."

"Can you hand me the fucking toilet paper?"

"How's your stump?" says Alicia, meaning his imminently gangrenous foot. Before he transitions from irritation into genuine anger, she gives him the toilet paper.

Remy wakes up in the middle of the night again. He hears a noise in the kitchen and yells at Alicia to come back to bed. But when he rolls over, she's still there.

Remy covers his mouth belatedly, afraid that his scream woke Jake. "Don't fucking smile at me like that!" he says. "What the fuck is wrong with you?"

Alicia's eyes are glassy and half open. She doesn't move for several seconds.

"Knock knock," she says.

The darkness prevents Remy from staring at her with precision.

"Knock knock."

When Alicia still doesn't move, he says, "Who's there?"

Alicia keeps smiling at him.

"Who's there?"

"Orange."

"Orange who?"

"Orange you glad I'm not bulimic anymore?"

"What the fuck?" He says her name a few times. He says it like he's asking if she's awake, and then he says it like he's asking if it's really Alicia he's talking to. "Who's there?" he says again.

"Someone's . . . in the kitchen," says Alicia.

Remy sits up in bed, listening to the darkened apartment. "Who's in the kitchen, Alicia?"

It takes a long time for Alicia to say the next phrase, and her smile becomes sweeter and her eyes tighter, as if trying to watch an eclipse. "Someone's in the kitchen . . . with Dinah . . . Strumming on the old banjo."

She turns over, and her breathing is slow and regular.

In the morning he tells her everything she said to him. Alicia doesn't remember any of it.

"Is this your way of telling me that you're bulimic?"

"You know that I went to a center."

"But since you were a teenager?"

"Not in any *systemic* way. I dabbled in college but never to the point where my skin got really bad again." Alicia elaborates with a convoluted metaphor about how recovery involves achieving "escape velocity": "You know what they say: You're going to have a few fires on the way out of the atmosphere."

Remy points out that ideally you really don't want *any* fires on a spaceship. Alicia ignores this and asks him if he's seen her work bandana.

Remy says, "Going into space has a negative connotation. You can't breathe there. Wouldn't it be better, for the purposes of recovery, to speak about *returning* to the atmosphere?"

"I don't know. They were therapists, not engineers."

He tells her on her way out the door that sometimes he feels as if he doesn't know her at all. His tone is meant to imply that he finds this sexually exciting. "Are you smoking more? Because you're acting different." By "smoking" he means weed. By "acting different" he means that she seems less anxious about getting on his nerves.

Alicia puts her hand on the doorknob and tells him that he should confirm with Jen about the upcoming trip. "Make sure you get time off."

"Very funny."

"I think you need to get used to the idea that we're going to Montauk. I don't want to have to bully you."

Remy smiles at her and Alicia smiles back. "You're stressing me out. It's not funny anymore."

"I'm not kidding. I don't want to have to threaten you, but if I have to take drastic measures, I will. Blackmail. Kidnapping. Torture."

The words *blackmail, kidnapping,* and *torture* sound ridiculous when Alicia says them in her squeaky voice. They both laugh, for different reasons.

On his laptop, Remy opens up a new message window with Jen.

Her most recent post is of people he knows, in a restaurant he's visited before. It shouldn't be difficult to find something to say about this. He looks at the messaging window, and sees their last exchange:

Are you going to Thirsty's tonight? I have a surprise for you.

At some point over that summer, Jen had made a passing comment about how she might have a protein deficiency from her "basically vegan" diet. He'd said, "Maybe you should drink more protein shakes," and she'd said *haha gross.* Several times, Remy tried to elaborate this small exchange into a more substantial joke, but failed. However, he remained convinced of its potential.

The last time he'd seen Jen was the night Belasco's closed, at a bar where the staff convened after shifts. It was a boxing-themed bar with a punching bag near the bathroom, next to a sign that said DECORATIVE! DO NOT PUNCH!

The night of this message, fraudulently sent before he'd even acquired the "surprise," Remy bought a whole tub of protein powder as a gift for her. He picked the biggest tub of the cheapest brand, because he thought it would only be funny if it were large, and carried it to Thirsty's Pub from a store six avenues over, his arms wrapped around it like a mast in a storm.

The scenario didn't go as he had envisioned. In his imagination, he'd thunked the jar of protein powder on the bar table, surprising Jen into laughter. He'd leaned an elbow on the jar to comically emphasize its size. The extravagance, the excess of the joke had endeared him to everyone who saw it. And in this fantasy, Jen asked to see him again, apart from these work-adjacent social gatherings.

But Jen was sitting at the bar when he came in, so he'd had to heave it up, and the drama of the act was undermined by the surprising lightness of the powder—it made almost no noise when it landed. Jen wasn't impressed, only confused. Carla smiled at him in a way that communicated his imminent failure, and asked him if he'd just come from the gym. A random British guy at the bar called him *mate* and said, "Are you selling that stuff or wot?"

"Remy, are you malnourished?" said Jen.

"It's for you." He reminded her of the comment she'd made. "And now you have as much protein as you need!"

"You're a fucking freak. The whole point of that conversation was that protein powder is gross." Jen covered her mouth with her hand, lowered it, covered her mouth again. "Am I supposed to drink this *now?*"

He didn't know what she was supposed to do. "Maybe there's something you can mix it with."

"I'm asking the bartender," she said.

"Please don't ask the bartender. It was a joke."

Jen told the bartender that her *friend* had brought her a special gift and could he creatively incorporate it into a cocktail of some kind?

The bartender picked up the tub with a huge hand and examined the label. He peeled off the price sticker and said something to Jen that Remy couldn't hear. Remy didn't know what to do with his arms now that he wasn't holding the protein powder.

"What did he say?" said Remy.

"He says that he knows how to make a whey white Russian but the quality of the whey protein matters."

"What?"

The bartender leaned over the counter. "You don't just want whey isolate. Ideally, you'd want hydrolysate and fewer hydrogenated oils and additives. I hate to say it, but you bought the lady some very cheap powder."

"How much was it?" said Jen. She looked at the price sticker on the bartender's immense finger. She looked at Remy. "Remy, you spent fifty-four ninety-nine on protein powder for me?"

Remy didn't say anything, caught being both too expensive and too cheap.

He rereads this last message several times and decides that if he contacts Jen it will be over a different platform, one without that last message hovering over their new beginning.

On the way to a dinner shift, Remy opens up a new text window with Jen. He takes care not to look at their previous messaging history.

Hey, he says, sending before he can think about it too hard. Then he types, Is surfing hard? He deletes this.

I don't know why we never hung out after Belasco's closed. Maybe because you were an asshole and never reached out.

He looks at this last sentence and evaluates its ratio of playfulness to aggression. He deletes it. I just feel like we let a really valuable friendship lapse and I'd like to rekindle it. It was so nice seeing you the other day.

Gross.

He types several other responses and deletes them. The only thing he's sent so far is Hey.

Jen responds: Remy what are you typing it's taking forever.

Remy stops typing. He starts typing. He stops again.

Jen: Y are you being weird.

Remy stops and starts again. He deletes, deletes. He types, Just wanted to pick your brain about your upcoming schedule—and then deletes. Is it ok—deletes. You're the weird one—deletes.

Jen says, are you contacting me about an exciting business opportunity.

Does she seriously think he's contacting her about an exciting business opportunity? Is she referencing something he's forgotten?

Any of the intuition that would have served him in the old days is inaccessible. If he hadn't started relying so much on Alicia for his social interactions, these instincts wouldn't have abandoned him. It's really Alicia's fault.

He types, Sorry I was weird at the apple store. I was having a weird day.

After he sends it, he realizes that he used the word "weird" twice.

Jen says, You were regular.

Remy stares at his phone, and then turns off all notifications. Even if she does say anything else—which she won't—he doesn't want to know about it. Jen is a genius. *You were regular.* It's ambiguous. It could mean *You were perfectly normal* or *You're always weird, so it was regular for you to be such a freak.*

Remy comes home around midnight, and Alicia, in bed but still in her work clothes, immediately holds up her phone to him. It's a picture of Jen eating Twizzlers. "So glad I'm an adult now and can eat as much candy as I want," says the caption.

"I never eat as much candy as I want," says Alicia. "I should be bulimic again."

The room smells of sweat and the wooly interior of the air conditioner. Remy glances at the phone, then says, "Listen. Even if I did want to go to the Hamptons, logistically it's impossible. I did some googling. You need a lot of expensive equipment."

"Jen says her boyfriend can lend us whatever we need. It sounds like he's loaded."

"What?"

"I wonder if it can get nerdy to have too much surf stuff, the way it is with other hobbies, or if it only gets more... *dank* or whatever." She laughs.

Remy says *what* a few more times and Alicia repeats herself. She says the word "boyfriend" again as slowly as possible.

"Did Jen talk to you? Did you contact her without talking to me first?"

"I just *continued your conversation* with her from your laptop. It sounds like you were really typing up a storm." Remy sits on the bed. He feels as if a dye pack has exploded in his chest. "Don't worry, she still thought it was you," says Alicia.

"I've had a really bad day at work. I can't believe this."

"I fixed your terrible conversation for you. Aren't you happy? And they're going to give everyone a ride up."

Alicia smiles at him, as if daring him to stab her. "It's only four days," she says.

"Alicia! I don't want to wear some wetsuit that rubbed against her boyfriend's balls! I don't want to be trapped in some beach house with a bunch of her crusty friends and their... *oat milk*."

Alicia explains to him that it will be warm enough that he probably won't even need a wetsuit. "But no one will make you take off your shirt. Don't worry. No one will make you *reveal your chest*."

"Fuck off," says Remy.

Alicia rolls her head around on her shoulders, and the next voice that comes out of her mouth is Jen's, but through Alicia's crazy face. "Remy, are you angry that I didn't fall all over myself when I saw you again?"

"Stop smiling at me like that," he says. Alicia-as-Jen smiles at him, and doesn't stop smiling no matter how much he insults her. He tells her she looks like the monkey in *Dead Alive* that bites the guy's mom.

"I'm not trying to be critical, *Alicia*," he says, "but you're always talking about how isolated you feel and I think that maybe that expression is preventing you from making friends. You make that face more than you realize."

He mentally prepares himself to act like this is a joke and not at all intended to hurt her. But Alicia-as-Jen isn't hurt. She crawls towards him on the bed, gecko-like, and says, "You can talk to Alicia like that but you can't talk to Jen like that."

"You really are brain damaged."

Remy goes to take a shower, but Alicia-as-Jen follows him into the bathroom. She presses her face against the glass of the sliding shower doors. "I'm *so* sorry that you're not as impressive as my *surfer* boyfriend."

Alicia gets into the shower with him, fully clothed, and Remy can no longer ignore her. "Please don't take it out on me," says Alicia-as-Jen, water streaming over open eyes.

Before Jen was such a large presence in their sex life, Alicia and Remy had other scenarios: home intruder, bad babysitter, vampire attack. This time, they get confused. Neither of them is sure if this is a Jen scenario or a home intruder scenario. Alicia-as-Jen's fingers slip against the soap holder and reach for his hair with a gesture somewhere between desire and self-defense.

They lie on the bed afterwards without speaking, until Remy tells Alicia that in a way, he's relieved she handled this. Alicia tells him again that the boyfriend probably sucks. "He's probably the type of person whose favorite book was assigned reading in high school," she says, although neither of them can remember the last time *they* read a book.

"Seeing her at the Apple Store really stressed me out. I felt caught."

"Like when you're speeding and you see a cop in the rearview mirror."

Remy doesn't have Alicia's driving experience, but nevertheless registers the correctness of this comparison. "That's exactly it."

Alicia laughs. She is always stooping to diminish her height, but when they lie on the bed together, she's unselfconscious about being the same size as him. She envelopes his body with hers. "Remy, I know what it's like to have a crush."

Remy puts off looking at the text conversation with Jen until Alicia is asleep, but she's deleted most of it, except for the address where they should meet Jen on Friday. When he asks her about it the next day, she says he shouldn't worry—that it's for his own good.

Part 2
Signifiers of Flow

On Friday, they take a train and a bus to the address Jen provided. By nine a.m., it's already hot, and they wander around a treeless row of warehouse apartments, sweat forming on their backs in the shape of their weekend-bag straps. Alicia complains that she just got clean and now she's getting dirty again.

"I told you not to take a bath. I don't understand why you're obsessed with baths."

"It's part of a new project I'm doing. Sort of a relaxation project."

Remy looks at his phone. The dot that represents them overlaps with the destination flag, but they don't see a building with the correct number. The destination flag sits right in the middle of the street. "I think that means Google Maps is guessing with this number and it doesn't actually know."

"Don't you want to know what the project is?"

"You realize you're already putting on your fake voice? Can you please not do that thing where you meet new people and agree with everything they say?"

"This *is* my normal voice."

"Just don't be like, 'Yeah, I totally agree!' to everything everybody says. I've never seen you be the same around other people as you are around me."

Alicia says that isn't how she sounds. "You think that because I act one way around you and a different way around other people that one of those is more authentic?"

Remy texts Jen that they're outside, and seconds later Jen says she's standing outside, but they look around and don't see anyone. They're never out this early. They can hear the crack of a baseball bat hitting a ball, but they didn't pass a baseball diamond on their way.

I'm waving at you, says Jen. They don't see anyone waving.

"Maybe it's an elaborate prank and Jen never wanted us to come in the first place," says Alicia.

The blankness of this neighborhood—with its blinding sidewalks and windowless warehouses in the place where Remy expected to see Jen—is unbearable. He turns around, and the dot turns too. This can't be right.

After some back-and-forth, it becomes clear that Jen mistyped one of the numbers in the address. Remy says, "The good news is that it's only a few blocks up!" Alicia looks at him and he says, "What?"

"You're just so completely fine with her fucking up the address," says Alicia. She isn't angry.

They get to the right address and Jen doesn't apologize. "You're early," she says, although they aren't. Her hair is wet, and she's wearing a long, square piece of clothing that she might have just dropped over her naked body (later, Alicia tells Remy it's called a *caftan*).

The apartment is large and humid, with high ceilings and a yellowed AC unit chugging in the corner. Beers sit on every surface. An abstract fiberglass structure hangs from the ceiling, swinging slightly, dirty where the sunlight hits it. In the living area, everything resembling dishware is in use as an ashtray. "Did you guys have a party last night?" says Alicia. She looks at the kitchen area, where polymer cutouts are scattered across a piece of plastic on the counter. The oven clock is *very* incorrect.

"What?" Jen looks around. "Feel free to sit wherever."

Jen's default expression looks different to Remy than it was two years and seven months ago. She seems sleepier and more relaxed, like a koala. Her voice and intonation have also altered, either with age or a change in milieu. In a voice as drawling and fried as a podcaster's, she says, "Sorry. I just moved in and we're in the process of getting my boyfriend's *useless ex-roommate* to come and get his stuff." She says *useless ex-roommate* while smiling. She either really likes or sincerely hates him.

"I'm so excited to learn how to surf!" says Alicia.

Jen leans against the counter, responding to Alicia's small talk in an entirely different rhythm. She tells them about where they're staying and that her boyfriend teaches little kids in Montauk and the Rockaways sometimes...that he's actually *great* at teaching little kids.

"It's so adorable. They follow him all over the beach. I call them his groupies."

"So he's a surf instructor?" says Remy.

"He works for his dad's company, sometimes. And he's helping me with my jewelry business. But we're both trying to resist the social pressure to get 'real jobs.' It's so fascist how society primes you to achieve self-actualization through these...very specific avenues."

"I totally agree!" says Alicia.

Remy says, "What's funny is that when we worked together, you *hated* kids."

"No I didn't. I just thought it was funny how much *you* hated kids."

"I just thought it was rude for parents to bring kids to a restaurant that's not kid-friendly. But I actually like kids."

"You do?" says Alicia. She looks at Remy. Her ass is on the edge of the couch.

"You'd be surprised, Jen. I've changed a lot. I actually love kids now. I always did."

"Okay maybe don't *shout* about how obsessed you are with children while you're on this trip, Remy," says Jen. Remy smiles, because Jen is smiling. He feels simultaneously bad and good.

Jen tells him that Carla's also coming and recounts some of her antics at Belasco's. Remy maintains intense eye contact with her, but then, to counteract this intensity, switches between staring into her pupils and staring at her feet.

"Is there something on my foot?" says Jen, lifting one foot and looking at the filthy sole.

In the days preceding this trip, Remy and Alicia have tried in vain to confirm this boyfriend's name or locate qualities in him that they can dislike. As far as they can tell, he has no presence on any platform. They aren't even sure they have the right guy.

Based on the few pictures they've located, they've both committed to the idea of his interchangeability with other Jen-adjacent men. But when they finally see him in person, they understand that he could never be confused with anyone else.

He comes back from the store while Jen's other friends are arriving, laden with grocery bags, flicking sweaty hair from his face, and smiling at everyone the way a kindly older man smiles at children who might be afraid of his dog. He knows everyone else in the room, but to Remy and Alicia, he says his name and makes as if to hold out his hand with the grocery bags. "Sorry!" he says, with many apologetic gestures.

The premise of this exchange is that he's struggling with the bags, but it's difficult to imagine him ever having struggled. His eyes are the mint color of Lady Liberty, and his expression is moneyed and free of pain, like a royal corpse. He sets down the bags. "Excuse me but I really have to shit," he says, and pumps his arms on the way to the bathroom.

After he shuts the door, Remy asks Jen to repeat his name.

He thinks that Jen says Horace, and he repeats back, "Horace?" but Jen says no, "H-O-R-U-S, like the Egyptian god."

"Ah," he says.

"Cool!" says Alicia, in her fake voice.

Alicia and Remy stand outside a circle of people who have only aimed a few initial, cursory questions in their direction. Horus approaches and says, "Remy, would you mind giving me a hand with the bags and stuff?" Remy assesses Horus's smile in order to understand if this is necessary or meant to be a social favor that will make him feel included.

He gets up and sees that Alicia's already putting on the expression she wears around other women. He looks away.

They take the groceries and bags outside, and Horus pulls a van around. The trunk is filled with boxes of trash bags.

"That's a lot of trash bags," says Remy.

"Whenever I go to the beach, I like to pick up litter and stuff. It's kind of a hobby of mine."

Horus considers all the grocery bags before placing them in the back. From within one of the bags, Remy can see the packaging of USDA certified organic rice cakes. "I always wondered who buys organic rice cakes," he says.

"Guilty!" says Horus. "Although to be honest, Jen's more the stickler for that stuff."

"The regular ones are about a million dollars less for the same thing. That organic stuff is a scam," says Remy, with certainty. "Rice cakes are mainly air anyways."

"You know how she is, though. She loves Hot Cheetos, so it's not like she's consistent." He laughs, and Remy isn't sure what this laughter means. Is Horus subtly drawing attention to the fact that Remy no longer knows *how she is*?

"You need money or anything?" says Remy.

"What?"

"For the groceries?"

"Oh I'm hosting! No sweat, no sweat," says Horus. He asks if Jen mentioned that it was his family house.

"She did," says Remy. Horus puts the luggage in the trunk first, groceries second, and organizes with evident pleasure, interrupting his graceful motions to consult Remy on placement.

"I don't want the clementines to get too smushed," he says. "We should put those on top of the luggage, probably. What do you think?"

"Whatever, man."

When they finish, Horus shuts the trunk doors but makes no move to get out of the heat.

"Should we go back inside?" says Remy.

"What an amazing day! Look at that sky," says Horus, lunging on the pavement, hands on hips. Then he's silent, looking at the streets and buildings, shaking his head like he can't believe what he's seeing.

Remy looks around. The silence is so long that he feels compelled to say something. The outside of Horus's warehouse apartment building is covered in barbed wire and security cameras. "Nice security cameras."

"Oh yeah! Don't worry, dude. They're all busted. I busted some of them out myself. No one's watching you."

"*You* did?"

"I'm not about that surveillance lifestyle. It's just taking the mystery out of life, you know?" Horus has a lot of opinions about this subject and launches into a sermon about the evils of technology. "And now if you don't know something, you just google it! You don't even have to work to know the answer."

"Yes, that's terrible," says Remy.

"I don't need to know *everything*. And I don't need to know what my friends are doing every second of the day, you know?"

"No," says Remy. "Definitely not."

Of the ten people on the trip, the only other person Remy knows is Carla, who arrives late and crawls over everyone else's legs to get to the most centrally located position in the van. She slaps his shoulder with her antique fan and says his name. "Remy! I never hear from you!" She jabs her fan at Alicia and demands to know who she is.

Jen turns around in her seat and says, "Isn't it *grand?*"

Remy says, "When you said I'd know some of the people on this trip, did you just mean Carla?"

"It all makes sense," Carla says. "You appeared briefly in a dream of mine." Carla's hands make a vaudevillian gesture around the word *all,* saluting some cosmic project that has *done it again.* Carla hasn't changed at all. She's put on a little weight, but her stomach is still exposed, and her collar still crowded by the same lethal tangle of gold necklaces. She still draws on the ugliest eyebrows Remy has ever seen, with great skill and fineness of line. But he doesn't know anything about eyebrows—maybe to other women, they look good.

Throughout the drive, Jen stays in the front seat, next to Horus. Unless she twists her torso around to participate in the conversation, it's difficult to get her attention without uncool effort.

As Remy is in the middle of telling a story that he thought would be more interesting, about how he was "pretty sure" a squirrel gave birth in the ceiling of his apartment, Jen interrupts him. "Oh my

God, I just remembered." She lowers her sunglasses. "Remy. I'm not sure that we brought enough protein for this trip!"

Jen and Carla laugh so hard that it makes it difficult for them to retell the story. Remy doesn't know most of the people laughing. They're all very attractive.

Remy says, "It was supposed to be funny. You win some, you lose some."

"What does that even mean?" says Carla. "What did winning look like for you, in this situation?" Remy laughs, but Carla doesn't drop it. "I'm really curious, Remy…what were you hoping to gain?"

"I've never heard about this," says Alicia, smiling and smiling.

"Leave him alone," says Jen. "I think this would be a great time to exercise a little *Karmic Intentionality.*"

Alicia waits for several seconds before saying, "You've read *The Apple Bush*?" as if she hasn't seen the picture of Jen in her bathtub. Alicia hasn't read it, but knows enough about it from Cassie to create the impression of having read it.

"We love it," says Carla. Carla and Jen enthuse about it in a way that makes Alicia feel she's missing something. It's not clear if they actually practice the self-improvement techniques, or if their interest is purely aesthetic.

"You guys see a lot of each other, then," says Remy.

Carla says, "I hate to say it—but the book works."

"It's *garbage,*" says Jen, her emphasis sending a small, thrilling amount of orthodontic spit in Alicia's face. "But that's why it's so great. I mean this seriously and truly! It's life-changing. But it's also—and I *can't* emphasize this enough—so incredibly dumb."

"Ah," says Alicia. Jen and Carla signal that they're interested in having a longer discussion, but Alicia's too tense to harness these cues, and the topic is dropped.

Horus's house is nicer than any house Remy or Alicia has ever stayed in. The design is nautical, with window seats hinged at the back, sailboat-style, and pointless bowls of shells on the end tables. A pool with a small waterfall is visible through sliding glass doors. Remy recoils when he realizes that the pictures on the mantelpiece are of Horus as a baby.

Jen's friends make nice comments about the house. Horus says, "I just wish I could come up here more. I recognize my privilege, and I feel like it's my responsibility to share it with people around me!"

"Thank you so much for sharing with those less fortunate," says Remy, looking at Alicia.

"Aw, you know what I mean."

"It's so clean!" says someone else, a girl with an unlocatable accent. She alludes to Horus's messy habits, demonstrating that she knows him well.

"That's because of Juana. She comes once a week. She's an amazing, just really amazing lady," says Horus, without offering any evidence that she's amazing other than the fact that she cleans the house.

Remy takes the first opportunity to escape to the bathroom as the more structured social situation of the van diffuses around the house. The claiming of rooms triggers intense anxiety in both of them.

"Do you even have to go?" says Alicia. "You always accuse me of doing this and now you're doing it to me."

Remy finds the bathroom down a dark taupe hallway. He stays inside longer than necessary, listening to the noise of people in the living room and scrolling on his phone. Already, people are talking about "making the most of the day." He might be forced to surf. Jen is shouting some story about how Horus took care of her when she had food poisoning in a hostel. She confidently includes too many details to tell the story well. "Honestly I wish he wouldn't be so nice to me. It makes me feel like shit!" It's not that funny, but everyone laughs.

Remy remembers how Jen used to walk around Belasco's with pens in her hair that *he* had put there. His masterpiece.

How did it happen? One night, she was the new girl who smoked too much. The next, everything she did hit his eyes with psychedelic tenderness. When he looked around the restaurant, with its antique light bulbs and pretentiously unpretentious paper tablecloths, the space around Jen was *activated* and different. When his eyes swept over the room and encountered Jen, the thrill was almost tactile, as if his fingers had brushed against an erogenous zone.

He has a mental picture of what they were like together at Belasco's. He's preserved this picture for over two years, consulting it whenever he wants to judge, by comparison, the beauty of a given situation. Jen's comment about disliking children was so evocative that when she'd made it, he'd had to concentrate on keeping his face neutral.

He remembered when a kid had come into the restaurant during the summer, wearing an orange T-shirt that said THIS IS MY HALLOWEEN COSTUME. Jen and Remy had exchanged eye contact.

The kid's mother replaced the restaurant's water glass with a plastic Halloween cup from her designer bag. Remy took their order and said to the kid, "You like Halloween, huh?"

"He's going through a phase," said the mother.

"It's the only good holiday," said the kid. "All the other ones are stupid."

The mother spoke about her child louder, in third person, as if that meant he couldn't understand her. "It's really fantastic. Especially when he gets sent home from school for biting the other kids with his fangs."

He told Jen about it while she was putting in an order, and she said that the child was probably going to be the next Jeffrey Dahmer or Ted Kaczynski.

But while they were talking, they saw the child raise his arms over his head, lifting his T-shirt and revealing a wet, bleeding gash on his stomach.

"Holy shit," said Jen. The mother saw them see and waved Remy over.

"Please don't overreact," she said. She said that it was fake blood—that he'd been gifted a kit for making different kinds of wounds. "Bullet wounds, axe wounds, ninja-star wounds... it's amazing. Do me a favor and tell your girlfriend it's not real. I don't want her calling CPS." Her laugh indicated she wasn't actually worried. The woman (who had a worked-on face like a soda can crushed and then carefully uncrushed) seemed to think that calling Jen his girlfriend would belittle him.

He told Jen what had happened, and she said, "What did the kid say?"

"Nothing. He was eating his sliders."

"Do you think the mom is hurting him and just telling people it's part of his whole Halloween obsession?"

"Is it fucked up that I had the same thought?"

"It would be the perfect cover."

Remy said, "He seems annoying. I'd probably hit him too."

They both tried to disguise their laughter while in view of their tables. At the time, they *did* share an inside joke about Remy's dislike of children, but the truth was, Remy didn't actually dislike children more than he disliked people generally. It was just something to talk about. Their manager that night was Harry the Homophobe, who came over and told them to *get to work and stop flirting.*

Everything about this memory pleases Remy. Back then, even strangers had perceived them as a unit. The current situation lies outside the picture, and he can't reconcile that Jen with this one.

No matter how shocking he was, he was acceptable to Jen. The best times with her were times like that—they were seeing something no one else around them could see, examining the expensive, unexceptional appearance of a Manhattan mom and looking for clues of cruelty.

When he washes his hands, he's confused about whether or not he's allowed to use the soap, since all of the soap in the dish is molded into decorative shapes like shells and cherubs, and the pump bottle turns out to be lotion. The wad of lotion sits in his hand, separated from his skin by a thin layer of water. He feels profoundly unwell. If he were home, he could be scrolling on his phone in his own bathroom instead of differentiating between real and decorative soaps.

When he finally rejoins the group, Jen looks at her phone and then at Remy. "Did you just like this photo of mine from last week?"

"What?" he says. Several other people turn around to look at him too.

"I've been waiting for the bathroom for like ten minutes! Were you just in there, scrolling away? Just liking photos of me?"

"No, I wasn't," he says. He doesn't bother to flesh out this lie.

Jen doesn't let go of this and continues to interrogate him for several minutes, calling him a freak and smiling.

Horus matches Remy and Alicia up with surfboards from the vast tangle of equipment in the garage. He looks back and forth between their bodies and the boards, smacking one that has passed an invisible test and holding it out to Remy. Remy has to stabilize himself with his back leg, as it seesaws unpredictably. The board is both heavy and hollow. A rubbery cord with a strap dangles from the back end, as if to prevent him from escaping once he's in the ocean.

"If I'm just learning, do I have to wear that thing around my ankle?"

"Why wouldn't you?" Horus makes movements implying that the selection process is over and it's time to get on with the process of drowning Remy.

As Horus and a friend of his load up the van, Remy asks Jen if Alicia's board seems longer than his. "I don't know if it matters, but obviously I'm taller than she is."

"They're basically the same size, dummy."

"Are you sure?"

"Everyone starts out on a longboard. When you get better you get a shorter one."

Alicia, who has been implicitly excluded from this conversation by Remy's low voice, says, loudly, that the waves "sound big. But I'm not an expert."

"We won't surf the ones you're hearing. We're going to Ditch Plains." Jen puts her arms around their shoulders, enclosing them in a configuration that mimics close friendship. "Don't worry, guys—Horus will only take you on baby waves. You're in good hands!" She releases them, taking the smell of her shampoo with her, and asks Remy if he's scared, walking backwards and smiling at him.

"I'm fine," says Remy.

Jen points between them and says, "I hope you both get *bit* by the surfing bug. Especially you, Remy." Jen makes her hand into a mouth and jumps at him, trying to bite him with it. She laughs and Remy is caught off guard, unsure what to do with his face. He's worried that he looked frightened.

"Are you high?" says Carla, fanning herself. Jen holds up a half-inch space between thumb and forefinger. Remy figures out what to do with his face. He laughs.

The beach is crowded, and Remy and Alicia stay close together once they get out of the van, suffering from the sensation of being on display. If Carla weren't also depending on a lesson from Horus, Remy is sure they would be forgotten.

Carla applies sunscreen, complaining about the fact that Horus's attention will be divided among the three of them. She says it like she's joking, but it's clear she really minds.

"Stop sucking in so much," says Remy to Alicia. "Just try to look natural."

"I'm not sucking in."

She's sucking in so much that the curves of her rib cage are visible under her skin. The twin curves look like a second, sharper pair of breasts. Alicia looks around at everyone who has come with them, bewildered to find herself among people like this. Everyone who isn't Alicia and Remy is moving around the beach without fear.

Jen draws a dick on Horus's back with sunscreen, and makes eye contact with Alicia for the first time, holding a finger up to her mouth. The attention is as special as a camp counselor's.

"Did you draw a dick on my back?" says Horus.

"No!"

"That's too bad. Because I was really hoping you did." Jen laughs and says she'll wipe it off, but Horus says, "No, I want it there."

"You'll get a tan line shaped like a dick!"

"Good."

"Stop it! Let me wipe it out."

"But I love your work so much!"

"Who are they performing this for?" Remy says to Carla, quietly. He monitors her face to assess if she's a likely ally or not. She doesn't respond.

Horus walks halfway down to the water with Jen. Alicia says to Remy, "Her board is long. That means she's probably not that good, right?"

Carla says, "Jen is fantastic. You'll see." The fact seems to irritate her.

Horus makes Remy and Alicia put their boards down on the beach and practice paddling, checking that their bodies are positioned correctly, and then teaches them how to stand up on a wave.

"Hey, Horus!" says a ten-year-old walking by. The ten-year-old glances at Remy and Alicia, but doesn't acknowledge them.

Remy puts his right foot down and then his left, as instructed. He wears an expression that implies none of this is news to him.

"Okay. Great job, but paddle first!" says Horus.

"I'll paddle when I'm in the water," says Remy. "I know how to paddle."

"It's all about making the connections in your brain! Just do it now, and it will be a lot easier later."

"*Carla's* not making the connections in her brain. She's just sitting there."

Carla blows her vape smoke into her cleavage, to hide it from the lifeguard, and says, "Just do what Horus says. Carla's done this before."

Horus circles them and only uses the words "Pop up!" and "Paddle." Sometimes he says "Great!" or "Faster!"

"Is there any real trick to this, other than the basics?" says Remy. "I feel like this stuff is kind of repetitive."

Horus kneels in the sand next to him, close enough for Remy to see the sun-bleached hairs growing on his toes.

"Remy, do you know what else is repetitive?"

"What?"

"Waves."

"Sure."

"*Life* is repetitive. Everything occurs in cycles. The waves just emulate the natural cycle of all living things. Don't *resent* the repetition—embrace it!"

"Yeah, man," says Remy. Horus laughs, as if it's a joke they're sharing instead of one meant to be at his expense.

Remy and Horus go down to the water together, leaving Alicia and Carla on the beach to wait for their turn. Remy's body is diagonal with the effort of holding the board, but Horus holds his as easily as if it were a Trapper Keeper. Horus, inscrutably, tells Remy to "give the right of way to the guys at the peak" and "be respectful to the locals. You're with me, but still."

"How am I supposed to know who's local?"

"You've got nothing to worry about."

"I'm *not* worried."

He steps into the ocean and remembers how much he hates sports generally. The water is cold and doesn't reliably confine itself to one section of his body. The spray hits his groin at the same time that it hits his face. Horus leans over and Velcros the cord to Remy's ankle.

"I can do that," says Remy.

"Too late!"

Remy follows Horus into the water, watching the sunscreen dick wilt and smear. They paddle the board forward against the waves, and Remy gets tired immediately. He's sure Horus can tell how out of shape he is. Horus keeps glancing back at him and Remy doesn't look back to see how far they are from shore.

The waves are massive.

Each one lifts Remy's board and pushes it like air catching a parachute, threatening to flip him backwards and trap him beneath.

Remy describes this scenario to Horus, working to be heard over the waves. Horus laughs and says, "Then just flip it over, dude. It won't sink, I promise." Then he slaps his forehead and says, "I guess I should have told you how to go over the waves. Sorry man, I kind of forgot."

He demonstrates how to lean against the waves at an angle, but Remy doesn't find it helpful. It's clear that it helps to be tall and strong. "Yeah, sometimes it doesn't work that well," says Horus.

"Are we far enough out?"

"We need to get to where all those people are."

"It seems a little crowded. Isn't that dangerous?" Horus looks back and takes the front of Remy's board. He tells Remy to stop paddling. "Relax. I'll take you out."

"I can paddle."

"Just relax."

"I'm not one of your nine-year-olds. I can paddle myself."

"And then what happens when you fall off your board and can't swim because your arms are all cramped up? Who do you think gets sued when you drown?"

Remy stops paddling.

Alicia asks Carla how she knows Jen, and Carla tells her *same as Remy we met at Belasco's* but doesn't continue the conversation. Alicia feels self-conscious with so much of her body exposed, especially the sun-and-moon tattoo on her back. Over time, it's come to irritate her with its smack-dabness, advertising to everyone who sees it that she got it at a mall when she turned eighteen. Her swimsuit, with its dryer-rippled elastic and faded color, looks like it starved to death in her underwear drawer.

She can see Jen in a different section of the water than Remy, who looks tense even from so far away. Jen's orange swimsuit—a bright slash in the water—is a difficult style, between a bikini and one-piece—the kind that bridges the top and bottom with a bandage-like connector.

Alicia has tried on swimsuits like this before. Normally, they don't work for people who aren't incredibly skinny, since the material's trajectory requires flat hip bones. But when Jen was walking around without a towel on, she didn't seem to know this. The unruly way that her boobs bulged out the sides made the *swimsuit* look inadequate instead of her body.

Alicia sees Jen slanting her board into every wave, floating easily over even the tall ones. Occasionally she makes large socializing gestures to other people on the water, as if she's on a stage.

"Damn, that's a big one," says Carla, pointing with her vape at a wave that's headed towards Jen.

The wave rolls in an intelligent way, like an alien moving beneath the skin in *Aliens*. It gets closer to Jen, and Jen, crazily, prostrates herself beneath it. She positions herself with unhurried strokes so casual that they don't even seem to propel her. When the wave meets her, she stands up in the whitest, meanest section and steers around everyone who didn't catch it in time. Teenage boys zip up the waves, levitating comically before they hit the water, but Jen is deliberate. She keeps her board in place and walks forward on it, then back, then forward, then to the side, as if approaching an animal that deserves caution but needs to see dominance. Her whole way to shore, Alicia imagines something jumping out of the water to bite her in half.

Carla claps, vape flopping in her mouth, and says *Yeah Jen,* although no one but Alicia can hear her.

When the wave gives out, Jen drops down and sits astride the board again, turning around and paddling back without even stopping to pick out a wedgie. Alicia says, "Am I crazy? She's doing it different than everyone else, right?"

"She's cross-stepping. Horus thinks anything on a longboard is lame, but if you can do it well, it looks good."

"It looks *so* good."

Remy sees the same waves that Horus sees, but their merits or disadvantages aren't apparent to him. Each wave is an ordeal, many of them sloshing into his face and filling his nostrils with salt water. Horus doesn't seem to notice a difference between the water and the air, inhabiting each with equal pleasure. He keeps submerging himself and throwing back his hair. It must hurt his face to smile so much. Remy realizes that Horus reminds him of Donny Osmond.

After dismissing ten or so waves, Horus says, "This one." He turns Remy's board around, insanely presenting Remy's *back* to the wave, and his motions are urgent, almost alarmed. "Paddlepaddlepaddle!" he says. "Harder, harder! Up now now now!"

Remy doesn't remember anything specific that he was taught on shore. He stands up, the board scoots from under him, and Remy is thrown into the water like soap off a dish. He inhales instinctively, filling his mouth and lungs. It's an ancient sensation that he associates with swimming lessons. When he surfaces, he feels five years old.

"Great effort!" says Horus. "Next time, remember: right foot, left foot, stand."

"I know, I know." He holds up his arms just in time to keep a wave from tipping the board over him.

"Right foot, left foot, up."

Remy doesn't answer him. He knows how to stand. He just forgot. Remy does worse the second time, and doesn't improve after that. He barely stands up, once, but falls off immediately.

Occasionally, through the sea of bodies, Remy can see Jen. She's wearing a swimsuit that he's seen in her posts before but never in real life. The eerie appearance of the swimsuit, combined with so much fear, is what makes him feel like he's in a nightmare.

On her first try, Alicia stands up on the surfboard and teeters almost the whole way to shore. She falls a few times after that, but catches almost half of her waves, her grin massive and visible at a distance each time she manages to scoot her way near the beach.

Later, when they're back in the van, Alicia isn't shy anymore. She tells Horus, "I felt completely in the moment!" "I didn't catch your name," she says to everyone in the van who hasn't talked to her yet. The guy who looks like he's chewing gum is named Joe. The couple is Daniela and Kiki. Joe's girlfriend is Sage. Rudy is the one with a tin of pomade that he's applying to his hair. Alicia stops sucking in.

"You're going to be a real surfer girl now," says Daniela. Jen turns around in her seat and asks if anyone wants a Hot Cheeto, rattling the bag at them. "Sage? Joe? Surfer girl?" She talks while chewing, and tells Alicia that she's *honestly such a natural.*

When Carla complains that she needs a Diet Coke or she's going to die, Alicia says, "Just hang loose!" and this joke goes over far better than it deserves to, in Remy's opinion. Remy, despite its logistical impossibility, believes that at some point everyone must have smoked weed without him noticing. He doesn't understand the voluptuous feeling in the van.

Horus asks if anyone is "up for wangs tonight," evidently referencing some shared experience in the past, and Alicia laughs even though this comment doesn't include her. Remy hopes that by pronouncing *wings* this way they're being either classist or racist and he can feel superior.

He texts Alicia: You're using your fake voice again

But Alicia doesn't check her phone. Carla is cradling Alicia's palm, complimenting her long life line. Alicia is totally still, as if trying not to disturb a butterfly.

At Horus's suggestion, they all go to dinner at an expensive pizza restaurant with outdoor dining. Remy and Alicia are seated with Carla on the farthest end of a long picnic table that deadens either end by consolidating the conversation in the middle.

Alicia, straining to be part of the central conversation, shouts, "Fuck Donald Sutherland, *marry* young Kiefer Sutherland, kill current Kiefer Sutherland!"

Remy tries to start a conversation with Carla, but her eyes move between her phone and Rudy, who monopolizes her limited attention with Sag Harbor whaling history.

"Oh my God!" Carla leaves her seat to show Jen and Horus something funny on her phone. When Jen gets up to go to the bathroom, Carla touches the table in front of Jen's seat, gradually taking her place next to Horus.

Jen returns from the bathroom and Carla looks up at her with large eyes. "Sorry I took your seat, Jen!"

"It's okay."

"I'll get up now."

She hesitates for an informative moment. Jen says, "It's okay, I'll go sit over here by Remy."

"Jen, no I swear! Look I'm getting up!"

"It's *really* fine. I want to."

Jen sits in Carla's old spot, across from him. Remy looks up from his phone. It's the first opportunity he's had since the Apple Store to study her at close range. He notices the tired hair elastic that disappears into her bun, and how three separate tan lines on her shoulders allude to three different swimsuits. "What were you looking at so seriously?" she says.

Remy says, too aggressively, "I don't know if I should lie to you or not."

"Are you liking my pictures again?"

Alicia's head flicks around and then flicks back before she can be accused of staring.

Remy turns his phone around and shows Jen that he's reading the Yelp reviews of the restaurant. He says he can't believe people like this place so much. He reads aloud a review that raves about the bacon ranch slice. The review calls the restaurant "authentic."

"Jen, what's authentic about a chicken bacon ranch slice? In what small Italian village did the classic *pizza with ranch dressing* originate?"

"Why are you talking like that?"

"Aren't these Hamptons people weird?" says Remy, indicating different groups of people with his eyes. Jen pretends to be stretching her back in order to turn around and observe the same people.

When she turns around, Remy asks her if she saw the birthday party in the corner. "That kid was wearing a suit. I've never seen a thirteen-year-old in a suit that actually *fits*. It's fucking creepy."

"You hate kids so much! I knew it! You're still the same."

Remy disputes this. He tells Jen that he's changed a lot in the past "however long," referring to the two years and seven months. "I know I could be kind of goofy back then," he says.

"How much can you have really changed? Aren't you, like, over thirty by now? And still working in service?"

Remy stares at her, controlling his face, but it doesn't matter because Kiki gets Jen's attention at this point, asking a question about someone that Remy doesn't know. Remy says, "I thought real jobs were fascist," but no one hears him.

It's possible that Jen registers how hurtful her comment was, because she turns her attention back to him and tells him something boring about an old coworker.

At the table next to them a woman says, "Connor! Bryce! Aidan! Sit down. You're giving me a headache!"

Remy and Jen smile at each other about this *unbelievable* succession of names. "Can't wait for Aidan to grow up and foreclose on my house," he says, in a low voice.

"*What* house?" says Jen. "The one you buy after your fortieth year as a server?" She laughs. After a pause, Remy laughs too.

Horus, several seats away from them, says something about the unconscionable use of extrajudicial drone strikes.

"This restaurant should get an extrajudicial drone strike," says Remy to Jen. Jen spits her soda back into her glass.

"What's so funny?" says Horus.

"Nothing," says Jen. "Just...drone strikes. I mean, obviously they're not funny. I'll tell you later." Everyone stares at Jen.

Jen stirs her soda with a straw and says in a whisper, "I will absolutely *not* be telling him later. Can you imagine?"

Later that night, Alicia touches Remy's arm on her way to the bathroom. Everyone else has already gone outside. She's holding a glass of pinot and the strange pleasure of carrying around a glass of wine, in her swimsuit, has made her smile all evening. She can't believe that before this trip, the closest thing she had to a social life was the prospect of helping Cassie move.

"Come outside," she says. "I think people are getting in the hot tub."

"*You* seem to be having a great time," says Remy.

"Do you want me to be miserable?"

Remy complains about how Jen and Horus got the master bedroom, and the other guest rooms are claimed. "It just seems kind of fake to me that Jen and Horus are…they have this whole generous *love and sharing and equality* vibe, but we're the ones stuck on the floor, you know?"

"Joe and Sage said that they'd trade with us at some point."

"I don't know why you like these people so much. They're so fake. Everything here is fake. Look at that." Remy points through the sliding doors, at the tasteful waterfall that feeds into the swimming pool, lit from below and beautiful in excess of any waterfall found in nature. He touches a wicker sun hat propped on the corner of the hall mirror. "Does anyone even wear this hat? Is this hat functional or is it just decorative?"

"It looks decorative to me. It's too small to wear."

"It's frickin' weird is what it is. There's some kind of…*farm* implement on the wall in the kitchen. I feel like I'm at a TGI Fridays."

"I kind of like it."

He tells her that even Jen is being fake. "For a second at dinner she was being herself again, and then when Horus asked her what she was laughing about, she got weird."

"Maybe she's different than she used to be, but that doesn't mean she's being fake."

The bathroom door opens and Rudy steps out. Alicia looks at the open bathroom, with its limitless white towels that Juana launders every week, and a child's drawing of a dolphin hung on the wall (*Horus, age seven*). "The self is mutable, you know?"

"Very true!" says Rudy, raising a glass at them.

Once Rudy has left, Alicia says, "People change all the time…Maybe Jen's trying to be her better self. I'd like to be *my* better self."

"'The self is mutable'? These people are brainwashing you already. Remind me never to let you out of the house ever again."

"Excuse me, I have to pee."

"She can't be that much better if she's being so rude to me."

"I thought you *liked* it when she was mean to you," says Alicia.

"It's different now."

"Because she has a boyfriend?"

Remy waits for Alicia to apologize, but she doesn't. She shuts the bathroom door.

Carla comes inside to make herself a complex mixture of alcohols, and Remy follows her into the kitchen, watching her work.

"It's better for my figure than beer," says Carla, without looking at him.

"Make me one too."

Carla gets a second glass from the kitchen cabinet. "Are you coming outside?"

"I don't feel like interacting with... everyone right now." Just as he says this, Daniela's laugh is audible through the screen door. It's slow, annoying, and accented, like a fortune-telling machine.

Remy asks leading questions about everyone on the trip, taking pleasure in Carla's blatant dislike for most of them. "I'm sure she's very nice," she says about Sage. "Her work is supposed to be amazing, but realistically, how brilliant could it be? Everyone's a photographer now. I bet this 'amazing work' is black-and-white pictures of birds on a telephone wire or some shit."

"Jen has kind of changed, hasn't she?" says Remy.

Carla laughs in a silent way that involves blowing vape smoke from her nostrils. "She hasn't changed at all. Don't get me wrong, though, I love her *forever*."

"You seem to be a big fan of Horus."

"He's a very calming presence. I'm naturally drawn to water signs."

"Isn't he kind of lame though? The whole *I'm so chill* thing is overbearing."

"You wish, Remy. What sucks for you is that he's such a *prince* of a man. It would be a lot easier if Jen were dating some asshole."

Remy laughs because this is the least guilty reaction. He says something noncommittal.

"It would be a lot easier for Jen, too," says Carla.

"What does that mean?"

Carla deflects several times, although it's clear that she wants to talk shit. Eventually she says, looking around to make sure no one has come in from outside, "You know how there's a type of guy who won't date women who are too funny because it makes them insecure?"

She goes on a tangent about how unfairly she's been treated in *her* dating life lately, due to her comic genius and unmatched insight into the human psyche, before making her way back to her point. "I think, similarly, some women get threatened when they're dating men who are too virtuous. Because culturally, women are supposed to be the vessels of virtue, you know? Jen doesn't always enjoy feeling like she's less than perfect."

"Whereas you're happy to be petty."

"I think she feels judged by Horus. It leads her to do weird things. Like invite her creepy former coworker on a surfing trip. With his girlfriend who she doesn't know at all." When Carla sees his face, she says, "I'm sort of joking. But you are a complete freak, Remy." She tells Remy not to take her too seriously. "It's just my opinion. Which is, you know, correct."

"Jen told you this?"

"Actually what she *said* would interest you. She said that if it weren't for what's-her-name—"

"Alicia?"

"I guess she didn't really *say* anything. She implied that she'd be down... if it weren't for your separate situations. And maybe she'd also like to teach Horus a lesson."

"A lesson for what?"

Carla assesses his reaction, and remarks that it seems as if Remy would be down too. “Interesting,” she says, without investment.

Remy tries to get Carla to be more specific, but she returns to her grievances about online dating, a subject that bears more directly on her own life.

Alicia doesn’t participate in the conversation in the hot tub unless she’s directly addressed. Eventually, Daniela turns her head and asks Alicia what she does, maybe because Alicia has been staring at her open affection with Kiki. Her answer receives more attention because she delivers it during a silence in the conversation.

“A sandwich shop?” says Daniela. “So you must be an artist, right? Like Jen and Sage?”

Jen looks in Alicia’s direction.

“Kind of. Not exactly like Jen, probably.”

“It’s awful,” says Jen. “Daniela’s never had a job that wasn’t in an office. She can’t understand our struggles.”

“You’re going to be *fine,* Jen,” says Horus.

The conversation diverts to discussion of Jen’s jewelry website. Jen complains about how difficult it is to run a business, and how she can’t wait to quit service forever.

Horus says, “At least you had help with the startup costs, though.” There’s a brief silence, and then he says, “Alicia, what kind of art do you make?”

“Um.” Alicia makes the not-exactly-swimming arm movements that people feel compelled to make in hot tubs. “I’m just working on this idea I had recently. It’s very early stages. I had this idea for a kind of... personalized relaxation module. Sort of like a hot tub, actually, but enclosed.”

Envisioning it as a hot tub had never occurred to her before this moment. Her face becomes suddenly blank with the perfection of this concept. It’s so perfect, it’s as if the universe dropped it into her head. Or as if meeting Jen that day in the Apple Store was the first of many signs intending to lead her to this moment in the hot tub, and thus to this inspiration.

"Like a sensory deprivation chamber?"

"Maybe. Not really. I just want to create a private space that meets all my needs. I thought I could even put shelves inside." She checks people's expressions and then looks back down into the water. "That sounds dumb."

Kiki says, "No, that's perfect. I get it. Like a commentary on our culture of instant gratification. A satisfaction chamber."

"Yeah!" says Alicia. "I mean. It's probably selfish of me, because I'm just building it based on what *I* would want. I have trouble relaxing or being in the moment, and I'm just trying to create this intimate space for myself."

"But that's part of the process," says Jen. "You just have to make a prototype and see what happens." Jen's face is flushed and generous. She understands. "And water in *particular* is so conducive to forces larger than ourselves."

"A prototype sounds great," says Alicia. "I was thinking of it as—like a spa, but in the form of a personal pod. A…'Spod.' Is that lame?" Someone laughs. She says, "I barely know anything about water treatment or plumbing. But I'm trying to learn. Have you seen *Collateral*? At the beginning, Jamie Foxx wants to create this tropical-themed limousine service. And we were watching it and I was like, *I* can't afford to go on vacation, and sometimes *I* just want my own little paradise." Alicia continues talking and hears herself describing a process of ongoing work and planning that's completely dishonest.

Horus says, "So you're like an autodidact? That's so inspiring. Are you learning how to hook up a filtration system? It must just be consuming your life, right? I can see it right now." Horus makes a frame with his hands, like a director. "Laboring away in your studio. Struggling with salination levels."

"…I'm not sure I would use salt water," she says.

Horus goes on to describe an interesting, dedicated person who in no way resembles Alicia. Alicia's face hurts from smiling. She can hear the ocean. The air doesn't smell of exhaust, the way it does in the city.

She looks through the sliding doors and sees Remy. He sits on the couch, beer in hand, staring into his phone as if something fell into it.

Remy wakes up in the middle of the night. He looks at Alicia's borrowed sleeping bag next to him and sees, thankfully, that Alicia is asleep. The light from the illuminated pool plays across the ceiling. He sits up and sees a figure watching television in the screened-in porch.

Remy goes to the bathroom, comes back, and looks at the figure. It's definitely Jen. Her head turns when he opens the fridge door, flooding the kitchen with light. He gets a beer.

He observes that Jen's head has turned back around, but opens the sliding doors and takes two steps down into the sunken porch, shutting the door behind him. It's the only messy place in the house—fishing tackle scattered in a mix of decorative and undecorative sprawl. Jen holds a glass with ice cubes up to her mouth.

"Are you crying?" says Remy.

Jen wipes her cheek. She gives him a wet, disciplinary look.

"Trouble in paradise?"

"God, Remy, you're such a tool."

They're quiet as they watch the preview for the next show. Jen says, "There's no story here. I'm just suffering from a general *malaise.*"

Remy doesn't say anything.

"Do you want to talk about something to distract me?"

"Uh."

"Anything, seriously. Tell me how you and Alicia met. That's gotta be a freaky story."

Remy tells her a version of the story that flatters himself and his motives. He adjusts the timeline between Greta and Alicia. "Wow," she says.

"Tell me how you and Horus met." Jen turns her face towards him fully, so that no part of her expression is lit by the television. It's a dark, blank oval.

"At this hostel in Croatia." The ice cubes in her glass clink. "I could just tell he was a really sensitive soul."

"Meaning?"

"I don't really want to say." He can hear from her voice that she's smiling.

Jen keeps refusing to elaborate, forcing Remy to beg.

"We—at least the Americans—were having an argument about this article we all read. It was about this guy who was in a sexual relationship with a horse. And everyone was being *really* judgmental."

Remy confirms that her objection is to the people who judged *the man* for having sex with a horse. "That's bonkers, Jen."

"If you read it you'd know what I mean! It was so heartbreaking and beautiful and he had so much respect for this mare—like, more respect, honestly, than I've experienced from a lot of men."

"Jen. A horse can't consent to having sex!"

"You can't anthropomorphize animal sex that way!" Jen registers the volume of the comment, and lowers her voice. "It's not like horses ask *each other* for consent."

"How do you know?" says Remy. "What if they communicate in some special horse language that people don't understand?"

"We don't ask animals for consent before we slaughter them for food, or inject them with sperm, or make their skin into leather!"

"So does *that* mean it's okay?"

"According to this article, there are ways you can tell if a horse is aroused." Jen angles her face towards the television, and Remy can see her expression again. This is an argument, but both of them are smiling.

"Like what?" says Remy.

Jen finds the article on her phone and reads aloud while Remy exaggerates his repelled reactions. He asks her several times to stop, and she refuses. There's a classic feeling to this interaction, and Remy wishes that Alicia were here so that he could offer this scenario up as evidence of Jen's teasing manner with him, of the way that things used to be. He *didn't* imagine it.

"Good to see the old Jen is still there."

She ignores him and reads aloud a graphic section about equine clitorises. "Is this getting you excited?" she says.

"I swear, I'm going to leave."

"Really, Remy? You've never wanted some *strong* lady to pin you against a barn door?"

"Stop making fun of me."

"I'm just teasing you! Would you rather I not tease you at all?"

He likes this a lot. He wants to say so, but doesn't know how.

Jen finishes her drink and says that she's going back to bed. He delays her for a while with questions about the restaurant where she's working, but she stands up and expresses annoyance with him when this goes on for too long.

"Thank you though, Remy. That was at least a very *distracting* conversation." She hugs him at light speed, the back of her wrist touching his shoulder inadequately, and leaves the porch.

Remy's performance anxiety is exacerbated early the next day, when Horus drafts him into making fried eggs. He breaks several yolks and says "Not my best work" as he puts the eggs on the plates. He blames his mistakes on the unfamiliar skillet, saying loudly that nonstick skillets give you cancer. Everyone he gives an egg to, he threatens with cancer.

Kiki says, "The egg is great, Remy!" and he says, with a viciousness he didn't realize he felt, "Don't *patronize* me."

Remy notices Joe and Sage exchanging glances. It startles him to think that other couples might share the same intimacy he has with Alicia, and he's suddenly aware of how exposed he is to their judgment.

The second day of surfing doesn't go any better. Whenever he stands up on the surfboard, his brain reminds him that he's being chased by unstoppable forces of nature, and he wants to use the board's surface to run away. He doesn't mind the moment when the wave catches him, sloppily, and he can fall off. The worst part is right before. He hates the infinitesimal silence that precedes the sound of the wave breaking—the moment when the board dips and he knows the wave is sucking up the surrounding water, darkening and fattening behind him.

He gives up quickly after further humiliation and sits on the beach with the cooler and a paperback from Horus's beach house, unable to locate Alicia in the water.

* * *

Carla and Jen take a break at the same time and sit next to Remy on their towels, telling him what a pity it is that he's given up already. It feels important to him, considering all his other failures during the day, to at least succeed in holding their attention long enough that Horus notices.

"You know, *you* should really read *The Apple Bush,*" says Jen.

"You're obsessed. Apples don't even grow on bushes. They grow on trees."

"If you read the book, you would know that's the point!"

Carla says, "It's about seeing the potential of yourself and everyone around you. There's all this invisible energy flowing around us all the time. What we don't realize is that all these little details—words we overhear or images we see in our dreams—are Signifiers of this universal flow of energy. If you learn to recognize these Signifiers of Flow, then you can channel your potential for transformation."

"You can laugh if you want, but that shit is *real,*" says Jen. She's smiling.

"It just sounds like 'manifesting success,'" says Remy.

"Manifesting is real too!" She sits up and lowers her sunglasses. "Energy speaks. It lets the universe know it can communicate with you. And then your greatest desires are possible. That's how you reach your Consummate Result—the ultimate version of yourself."

"I can't tell if you're joking or not."

"I'm not! When Jim Carrey wanted to be successful, he wrote himself a ten-million-dollar check and gave himself three years to cash it. And within three years, he made his first big break and got paid ten million dollars for a movie."

"Yeah, but he's still Jim Carrey. If that's his best self, then that's gotta suck."

Carla interrupts to say that Jen is mischaracterizing the point—it's not just about personal success. "That's how they sell books, but I think it's more valuable to think about recognizing all the possibilities around you and not getting hung up on self-doubt. It's like meditation—it's about the process, not the goal."

"It's not about personal gain for you? That's surprising," says Remy. Carla ignores him.

Jen contradicts Carla, and Remy perceives that they've argued about this before. "But the book talks about following all the signs towards your Consummate Result, so obviously the point is to reach your potential. Personally, I don't think there's anything wrong with striving to be your best self."

"I'm sorry. I forgot I was speaking to a *female entrepreneur,*" says Carla. She slants her eyes at Remy, trying to involve him in her disdain.

"The point is," says Jen, shading her face so she can make better eye contact with Remy, "that you have to be willing to accept the Signifiers directing you towards your destiny. And you have to abandon the mindset that you, Remy, are so married to—that paranoid, the-world-is-out-to-get-me-and-failure-is-inevitable mindset. The truth is that the universe *conspires* to bless us."

"Just in general, Jen, I would imagine the universe conspires to bless you a lot more if you're hot and your boyfriend is loaded."

Carla laughs. Jen doesn't, but she doesn't exhibit anger. "You can attack me for being lucky and beautiful, Remy, or you can decide that maybe that's how I've allowed the love of the universe to express itself in my life."

"I still can't tell if you're joking or not," says Remy, because Jen is smiling again. The longer she observes Remy's face, the more wicked she looks.

Carla says that Jen has a point. "You have to concentrate on what you have, not what you don't. Of course there are obstacles to realizing our desires, but those obstacles—A. B. Fisketjon calls them Toxic Antagonists—are almost always self-generated."

Remy watches Jen while Carla speaks. "That implies that there are other Toxic Antagonists that aren't self-generated."

"Yes, of course."

"So this author is admitting that sometimes there are real obstacles to achieving your destiny. Maybe material obstacles. Maybe if you don't have money or connections, then this book isn't going to help you."

Carla says he's misunderstanding. "That's not what she's talking about. In her Author's Note, she explains that non-self-generated Toxic Antagonists are too controversial and specialized to talk about. Her publishers wouldn't let her."

"I'm sure," says Remy.

Carla complains about the heat and walks down to the water to put her feet in. While she's gone, Remy says, "You and Carla are nuts." This Jen is unlike the Jen he spoke to the night before, and he wonders if this is intentional.

Jen puts her hand on his arm and taps it in time to her emphasis. "I see how you're looking at me. But cynical, *quote-unquote smart people* always underestimate the power of something as simple as a positive mindset and openness to the world. Lots of good things have come my way because of it."

Jen says she's serious, but smiles in a way that implies she might not be. She leaves him shortly after, and Remy sees her briefly tangled in an embrace with Horus on his way to the water. He gives her a kiss that distorts her mouth, as if he doesn't know his own strength.

Horus and Joe make paella for lunch, Horus lecturing Remy about how much he's missing by spending so much time on the beach and not enough in the water. "I *get* that it's not for everyone," he says, "but when I saw you out there, it looked like you gave up. You had a wave for a second, but then you just went limp."

The TV is playing *South Park* and Remy pretends to watch it. When Horus doesn't get a reaction, he keeps repeating himself, louder.

"Leave him alone about being limp," says Jen.

"I *said* that I understand it's not for everyone."

"*Do* you understand?"

"Is it a crime for me to want someone to succeed?"

"I really do appreciate all the time you've spent teaching us," says Alicia. She looks sunburned and she's wearing a light sweater that Remy doesn't recognize—it must have been borrowed.

Horus holds forth about the primal satisfactions of surfing and its ability to transcend language. Jen asks him pointed questions about the status of the paella, either to assert how hungry she is or to change the subject. Horus doesn't hear her. "I first learned in Malaysia from a one-armed man who didn't speak any English! That's how powerful it is."

"Is it important that he was missing an arm?" Remy says. "Or did you just include that detail to make him sound more exotic?" Even Joe, who is Horus's closest friend, smiles.

Horus doesn't seem to notice any laughter at his expense. "I think a shark bit it off. But I'll actually never know because we never spoke to each other."

"Was he...aware that he was teaching you how to surf?"

"I didn't pay him anything if that's what you mean. We had a connection out on the water and after that he created space for me to watch him. I would go to the beach every day and try to imitate him. At a respectful distance, obviously."

"Sounds like you might have been exploiting him."

"I never thought about it like that!" says Horus, generously. Horus keeps making the paella and Jen and Remy look at each other. Jen rolls her eyes for him alone.

The group splits up in the afternoon between those who want to keep surfing and those who want to nap or watch TV. Alicia surprises herself by going to the beach without Remy.

She has no opinion about any of the subjects mentioned in the van on the way there, but tries very hard to contribute. She knows that she *would* have an opinion about these things if she were able to relax properly, or if she didn't have brain damage. She smiles while they discuss the retrospective of a painter who sounds familiar, confident at least in the knowledge that in some other iteration of herself, or in different circumstances, she might have an opinion. The conversation moves to a story about doing coke in Berlin. Alicia inhales, exhales, and then interjects to say that she's only done coke once. She had hoped that by saying it with enough force, this factoid might become interesting.

"Hmm," says Rudy, kindly.

"But, I'll be honest, I really had to—it wasn't good because—I had to, like—" Alicia remembers Horus's declaration about having to shit in the first moments after they met, and gathers courage: "—I had to, like, *run to the bathroom* after. It seems like generally they cut that stuff with laxatives."

"Oh honey," says Jen, twisting her torso and almost, but not quite, touching Alicia. "Maybe they cut the coke *you* did with laxatives. I'll have to take you out sometime. I know how it sounds, but I don't think you've *really* done coke unless you've had the good stuff."

Carla accuses Jen of being a snob, but Alicia is hardly listening. Jen's invitation, real or not, suffuses her body. Could it be real and not a joke? Could she, maybe, "go out" with Jen sometime?

Rudy exhales smoke from one of his fancy cigarettes and says to Jen, "Did I tell you that my stepmother just bought a *gorgeous* George Condo?"

"I don't know that *gorgeous* is the right adjective for a Condo."

"Ooh, where is it?" says Alicia.

"What?" says Rudy. It becomes clear they aren't talking about a condominium. The conversation turns to whether or not it's nice to have artwork in the house (Rudy says, "I think a *few* pieces can be nice"), and Alicia is once again at a loss.

Whenever Alicia catches a wave, she looks up afterwards to see if Jen saw it. When Jen catches her looking for this approval, Alicia is careful not to look at her again.

She and Carla end up close to the shore around the same time, and Carla paddles next to her, complaining about her own skills in order to extract reassurance.

The waves are smaller in this section, and they look crispy and different in the afternoon light. It astonishes Alicia that at this very moment, she is here and not at the Hungry Goat. It's difficult for her to believe that the stuffy sandwich shop, with its perpetually wet kitchen tiles and rank cooking odors, can continue existing at the same time as a place like this.

Carla says, "God I'm exhausted. I just want to catch my breath." She adjusts her swimsuit to show more of her ass, not less. "Hang out with me for a second."

Alicia has often noticed that even strangers adopt a commanding tone around her, sensing that this is a mode she responds to. Carla puts her face on the board and closes her eyes. She says a few inane things about the weather and the discomfort of her swimsuit, yawning. Then she says, "So how did you and Remy meet?"

Alicia lies on her board, in the same position as Carla. "He was dating my roommate."

Carla opens her eyes again. "No shit."

"I guess that's an overshare. Sorry. Sorry."

"I *asked.*"

"I didn't know her well. It wasn't a good relationship. But then we hooked up while she was at work, and she found out. And then she didn't want to live with me anymore, so she left and Remy moved in."

"How does that just *happen?*"

"We... watched a lot of movies together when she was out of the house. I don't know. She worked a lot." Alicia laughs. "I had just moved here, so I didn't know anybody. She was driving us both crazy. She had really bad foot fungus. It was disgusting."

"Aw. That's sad."

"No! You don't understand. She wouldn't go to a doctor. I can't even—she was really annoying." Alicia considers whether to say how she really feels: *She deserved it.*

"Relax. I'm not judging you. I'm just interested."

"She was one of those people who thinks that the answer to every problem is apple cider vinegar."

"I always wonder about relationships like that."

"How do you mean?"

"Where the reason you're together is because one of you cheated." Carla holds up her hand, propping her elbow on her surfboard. "Again, I'm not judging you. But can you ever trust that person?"

Alicia doesn't say anything.

"For example, Remy used to have a huge crush on Jen. He still acts like a total *goon* around her. You must have a really strong relationship if you're fine with it."

Alicia puts her hand in the water and says, "Remy likes to say we have a mystical connection."

"I will say, the energy between you two is insane."

"Really? Like good or bad?"

Alicia wants to hear more, but Carla has already moved on. She laments her inability to sense good energy in her own romantic life and complains about a guy who machine-washed one of her cashmere sweaters. She doesn't return to the topic again.

Alicia finds Remy while everyone else is making dinner. He's sitting with his feet in the pool, staring at nothing and holding a hand of cards left over from a game with Kiki and Daniela.

"You hate cards," says Alicia.

"It's better than surfing."

She considers pointing out that he's sent her fewer texts than the first day, but anticipates that this will make him defensive.

"I feel so relaxed," she says. She tells him how Horus told her that there are "all these studies" about the therapeutic effects of surfing.

"Horus is driving me crazy. I swear, I want to peel off his face and wear it." He does an impression of Horus saying *paddle paddle paddle*.

"I know it sounds corny. But everything I'm feeling is so urgent! I wish you could understand. I feel like I need to tell you all about it, but I can't explain."

"I suck at surfing."

"You'll get the hang of it soon!"

"So you agree that I suck?" Alicia doesn't engage. Remy examines his cards. Alicia talks about a long conversation she had with Jen about the travails of being an artist.

"She's being so sweet to me. I don't know what you mean about her being a bitch."

"That's because she's got all this crazy New-Agey shit going on." He tells her about the conversation they had on the beach earlier. "She said I need to be more open to the world and a bunch of other shit...which is extremely not like her. I would just like to point out that we're *still* sleeping on the floor. Despite the fact that she suggested a trade at some point."

"That's not Jen's fault."

Remy looks at his hand of cards, again, pointlessly. "Carla told me that *Jen* said she's still attracted to me. Did I tell you that we hung out last night after everyone went to bed?"

Alicia doesn't say anything.

Remy laughs and says, "How fucked up would it be if I broke up with you in the middle of this trip?"

Alicia looks at him and drinks from a water bottle. "Pretty fucked up."

After dinner, Horus hooks up a karaoke machine in the living room. "I'm not embarrassed to start," he says. He sings "Toxic" by Britney Spears, sober, with a sincerity instantly available and startling. In order to get on his level, everyone drinks a lot very quickly.

Alicia sings the song about being a bitch and a lover, a child and a mother. At one point she sees the tag sticking out of Jen's caftan and tells herself *not* to tuck it back in.

She tucks it back in.

Jen jerks away. "Your tag was sticking out." Alicia stands there, weirdly. She doesn't know what she's waiting for.

Jen sings "Material Girl," and when she finishes, she sits down in the only open spot, between Alicia and Carla. Her leg touches Alicia's. Carla says that she *killed* it.

"It's crazy," says Alicia, "because you're such a material girl!"

"What do you mean?"

"I mean, because you're right here in front of me! You're completely real!"

"That's so weird of you to say," says Jen, but her face is pleasant. Sage sings a song with a wide, loud range that's tough to listen to, and Carla suggests that they go outside for a smoke.

"Me too?" says Alicia.

When they're outside smoking, Alicia holds the cigarette awkwardly, as if it were a crayon.

"Don't Remy and Alicia have such intense energy?" says Carla. "The two of them together are like some kind of *crazy* magnetic field. Like some haunted portal."

Jen steps close to Alicia to light the cigarette. Alicia looks involuntarily at the part of her midsection visible through the caftan's oversized armhole. Jen's sunbaked body smells as good as a carb.

Carla looks at Alicia and says, "You probably had a really fucked-up childhood, right? I have a good feel for these things."

Jen pushes Carla and tells her to stop.

"I don't mind!" says Alicia. "It's nice to be looked at. To be perceived."

Carla says, "I don't want to brag, but I kind of have *the Sight*. I can tell what people were like in their past lives and stuff. It's always been in my family, on my mother's side."

"Who was I in my past life?" says Jen. Carla ignores her.

"I feel like you and Remy might have been together in a past life," says Carla to Alicia. "That's what the *energy* is like."

"I feel the same way!" says Alicia.

"I think you two were, like, traveling magicians around the turn of the century. Remy was the magician and you were the girl he sawed in half. Or tied up in a water tank."

"The assistant!"

"Don't take Carla too seriously," says Jen. "She's just thinking about that movie with Christian Bale."

Alicia stands there, listening to them argue, like a regular girl smoking a regular cigarette, listening to a regular (if inane) conversation with her regular, hot girlfriends. If someone were to take a picture, no one would think any different.

Later in the night, Carla plays a game in which she psychologically profiles Sage and Jen and Joe by looking through their wallets. She reiterates her claim about having the Sight.

"A wallet is one of the most intimate objects a person can possess. Besides containing the objects that define a person's identity, it also absorbs all their energy."

She goes through Sage's wallet first and claims that her lack of receipts demonstrates her willingness to "live on the fly." She counts out Jen's library cards from five different cities. Remy refuses to hand over his wallet, but Alicia gives Carla hers. It's fat with receipts. There are also business cards for eyelash extensions, and little cards with codes for credit on rideshare apps.

"This wallet belongs to someone who can't resist taking a flyer," says Carla. "Either that or she is really interested in eyelash extensions. My instincts," says Carla, looking at Alicia and her unremarkable eyelashes, "tell me that she has an idealistic, even unrealistic, view of the future."

"Oh my God, that is so true!" says Alicia. "It's, like, *such* a problem."

"Alicia," says Remy.

"What's this?" says Carla. She holds up a tiny, folded piece of paper that has attained lint-like hardness. She unfolds it. There's a name and number on it.

Alicia leans back on the heels of her hands and explains that it was a therapist her parents tried to make her see. "It makes them feel like they're looking out for me so that if I'm hospitalized again they can at least say that they tried."

There's silence that Alicia tries to make less uncomfortable by laughing. It's not the kind of laughter that puts people at ease.

"Why were you hospitalized?" says Jen.

"I was actually"—and here Alicia raises a finger as if bragging—"one of the youngest bulimic patients at the recovery center! In fact, I deprived myself of so many nutrients during my developmental years that my mom thinks my brain was permanently damaged!"

People make apologetic sounds. Sage says that she didn't know you could be hospitalized for bulimia. "Everyone's a *little bit* bulimic. I've never known anyone who was *hospitalized.*"

Alicia's body language is wild and large. "I think they overreacted, totally. The hospital didn't keep me—they just recommended that I go to recovery. But I do still have the videos."

Remy says, "What videos? You didn't tell me about this."

Alicia continues laughing as she talks. The timbre of her laugh has silenced the other conversations on the deck. "When I was little, I used to throw tantrums. And every time I threw a tantrum, they'd film me—I guess that's some kind of child-rearing technique they'd read about. And then afterwards, they'd show me the video so I'd see how 'embarrassing' I looked when I cried. I'm a *really* ugly crier."

"Jesus," says Jen.

"And they kept doing that, off and on, whenever I threw a tantrum. And when I was thirteen, I clogged up the toilet and my mom freaked out. So every day before they sent me off to recovery, they videotaped me so I would see how puffy my face was and how much acne I had."

Alicia scratches her nose.

"Sorry, I know that's . . . heavy or whatever. I think it was coming from a place of love." Alicia laughs. "It was a good call though, because now when I look at the videos, I *do* think I look wrecked!"

Sage says *Woof.*

"I'm sorry! I just feel so close to everyone here. I feel like I can really open up. I feel like you all *accept* me."

"Yeah," says Jen. Then silence.

"I'm sorry. Is that weird? I'm just—you know—trying to be more open to the world."

"Can I get anyone else a drink?" says Jen.

Remy follows Jen into the kitchen. The house is quiet and uncomfortably air-conditioned. Jen sees him and hands him a beer. They stand in front of the kitchen island.

"I'm not in a hurry to go back outside again, if you'll believe it," says Remy.

Jen doesn't react. Remy starts to apologize for Alicia, but Jen tells him not to.

"I have to say something," says Remy. "I feel like—except for last night—we don't interact the way we used to, and it makes me really sad. I've been having a hard time describing it to myself, so I don't know if I can explain it to you."

"Is this really the time?"

"There are always people everywhere. When else would I talk to you? It's like there's a *barrier* there. It bothers me."

"Why? Because I don't shit on people as much anymore?"

Remy checks himself before he physically puts his body between Jen and the door. He says, "You've been giving me endless shit since I got here."

"That's just how I talk to people. You know that."

"When I think back on the time we spent at Belasco's, it's like I can see this picture so clearly. And it feels like it would be really easy to step into the picture. But then it's *not* easy. And everything—" Remy makes a gesture that includes her, the house, the ocean, the world. "It all feels *off.*" Remy says that this didn't come out sounding articulate. "You're *different,*" he says.

Jen imitates this phrase back at him mockingly. "You sound like you came back from a war."

"Well fuck me for trying to be earnest for once."

"Maybe it makes me uncomfortable that you flirt with me in front of your clearly very disturbed girlfriend!"

"I'm not flirting!"

"I'm not saying I *mind* necessarily."

"You don't?"

Jen sits on the island, flicking her eyes at the window and then back to Remy's face. If this were a porno, she would be at the perfect level for sex in the kitchen. "I've always known that despite all your defense mechanisms—all of these emotional walls that you put up—you're really a compassionate person. Maybe I tease you, but that doesn't mean I don't like you. You're clearly very supportive of Alicia, and honestly, it's sweet to see that side of you."

"Okay. But have you *really* seen that side of me?"

"I have excellent intuition. I can see there's kindness in you, even if no one else does."

"Uh. I don't know." Remy is aware as he says this that by doubting her, he's in fact feeding into Jen's narrative of a tough guy with "emotional walls" and allowing her to continue believing that there's something good about him that he can't accept. He says again that she's been nothing but mean to him this whole trip.

Jen says, "But if you were ever really in trouble, or hurt or something, I'd be a really good friend to you."

"I'll keep that in mind."

In the middle of the night, Remy wakes up to a loud sound. He sits up in his sleeping bag. He looks over at the porch, but the television screen is dark.

Knock-knock-knock-knock—and then silence for several beats. And then again: *knock-knock-knock-knock*. The tempo is faster the second time.

He looks next to him and sees that Alicia isn't in her sleeping bag. He gets up and goes to the front door, pulling back the prissy gingham curtain in front of the window. He doesn't see anyone. All of the shadows seem suspicious. He watches the lawn for a moment, but nothing moves.

Knock-knock-knock-knock.

It's impossible to tell where the sound is coming from. Now that he's next to the door, he doesn't think the sound is anywhere close. It seems to be both far away and all around.

He goes to the sliding doors that lead out to the pool. When he looks out, he does so at an angle that makes him invisible to anyone who might be on the deck. He's reminded of the scene in *Godfather II* when Michael Corleone is shot at through his big bedroom window.

The pool is turbulent, as if someone just did a cannonball in the deep end.

Remy pulls back the sliding door and runs outside. He scans the bottom of the pool for Alicia. He doesn't see anything.

Knock-knock-knock-knock.

The sound definitely isn't outside. He sits in the silence. He hopes that when he hears the knocking again, it will be recognizable and mechanical. He'll realize the neighbor's garage door is stuttering on its tread, or an engine is misfiring. But each time he hears it, he can't deny that the knocks are subtly, rhythmically imperfect, as if made by a human hand.

He scans the bushes, looking for movement. And what he sees, briefly, amid the greenery, is something blue-green and iridescent, like a beetle. Wet. Rubber, he thinks, maybe a pool toy—but then it moves. An animal, maybe, except then he sees its face.

Its eyes are impossibly large, and black, without pupils. It stares, one side of its mouth upturned. Remy's first thought, empty of fear, is that it's an art installation. His second thought is that the face seems familiar.

He hears screaming.

Remy runs back inside, towards the sound. Sage has opened her bedroom door. He turns on the hall light and follows the sound down the hallway, to the master bedroom. He doesn't know what he saw, but the scream takes priority in his thoughts, and he shunts the face into the category of things *to be dealt with later.*

The screams are words now, like *What the fuck.* Remy opens the door, turns on the light, and sees Jen grabbing her throat, and Alicia on the floor, holding her head. She's soaking.

"She was choking me!" says Jen. She looks at Alicia. "What the fuck is wrong with you?"

"Let's all calm down," says Horus.

Alicia is unintelligible at first. Then she says, "I sleepwalk sometimes. I didn't know it would happen."

Jen says, "Do you normally sleep-*choke* too??? Do you sneak into strangers' rooms at night and attack them?"

Alicia is crying. "You're not a stranger," she says. Her eyelashes are damp, and unlike Jen, she doesn't look sexier when wet.

Horus looks at Jen's neck and says he doesn't see any bruises.

"Oh, so it's fine then, because she didn't break skin?"

"Most of the time it's not this bad," says Remy. "I'm sorry. She hasn't done it in a while." Sage and Joe and Carla are in the doorway now. There's a damp imprint on the sheets where Alicia was curled up next to Jen.

Sage says, "Did she jump in the pool?"

Jen says, "Why me? Why not choke Remy?"

"Maybe *no one* should be choked," says Horus. "I think this is the real takeaway."

"I'm sorry," says Alicia. She cries, carefully keeping most of her facial muscles still and contorting her mouth as little as possible.

Horus says, "We know you didn't mean to, Alicia."

"Well aren't you so *fucking* understanding?" says Jen.

"That's pretty messed up," says Joe.

"I wasn't choking her! I just had my hand there. I swear!"

Horus tells everyone to get out of the bedroom. Remy takes Alicia by the hands and tries to lift her.

Jen says that she's read articles about people getting murdered by sleepwalkers. "I could have been one of them!"

"But you *weren't,*" says Horus.

Alicia's crying in a way that makes it difficult for her to stand up. Jen calls her psychotic. She says that Alicia was *smiling* at her.

Carla is in the doorway now too. "She can't help what she does in her sleep. In another life, she might have been a shaman."

Remy can't help himself and laughs, but Alicia, previously insensitive to everyone but Jen, gives Carla a look of pure love.

Remy puts Alicia in a hot shower and goes back into the kitchen. Joe and Sage go back to sleep in their guest room, exchanging private expressions. Remy wonders if they, too, text each other. Horus asks Remy if he wants a drink. "I'm making one for Jen."

Carla doesn't go back to sleep. She remarks that Kiki, Daniela, and Rudy didn't even wake up.

"You seem disappointed," says Horus to Carla. Remy takes a glass but doesn't say anything. "Jen will calm down. From what I saw, it didn't look like she was really choking her. I think Jen was just freaked out."

"Aren't *you?*"

Horus drinks from his glass of scotch. "Jen can be dramatic sometimes. I know it sounds sexist, but with Jen—"

"That's *very* true," says Carla. "Remy, you know how she is."

Remy says, "This might be a strange question, but did you hear knocking earlier? I woke up because someone was knocking…not on the door, but on *something.*"

"That's not funny."

"It's not a joke."

"I heard it too," says Carla.

Remy says, "I could be crazy, but I think I even saw something in the bushes, when I was looking for Alicia." He's only just remembered, and he wishes he hadn't said it out loud, which makes it more real. If he'd seen something he'd understood—a man with a butcher knife or a ski mask or a gun—then he'd know what to do.

"What kind of *something* did you see?" says Horus, his glass stopped in midair.

"I don't know. Weird. Kind of shiny. Maybe an animal?"

"Shiny? What does that mean?"

"Forget it," says Remy. "I think I was just freaked out." As he says this, Remy is ninety-five percent convinced by his own explanation. Wasn't there something familiar about the face? Couldn't it have been someone's reflection in the pool? Couldn't he still be a little drunk? But already Horus has put his glass down. He circles the house, checking doors and windows. He goes out onto the patio and looks behind lawn chairs and potted plants, his long hair falling in a dark silhouette against the pool. He bends over the hedges and looks behind them.

Remy, his eyes on Horus, asks Carla if she really heard it or if she's just fucking around.

"Of course I heard it. I'm *tapped in* to that kind of thing. It wasn't ordinary knocking."

"Stop fucking with me," says Remy. "If you really heard what I heard, you'd be more creeped out."

Carla drinks from Horus's glass while he's gone. "Fear is the greatest impediment to communing with things greater than ourselves. It's the least productive response to ignorance, and ignorance is a given in the spiritual realm."

Horus comes back inside and says that he didn't see any footprints. "If there was anything out there it would have had to leave tracks."

"I told you," says Remy. Then, unsure what he's arguing, he says, "I'm not crazy though."

"I believe you," says Carla.

At breakfast, Alicia comes into the kitchen and Joe, Sage, and Rudy stop talking. Kiki and Daniela look at her. They pass her the cereal politely.

On the way to the beach, only Carla talks to Alicia. Remy suspects this is out of a desire to annoy Jen. He dozes on the wheel well while Carla asks Alicia about her astrological sign. Carla looks something up on her phone. "I don't have your whole chart, but based on your rising sign, you're going to have a sudden change in your life soon. I also, personally, have a sense about you. Unrelated to"—and she indicates the astrology app open on her phone—"*science* or whatever. I can see *slightly* into the future. A few weeks or months."

Somehow, despite the noise of the other conversations, Horus hears this from the front seat. "Can you please stop bullying her?"

"This is a private conversation, Horus!"

"Don't believe anything she says," Horus says to Alicia.

Carla says, "I have a sense that *soon*... you're going to experience a release of some kind. Either a sexual release, a creative release, or a release from a situation. A job, maybe. Or a person."

"Really. A person?"

Remy pretends to be asleep. Carla says, "I sense that the color blue will be involved." Remy has a memory of that blue-green patch of *something* that he saw in the bushes. "Did Remy tell you about the knocking on the door last night?"

"No!"

Carla tells her what happened, recounting the incident differently from how Remy remembers it. "The sound was powerful, yet, in its way, benign. I suspect that the sudden life change I was talking about is nearby, trying to get to you. And that what we heard, knocking on the door, was your personal transformation."

"Jesus, Carla," says Remy, no longer pretending to be asleep. "Alicia is superstitious enough. You don't need to fuck her up more."

When it's just the two of them by the van, Remy says to Alicia, "Why is Horus being so nice to you?"

"I didn't realize you were listening."

"Not that I *don't* think Jen was being hysterical. But, devil's advocate: If she's his girlfriend, should he be so nice to the person who choked her?"

"I really wasn't choking her. You have to believe me. I was just sleeping next to her."

Remy holds up his hands to indicate he doesn't want to get involved in an argument. "At least it's the last full day."

Alicia doesn't surf as well as before and keeps falling off her board. Remy sits out on the waves but rarely tries to catch one. He comes back to the beach when this becomes boring.

Alicia and Horus come back to get some water just as it starts raining. She covers her head and says, "I don't understand how everyone else can drink so much and still surf so well! I think I'd do better if I weren't so hungover!" Her voice is forced, and full of hope that everything will return to the way it was before. It embarrasses Remy.

Horus says, "Remy, want to give it a shot with me again? Last day? I've got a good feeling!"

"It's raining." Remy is hungover again.

"What are you afraid of—that you're going to get wet?"

Joe and Horus laugh at this for so long that Remy feels humiliated and consents to going out on the water again.

Once they're in the ocean, Remy pees in the water next to Horus. He imagines Horus confronting him about the warmth, and imagines his own response: *What, are you telling me that you don't pee in the ocean? Are you saying there's a substantive difference between peeing next to your leg and a few feet away? Isn't this more about some ephemeral, psychological discomfort than an actual hygienic issue?*

But Horus doesn't seem to notice—or if he does, it only makes him smile more. The farther out into the water they travel, the more *pumped* Horus gets. It's as if, Remy decides, he *gets off on fear*. Horus looks back at him and says, as if this is funny, "Now's the time for any questions about the craft!"

Horus picks a wave for him and, predictably, Remy falls. He has intense vertigo. Horus says, "Remy, I've got to be honest. It's like you *want* to fail."

Remy blows water out of his nose—water that potentially contains his own urine. He disputes Horus's assessment.

"I think your biggest issue is fear of the wave. You're treating the wave like an obstacle, when really it's an opportunity. The obstacle, man, is the occasion. And that's not just surfing advice, that's life advice. The cliché is true: You have to go with the flow."

Remy tries to demonstrate that he wants to succeed. "Is there a different way to approach different waves? Should I adjust my approach depending on the, like, personality of the wave?"

"Personality! I like that."

"Should I paddle faster or slower?"

"I would say that it's important in all things"—a wave rolls over both of them and Horus resumes this thought without even reacting to it—"to respond to your environment intuitively and honestly.

Don't plan for an environment you can't predict. You wouldn't strategize about how to talk to someone before you talk to them. You'd want to be honest in the moment, right?"

"... Right."

A surfer appears over a wave and careens to the side, narrowly missing Remy's head. Horus yells at the guy, who is already gone. "He could have killed someone! This is why locals have to be dicks. These people come here and they aren't courteous!"

After several more attempts, Remy catches a wave. He didn't intend to. This time, when Horus says to "pop up," he does. He stabilizes himself: right foot, left foot, stand. The wave, as if making the decision for him, nocks into the blade beneath his surfboard and throws him forward, compelling him to subtly adjust his weight. Remy is standing so barely that his knuckles periodically graze the board, but he is surfing.

Briefly, he understands the big deal.

The water is a floor beneath him, and the sensation is like dream-flying. He's afraid, but it's the opposite of the fear he experienced while on his belly, waiting for the wave's arrival and unable to see what was coming. His desires have total clarity: He doesn't want to fall. He can't steer and people scatter in front of his board.

In his suddenly spacious, blank mind, the desire to stay in this stream of movement is the only thing that matters. But this thought, like a cell mitoting, elaborates into a more complex thought. After the initial attention required to control his body, Remy's knee-jerk anxiety about imminent failure reasserts itself. He's too hungover to keep this going, and this is clear in a way that most things in Remy's experience aren't.

Just as clearly, he perceives how humiliated he will be when he's unable to accomplish this again. He sees a bit of orange in his peripheral vision. It's probably Jen, watching him succeed badly.

Each of these thoughts is half formed, unlike thoughts on land; they're interrupted and whipped apart by his need to balance. In this state of mind, it's easy for a bit of fantasy to escape the area where dangerous ideas are normally sequestered, and—catlike—present itself without warning.

Another surfer, with a pointed, short board, appears alongside him. Even his *knees* are muscular. The guy smiles and shows him two thumbs up. This tiny incident—this patronizing *yeah man thumbs-up*—is what Remy later identifies as the main catalyst for what he does next.

Remy thinks, *I am losing my balance. I can't be expected to have expert control over the board.*

He relaxes the small amount required to pitch sideways into the path of the other guy's surfboard, at the last moment trying to take back this action by covering his head with his hands. He's surprised by the pain that follows—a confusing series of impacts, as difficult to parse as counting gunshots fired in quick succession.

Remy inhales water. He isn't sure which way is up. Arms embrace him and he immediately embraces them back as they pull him to the surface. He keeps hearing *what the fuck man what the fuck.*

Remy makes a nonverbal noise and prioritizes breathing. He refuses to open his eyes. On some level, he's aware that he's likely being held by exactly the type of surfer dude he dislikes, but Remy allows himself to grip the arms, astonished by the sweetness of being cradled.

Horus, Joe, and Jen debate over whether to take Remy to the hospital. Horus uses the flashlight on a plastic-baggied iPhone to look into his eyes. A lifeguard stands nearby, clutching his rescue tube and saying, "I'm happy to call an ambulance. Happy to."

"Mostly he just seems scraped up, although I think his shoulder might be dislocated."

"Am I dying?" says Remy. His ability to be fraudulent even now informs him that he's alive.

"You know perfectly well you're not dying," says Alicia.

"Am I too injured? But I was just getting the hang of surfing! Can't I go back out?" Remy can't see Alicia's expression, but he can feel it.

Horus says that he despises hospitals and medical personnel. Remy says, "I can't afford an ambulance. My insurance would really fuck me."

"I understand, man." Horus tells him that he doesn't even have insurance. "Until every American has free health care, I refuse to buy insurance."

"That's the dumbest thing I've ever heard," says Remy.

"I'm going to put your shoulder back in place. Just breathe in and out."

What Horus does next, Remy remembers as an awful bit of pure magic. He blacks out, briefly. He hears someone say, "Do you think he even realizes that he could have hurt Kyle?"

* * *

Jen and Horus have a tense conversation out of earshot, and then Jen volunteers to drive Remy and Alicia back to the house. "Me too?" says Alicia. She stands there. She doesn't point out that it's her last day to surf.

"You can ride shotgun," says Jen to Alicia. They put him in the back of the van and Alicia, after a lag, gets in too.

Jen tells Remy, "You're going to be fine. Horus was a volunteer EMT in high school. If he says you're fine, then you're fine."

Alicia says, "I think he's just hurting so much because he's hungover."

When Remy expresses pain again, Alicia tells him to stop being so dramatic.

"Babe?" says Jen.

She has never before used this word to refer to Alicia. Alicia changes color.

"Babe, I say this with respect and empathy in my heart, but this attitude is not super helpful. What *would* be helpful is if you could locate your compassion for Remy right now, and access that." Jen doesn't look at her as she says this. She concentrates on shifting gears. She doesn't rush between gears like most people do.

Alicia stares ahead, at the road. She takes her phone out of her tote bag and texts Remy:

> That was kind of bitchy. She didn't have to talk to me like that.

Remy pretends to be delirious and says, "Jen, are you locating your compassion for me right now?"

At the house, Jen puts rubbing alcohol on a cotton ball and leans over Remy on the couch. Her closeness to him could be justified as a medical necessity.

Alicia makes a lame comment about how Jen is doing a lot more than she is to help Remy. There's a long silence.

"Ugh, my head!" says Remy.

"No one forgot about your head," says Alicia.

Alicia watches this scene for a while, following Jen's orders whenever they're given in her pissed-off, clipped voice. Maybe Alicia is wrong and Jen isn't thinking about what happened last night. Maybe she's just really on task.

Alicia goes to the kitchen. She gets two beers from the fridge and opens them. She brings them to Jen and Remy. "It's been a stressful day," she says. They both look at the beers.

Jen says, "On the off chance that Remy has a concussion, it's probably better for him not to have alcohol."

"They're already open."

"I don't have a *concussion,*" says Remy, "I mean, I *might,* but I want to have a beer."

"Where's *your* beer?" says Jen.

"I think the alcohol makes my sleepwalking worse. It's probably better to abstain." Jen looks at Alicia without saying anything.

Alicia's impulse is to apologize again for the night before, but she doesn't. Jen is being such a cunt that maybe she deserved it. Even though Alicia *didn't* choke her.

Jen says, "You know, I get the opportunity to surf all the time. I get the sense... that you'd like to take advantage of the beach while you have it." Jen looks down at her cotton ball. "If you're comfortable with it, I could hold down the fort here—make sure Remy doesn't exhibit any signs of a concussion. *If* you felt comfortable driving the van back. You *do* drive, don't you?"

Alicia has the sudden need to tell Jen more than necessary about how she used to drive a van for a bakery—to assert herself and her history one last time before she leaves. She doesn't.

"And we're drinking and you're not, so..." says Jen.

They discuss the logistics of getting back to the beach. Alicia takes the van keys, and leaves.

Once Alicia is in the front seat of the van, she considers texting Remy something that would embarrass him if Jen accidentally saw it—maybe something that alludes to their role-play, or Remy's encyclopedic knowledge of Jen's photos. But she can't think of anything that would lessen rather than increase the sexual tension.

Remy and Jen finish their beers and open two more. They both agree how nice it is to be away from the group. Jen says, "I love Carla, but she's just a *lot*."

Remy agrees. Jen complains about Sage and gushes about Kiki. She seems more relaxed. He asks her how things are "going" with Horus. "It seems like you were annoyed at him about what happened last night. I would be too, in your position."

"Thank you! Like, you're her *boyfriend* and you're basically on my side." Jen says she *knows* what she saw. She says something cursory about how she's sure that Alicia is a really nice person but *No offense she's been acting in a bona fide dangerous way* and frankly she doesn't know how he puts up with it. "I think I was *very* understanding considering the circumstances. She could have really hurt me."

"For what it's worth, I don't think so."

"Has she ever been dangerous before?"

"She just sleep-eats or tells knock-knock jokes."

"Excuse me?"

Remy tells her about the knock-knock joke.

"If I were you, I'd be terrified about sharing a bed with her."

"She's really fine. I mean... sometimes I do think about what it would be like to be with someone different. Maybe someone a little less needy. I mean, of course I care for her, but—"

"I'm going to get the scotch. I'm not supposed to."

Remy is annoyed. "You're not supposed to?"

"Horus doesn't get mad, necessarily... He implies that my palate isn't refined enough for the good stuff. I'd rather drink it when he's not here because I don't want to be *watched* while I drink it. It's too much pressure."

"That sounds really fucking annoying."

"It's fine, it's just—how am I supposed to take pleasure in something if I'm being neurotic about how I consume it?"

Jen disappears for a long time, and then comes back with the scotch. Remy wonders if she put more makeup on, but he isn't positive she looks different. Briefly, he wishes that Alicia were here. She would know.

Jen pours him a glass and says, "I hope we finish it. I hope he comes back and sees the empty bottle."

"Would that really bother him? He seems like an easygoing guy."

"Which is exactly why it's so ridiculous when he won't allow himself to react! It's funny, actually. I want to be like, *Just fight with me!*"

"You're one of those people? You like fighting?"

"When we do fight it's very— He gets very passionate." Jen says this in a way that Remy dislikes.

Later, they sit outside, still sharing the scotch. Remy strategizes about returning the conversation to the shortcomings of their respective partners. He reintroduces the subject, but Jen says *Hang on* because she's just gotten a text from Horus. She asks Remy to roll a joint, and without thinking about what this entails, he says yes.

"Everyone is going to happy hour in a little bit. Horus is wondering if he should pick us up." Jen describes the bar, and they both laugh at her undisguised lack of enthusiasm.

Remy says, "Tell them I'm *extremely* injured."

"I'll say I don't feel comfortable leaving you by yourself. Or something."

Jen types, backspacing and restarting often.

"It doesn't seem to me like...you're always comfortable being yourself around Horus."

"We're very comfortable around each other. We shit with the bathroom door open at this point."

"Just because you're free of one type of judgment doesn't mean you're free of other types."

Jen finishes what she's typing and puts her phone down.

Remy says, "Like you didn't feel as if you could joke about drone strikes with him."

"Maybe that's not something I can share with Horus, but I have other people in my life. That's what I like about you, Remy. Horus doesn't have an evil bone in his body, but you do."

"I would *agree* that I have an evil bone in my body."

"I think it's a good thing that he's someone who wants to bring out the best in me. And challenges me to be better."

"That sounds awful, actually."

"I genuinely want to be a better person." Remy doesn't say anything. Jen says, "Relationships are work, you know?"

"Mine isn't."

Jen looks at her phone.

Remy says, "I don't think you should feel like you have to present yourself...or perform a certain way. You should feel completely accepted."

"That's very sweet, Remy." Jen notices the result of his efforts to roll a joint, and puts her hand over her mouth. "Have you ever done this?"

"I normally use a bowl! I haven't done this shit since high school." Jen takes the rolling paper and starts over. Remy comments on how filthy her fingernails are.

"Stop trying to neg me because you feel insecure about what you just did here." She laughs and says that she should send him back to high school so he can relearn. "You're such a child."

* * *

A few drinks later, Jen looks away from Remy while delivering a string of qualifiers about Horus. He recognizes this as the beginning of a complaint.

"But the thing about our situation is that I think things would be perfect, really perfect, if I didn't *need* him in quite the same way."

"I'm sure you'd be fine without him."

Jen shakes her head, smiling. "I wouldn't be. He basically owns my business." She acts as if this is very funny. "A relationship can mean freedom in a lot of ways. With Horus, there's the obvious financial freedom. I can travel more. I have more options. And don't get me wrong—I want to be with him. But that freedom itself is weirdly...circumscribed. If he has an idea about the website, he won't force me to do it, but for something that's supposed to be my business, it doesn't feel like my choice."

"You know how to get your way most of the time."

Jen laughs. "It's one of my worst qualities." After a long pause, she says, "I don't even know what freedom would look like to me. It sounds corny but I guess what I want is to, like... *live in the now*. Which you can't really do if someone is always reminding you of the ways in which you're not only accountable to yourself."

"What else are you supposed to be accountable to?"

"My relationship obviously, the environment, future generations."

The scotch is supposed to be good, but to Remy, it tastes like chemicals and burnt hair. Jen gets up and stretches. "It *is* nice to let loose a little. I think I just needed to talk shit for a second." She loses her balance and catches herself on Remy's shoulder, letting her hand stay there, and laughing. "I *really* hope you don't have a concussion, because I feel useless." She examines his wounds again, touching his face a lot in the process.

* * *

Jen complains about how disgusting she feels, and takes a shower. She trips on her way to the bathroom and laughs for a full minute. Remy sits in the living room and looks down the hall, at the bathroom door. The shower is running, and the door has been left slightly open.

He looks at the door and remembers Alicia-as-Jen, asking him what he would do if Jen were taking a shower. He remembers asking, "Am I me? Or am I the gardener?"

He wishes he *were* a gardener. It would be safer to be a gardener. To be himself in this moment is unbearable—it's too much responsibility. Remy is certain that Jen left the door open on purpose. And then, he's not certain.

He looks at his phone, idly wishing that he could ask Alicia for guidance. He doesn't have any messages.

The shower turns off. Jen's footsteps travel back and forth in the hallway. A door shuts, then opens again.

Jen comes out to the living room, a towel wrapped around her body. The towel technically covers more skin than her swimsuit does, but seeing her in a towel is much more intense. The front of her chest is red from the shower.

Jen moves around in a self-conscious way. "I left the door open," she says.

Remy feels embarrassed on her behalf. He laughs.

"I left it open for a reason." Her mouth moves strangely, like a tide-pool creature.

"Are you teasing me?"

This comment makes Jen perform more. She mocks him with over-the-top sexiness. He's never seen anyone *mince* off screen. Her natural confidence has been replaced by bad acting that makes her both overwhelming and strangely pathetic.

"Stop. Don't say anything," he says, when he can tell she's about to try to make him laugh again. "Don't be funny."

She sits on his lap and pulls his head towards hers, like a high-schooler. Instinctively, he supports her back with his arm.

Alicia listens to the boring conversations around her. Joe is complaining that he always wants to cook fish at home but hates how it stinks up the house. Everyone at the table is suggesting different strategies for preventing fish odors, and Joe is rejecting all of them.

The happy hour place is too expensive for Alicia, and she orders a strong drink instead of food. The bar is situated at the manicured edge of a lawn that looks like it belongs in suburbia, before it gives way to sand.

Alicia has never seen people like the people at the other tables. The men smell of aftershave and the women wear sun hats. She checks her phone. No messages.

There's a cracking sound and everyone at the restaurant looks in the same direction. Fireworks originate at a distant point along the beach.

Joe says, "I guess someone had them left over from the Fourth." The entire bar is confused. More than one person points out that you need a special permit to set off fireworks.

Alicia watches a seedlike spark squiggle into the air and transform, caught unawares by its own explosion. The confusion and surprise lift the social barriers between tables. People make amazed spectator sounds. A man at the next table says something corny about how fireworks don't get less amazing in old age, and looks around, waiting for his wisdom to be appreciated.

Alicia looks at the unexplained fireworks and has the type of emotional reaction that would really embarrass Remy if he were here. She makes sure to keep her face still even though her eyes are wet.

She involuntarily remembers a scene from the very beginning of her relationship with Remy, when he was still dating Greta. Alicia was yelling into her phone, trying to cancel a gym membership. She opened the door expecting a food delivery, but instead *he* was standing in the doorway, a magazine rolled up in his hand like a nightstick. The patterns of distress around his jean pockets were not yet overfamiliar, but already she could have recognized his bad posture at a distance.

She stared at Remy in the doorway and said to the guy on the phone, "No, you're *not* going to charge me a cancellation fee because I paid for the whole year up front and I was told *specifically* that the payment wouldn't renew automatically." Then, influenced by the amused expression on Remy's face, she added, "You little shit."

Remy said, "Yeah, Alicia. Give 'em hell." It was the first time he'd said her name.

Alicia stepped back from the door and turned away. "I'm sorry, I know it's not your fault," she said to the Eeyore-voiced man on the phone. "I'm sorry." She glanced up at Remy again. His attention at that point was *too much.* He looked at her neutrally and yet with care, as if she were hanging on the wall of a museum. Then he went to Greta's room and shut the door.

When the fireworks are over, Carla drunkenly throws an arm around Alicia's shoulders and says, "Alicia, whatever happens in the next few months, keep me in the loop. I want to know how my predictions worked out."

"I will." Carla forgets to retract her arm and they sit there, like sisters, for the rest of the evening.

* * *

Remy is unable to process what's happening, and decides he may actually have a concussion. He takes note of each disparate sensation: Jen's braces interacting with his teeth, the fancy smell of the products on her wet towel, the singed smell of scotch, and her kissing speed and technique—so strange after over a year of kissing only Alicia.

He examines each sensation again, mentally toggling between each place where her body touches his, switching between her mouth, her body, and her odor, evaluating the degree to which these things give him genuine pleasure or barely exceed tagging as sensory inputs.

The knowledge that he's touching Jen doesn't snap into place. It's like flying a kite on a windless day. He visualizes the two of them on the couch. He can imagine what they would look like on a screen, but he's not inside the picture. If he had more time, if there were less pressure, he could relax.

"Why are your eyes open?" says Jen. "You're freaking me out."

Remy answers out of an impulse that at first he doesn't recognize as a desire to make Jen jealous. "I'm thinking about Alicia. I guess I feel weird."

Jen leans back. She wipes her mouth. Remy is silent, expecting her to talk, and she's silent, expecting *him* to talk. She stands up and monologues about the logistics of when people are likely to return. She looks for her phone.

"Are you mad?" says Remy.

"I'm trying to be respectful."

"It seems like you're pissed. Can't we just— I feel like there's this barrier between us."

"You've mentioned."

"I think I might have a concussion. I feel really weird." They have a tense exchange about who is to blame for Remy not going to the hospital. Remy insists he isn't blaming her, he's *just saying.* "Can't we put a pin in this? I can't relax right now."

"Sure. I'll put it in my calendar."

"I'm trying to explain! *Jen.* I feel really weird."

"Remy, you're taking things too seriously. We're just messing around. I know how you can get neurotic sometimes."

Remy inflicts the last bit of his scotch on himself. Neurotic is a word that applies to Alicia, not him. "Really? Would Horus not take this seriously at all? Would he consider it just 'messing around'?"

"Why would Horus care? Can you please be cool."

"I'm not 'cool'? I'm sorry if I'm not 'cool.'" Remy is out of breath. "Maybe I'll let Horus know that his girlfriend was just 'having fun' with me, and see how cool he is about it."

Jen holds the towel tightly around her torso. "I'm confused, Remy. Have things changed since we talked? Because you led me to believe that you and Alicia were open too."

Remy stares at Jen. "When the hell did I say that?"

"When we were texting! I'm sorry, I guess you didn't say *open,* but you implied it."

Remy remembers the texts that Alicia deleted. This only makes him more angry at Jen. "So I'm not *cool* for not being open?"

"That's *not* what I said. Based on your behavior, I think you have some unrealistic expectations about what's going to happen here."

"Wow, you guys are so *cool,* with your open relationship and weekend house, and your one-armed surf instructors, and your horoscopes, and your... endorsements of bestiality! You're so open that Horus is even fine with you hooking up with someone in his *mom's* house while he's at happy hour?"

Jen observes Remy before saying, "Yeah, actually, I think he would be fine with it."

"Wow, Jen. You're so open-minded. Just be careful that you're not so open-minded that your brain falls out."

"Are you quoting Harry the Homophobe at me?"

Remy has briefly forgotten that Jen knew Harry too. Stripped of context, Harry's motto seemed apropos.

Jen goes on a didactic tangent about how it's perfectly natural to want more than one partner, that even animals that are commonly believed to be monogamous are only socially, not sexually, monogamous.

"What the fuck is with you and animal sex?"

"Like it's a myth that penguins mate for life. Neither do swans." She lists animals on her fingers. Then she goes to the bedroom, puts on clothes, and calls Horus to see when he's coming back.

Once the van returns, several people complain about the price of food at the bar and collaborate on ordering a pizza. They ask Remy how he is. Alicia can hear Jen using a blow-dryer somewhere in the house. She looks at Remy as if the past will be revealed to her, and notices Carla watching her watch Remy.

Jen emerges and requests olives on the pizza, her face impassive. Beers and whiskey glasses surround the couch where Remy is resting.

Carla leans on the marble kitchen island next to Alicia. "Not to stir shit, but are you doing okay?"

Alicia doesn't say anything.

"Maybe it's in my head," says Carla. "Sorry. I'm just being an asshole."

Alicia smiles. "I may not be playing with a full deck, but I'm also not *completely* stupid."

Carla touches Alicia's arm and says with as much kindness as Horus might use, "Remember what I said. You have a destiny so strong, it's knocking on doors."

Alicia looks at Jen. Jen doesn't look at her. Alicia has the superstitious sense that if she can just *touch* her, in the same way that Carla is touching her now, she will know what happened. Like Christopher Walken in *The Dead Zone.*

Alicia concentrates on not indulging this impulse. But when Jen comes into the kitchen, Alicia says to her, "Thank you so much for looking after Remy! I really appreciate it!"

"Of course. Anytime. I'm just glad he's better."

"I mean it! It was just so nice of you. So nice." She entangles Jen in a hug like a hot bedsheet.

Jen pushes Alicia away. Without lowering her voice to spare Alicia embarrassment, she says, "In general? You touch me too much. We do *not* have that kind of relationship."

The kitchen is quiet, and Jen's face, even now, is beautiful.

Jen walks away and Alicia remembers a rare video Jen once posted to her Instagram, of someone coming behind her and pushing her into a lake, as a prank. Jen's expression, before she hit the water, was incredulous at the betrayal. But when she emerged from the water, she was laughing. Everything was forgiven. Right now, she badly wants to push Jen into a lake.

Alicia and Remy are put in one of the bedrooms for this last night, instead of in sleeping bags on the floor. Ostensibly, this is due to Remy's injury, but the solemnity with which Horus approaches them to propose this sleeping arrangement, as well as the triangle formation of Horus with Jen and Joe behind him, makes it clear that this was the result of a private conversation.

This guest bedroom is obviously intended for children, since it contains two twin beds. They're forced to sleep apart, like siblings. Remy goes to bed as soon as he finishes his pizza. Briefly, in the hallway, he hears a low argument between Jen and Horus, but he can't make out distinct words.

Much later, Alicia comes in and sits on her own twin bed. The rest of the house is dark. She hears swishing in the front room, where Joe and Sage are rolling out sleeping bags. "Are you awake?" she says.

Remy doesn't answer.

"I can tell you're awake. Don't forget that we have a mystical connection."

Remy's eyes are open but he stares at the wall.

"Did you and Jen hook up?"

"What?"

"You guys were alone for a long time."

"Because *you* left."

"*You* didn't want me to stay. You weren't even talking to me."

"I was injured!" Remy sits up in bed, gratified by the pain this swift motion causes him, because it reminds him that he's the victim. "Okay. I guess we're doing this now."

Alicia doesn't say anything.

"The funny thing is, Jen seemed to think we were in an open relationship. Someone must have told her that. Isn't that *so* funny?"

"Remy."

"It's almost as if someone misinformed her. Why would someone do that? Did I miss something? Are we in an open relationship? Have you been sleeping around and I didn't notice?"

"It was a prank. I was messing around. I didn't know you would take it that far!"

"Maybe Jen and I were just *messing around* too."

"Can you talk a little quieter?"

"Let me tell you what happened here. *You* set a trap and I fell into it. You won—I'm the bad guy. Are you happy?"

Alicia turns on the shell-shaped bedside lamp and he tells her to turn it off. She doesn't. She starts several sentences with "I thought" or "I wanted" but doesn't complete them. She says, "Can you at least tell me how it went?"

She sits in this beautiful bedroom, in her yellowed nightshirt with her wet face, looking completely wrong—like a piece of toilet paper stuck on a soufflé. "Just give me the details? Make it like I was there. Don't you think that would be kind of hot?"

Remy asks her, again, to turn out the lamp.

"Did you have sex? Or did you just make out?" When he doesn't respond, she says, "Can people with braces give blowjobs, or is that dangerous?"

Remy says *fuck you I'm not talking to you* and Alicia, with increasing aggression, tries to make him laugh.

"When you got hard, did she say, 'Surf's up'?"

They take turns telling the other one to quiet down. They don't stop arguing until they hear a noise.

"Did you hear someone knocking?" says Alicia. "Or, like, a bang?"

Remy doesn't say anything. Alicia stands up.

"Don't open the door!" says Remy.

Alicia turns around with her hand on the doorknob. She smiles and opens the door.

Silence.

Now the noise is louder. They look at each other. Alicia keeps smiling. "Oh my God!" she says.

"That... asshole," says Remy.

"Should we go ask if we can join?"

"She's doing this on purpose! She's doing it specifically to humiliate me!"

"Why are you mad? You had your turn."

"I didn't, in fact. You don't even know the worst of it. She was such an asshole."

Remy shuts the door. They can still hear the noises through the wall. Jen's sounds of pleasure have a distinct beginning, middle, and end, like bus brakes, or a taffy machine on a rusty spindle.

Remy doesn't sit down. He says how self-absorbed and delusional Jen is. "She said I had 'expectations'! She's so patronizing."

The sounds stop suddenly. Remy drinks the warm remains of a beer on the nightstand.

"She's probably giving him head," says Alicia.

"Right in the middle? That doesn't make any sense."

"It's plausible." They argue about how plausible this is. "We've done that before," says Alicia. "Sometimes you need a little booster."

"I'm glad you're enjoying this so much." Remy tells Alicia that Jen is a fraud. That she enjoys manipulating people. He assigns many of his own qualities to her.

"Shhh!" says Alicia.

They hear Horus make a sound of total sincerity, one that Remy would never allow himself to make.

Remy points at the hallway and says to Alicia, "She's telling him to be that loud! She's purposely trying to piss me off!"

He opens the door and goes down the hallway, towards the sound. He's drawn there inevitably, just as Alicia was the night before. The door to the master bedroom isn't locked, and the movement that Remy intended as a doorknob-rattling expression of his anger modifies into swinging the door all the way open. Jen and Horus scramble to cover themselves with the bedspread. Remy has a clinical view of Horus's definitely—probably—average-sized dick.

After a microsecond, Remy says, "Oh I'm sorry, guys. Is this not 'chill' of me?"

"What the fuck!" says Jen. Horus says *C'mon man.* Jen's face is flushed. She's clearly been holding her head at an unnatural angle.

Remy says, "Horus, I know your mom's house is supposed to be so amazing and expensive and all, but the walls are surprisingly thin."

"You're psychotic!" says Jen.

"Folks, let's calm down!" says Horus. "Let's all just take a *deeeeeep* breath."

"I know what you're doing, Jen. You can't just let people sleep. You have to wake everyone up with how *liberated* you are." He says to Horus, "Did she ask you to be that loud? Did she coach you?"

"Get out of here!" Jen hobbles to the door under the bedsheet. She tries to shut it, but Remy won't let her.

Horus rubs his face and says, "Remy, I'm sensing that whatever this is, it could best be resolved in the sober light of morning."

Jen turns around to Horus, covering her ass with the sheet, and says, "Aren't you so fucking mature! Aren't you *so* rational!"

Jen and Remy yell at each other and Horus makes quelling

motions with his arms. He says "Guys, guys. I think I'm missing something!"

Remy says, "Nothing at all. Jen and I were just *making out* on your mom's couch earlier." Horus's expression doesn't change.

Jen says, "We had an *encounter* today that he's wildly exaggerating."

Carla appears in the doorway, picking encrusted makeup out of the corner of her eye. "You guys *are* being kind of loud," she says. Joe shouts from the living room, asking if someone is getting strangled again.

"Get your *goblin* girlfriend out of my bedroom!" says Jen when she sees Alicia standing in the threshold, smiling in her private way. Jen and Remy both call each other delusional until Remy leaves and shuts the door.

Joe and Sage are awake and watch Remy and Alicia return to the bedroom, with the suppressed faces of people trying not to laugh at a funeral.

Remy and Alicia hear Jen raise her voice, several times, but never hear Horus raise his.

They talk until morning, eventually moving into the same twin bed. At some point, Remy suggests stealing the scotch, since he now knows where it is, telling her it might get Jen in trouble with Horus. When he retrieves the scotch, Alicia doesn't like it either, so she sneaks into the kitchen at two a.m. to get a bottle of red wine.

They look out the window, at the moon. The sand and the silence of the house make it seem like they're on their own island. "You never drink wine," he says. "You look like a housewife."

"Or like Jen."

He tells her everything that happened. "Can you believe how stupid she is? First she tells me you *can't* make an equivalency between human sex and animal sex, and then, as soon as she's talking about open relationships, she makes that *very* equivalency!" Alicia agrees, easily now, that she's stupid, and a liar.

He says, "She's kidding herself if she thinks she's changed. She's just the same asshole she always was."

"Do you think they're really open?"

"I don't believe anything she says. Everything she's said on this trip could be a lie."

"Maybe they didn't even meet in Croatia. Maybe they met on Seeking Arrangement."

They both laugh at a low volume. They agree that Jen and Horus must be very unhappy, and hiding it for the sake of appearances.

Alicia can already tell that she's making a happy memory. It occurs to her that decisions that at the time felt wrong—leaving Remy alone with Jen, for example—were in fact so easy to make because they were actually correct, leading her to this moment with Remy, listening to the waves and bound together by the theft of the alcohol. Although she doesn't completely understand the mechanics of *The Apple Bush,* she believes she was intuitively following some sort of Flow.

At the time, she didn't understand her sudden desire to leave them alone, or even, necessarily, her desire to go on this trip at all. Now, she recognizes these instincts as not strictly her own, but rather belonging to some cosmic hand, guiding her towards a state of being that she couldn't have accomplished through her conscious volition. She says, "At this point she's pretty much available to us forever. We know what she's really like. We've figured her out."

"You're drunk. Your mouth is completely red. It looks like a *literal* asshole. Like a hemorrhoidal asshole."

Alicia kisses him with her asshole mouth. "She can be as awful as she wants. She can even block us on Instagram. But we've had time to study her and figure her out. She can't keep herself out of our sex life."

Both of them are pleased by this idea, to which they return

often before the sun comes up: the image of this arrogant girl continuing with her life, thinking she's free, with no idea that they can humiliate her whenever they want.

The next day, when they finally get home, Alicia checks the mail. The earrings she ordered from Jen have arrived.

Part 3

A Spod of One's Own

On Alicia's first day back at work, Cassie tells her she seems different.

Alicia says something about the therapeutic effects of surfing, but changes topics when this fails to keep Cassie's interest. "Honestly, I think it's because Remy and I have been role-playing more." She pulls at her halter-top and throws back her hair. "It's a shame how most people don't explore their desires. We like to think of this country as progressive, but it's really puritanical in a way, don't you think?"

"You just switched things up in the bedroom?" Cassie makes a face like Obama's *all right then* face.

Cassie asks if she's still down to help her move this weekend, and Alicia says, "Of course—it'll be amazing! I'm actually really pumped."

"I don't know *why.* I hope your expectations aren't unrealistic. It's three flights of stairs."

Later, apropos of one of Cassie's traveling stories, Alicia tells a long story about how an old boyfriend of hers took care of her when she had food poisoning. She laughs too much telling it, and Cassie doesn't laugh even to be polite. "Is this going anywhere? Because Jorge wants me to wipe down the shelves in the ready-to-go case."

But when she stops talking, Cassie doesn't immediately go and clean the ready-to-go case. Instead she spends five minutes slathering a specialty skin lotion—which she insists on keeping under the counter—on her hands and elbows. She bores Alicia with details about the cream and what would happen to her skin if she didn't use it.

"Is *this* going anywhere?" says Alicia-as-Jen. Cassie glances at her, and Alicia is too chicken not to act as if she was just joking.

Every order that Alicia takes that day, she smiles at the customer as if it's her greatest pleasure to serve. She imagines how pissed Jen would be if she knew that she were stuck in a humid sandwich shop, compelled to be cheerful even to the lady who sees a friend while ordering at the counter and holds up the entire line with her conversation. The woman puts a shopping bag and her other possessions on the counter. It's Alicia's pet peeve when customers crowd the counter with their stuff. *Smile, Jen,* she thinks, sadistically, stretching her mouth even wider.

Jen has posted several pictures since the weekend, and they're all of people other than Remy and Alicia. Remy asserts that this is a calculated attempt to erase them from the trip.

"Can you blame her?" says Alicia.

"How did they take a group photo without us there? When did that happen?"

"She was taking a lot of pictures. There was bound to be one without us."

"She knows exactly what she's doing. We were there, though. She can't change that."

The posts are distributed across several platforms. Here is Joe wearing a hat that was kicking around the bottom of the van all weekend. Here is Jen next to the pool with Horus.

Remy says, "Don't you think it's interesting that she didn't block either of us?"

"She doesn't even know my handle."

"It's like she *wants me* to see this. She's *taunting* me."

Alicia takes Remy's phone. "I don't think she's even wearing makeup here." This is annoying, since it limits the ways in which Alicia can approximate Jen's appearance. "She really tricked me."

"How do you mean?"

"She was so nice at first. But you see someone's real *essence* when they're angry. The Jen I saw before would never have called me a goblin."

"That's what I've been saying. She's *fake*."

"I'm not sure if Jen's *fake* so much as she's...other than how she imagines herself."

"What's the difference?"

Alicia says something only half worked through about how it makes her more relatable. She looks at several more photos. "I think, on some level, Jen and I aren't that different. Otherwise she wouldn't have been so cruel to me. Like how she said in front of all those people that I 'touched her too much.' Maybe I remind her of herself."

"You seem very different to me."

"We both care what people think about us. And we're both a little lonely, in our way."

Remy says that Jen doesn't seem lonely at all. "It sounds to me like you're projecting."

Alicia tells him that he doesn't know anything about how women work. "I think we're connected, and she hates it."

On Saturday, Alicia meets Cassie at the gas station where they dispatch U-Hauls.

Cassie is unpleasant and impatient during the move, just as she promised. Whenever she's at work, Cassie veers quickly from complaining about customers to sudden charm as they approach the counter, and this changeability turns out to be a trait that's not confined to the work environment, as it often is with people in service. "I thought you had fucking moving experience!" she says when Alicia searches for a place to put her dresser drawers.

"All I said was that I used to drive a van."

"Just put them up there. It's common sense!"

Alicia tries to imagine how Jen would act in this situation, but it's difficult for her to imagine anyone speaking to Jen as Cassie is speaking to her.

As soon as Cassie's stuff is loaded and they're in the van, Cassie is laughing and happy again, pointing her phone at her face and scanning it over the cityscape outside. Cassie's Instagram stories are the routine, dull content that only a truly confident person could post. She doesn't include the driver's seat in her video.

"What are you doing after this?" says Alicia.

Cassie gets a call and says *Hello, yes I'm moving, no it's been easy so far, yeah maybe I'll meet you there if I don't pass out.*

When she hangs up, Alicia asks if she's meeting someone afterwards.

"I don't know. Maybe if they beg me."

"Where?"

"But I might not go. That was *so* easy, wasn't it? I knew I planned it well."

Cassie's new apartment is filled with paintings, dismembered mannequins, and dirty, lurching roommates whose eyes pass over Alicia as if she's part of a shadow world. The roommates help them carry boxes upstairs, slowly.

"I didn't know you knew so many artists," says Alicia. She understands now that she's miscategorized Cassie. She's from a similar flyover-state background, so Alicia assumed that they shared the same trajectory—the same dearth of connections, and the same uphill battle to make friends. But Cassie, despite her antisocial behavior, does not lead a solitary life.

Cassie points at someone passing by with a box. "This is Marvin.

He's a good person to know if you ever need anything weird. A samurai sword. A gas mask." Cassie talks for a long time about Marvin and Marvin picks up a box. He doesn't seem to notice he's being talked about. "He has an auctioneering degree," says Cassie.

"That's fascinating! I didn't know you could get an auctioneering degree!"

"You can. I have one," says Marvin.

"I wasn't doubting you at all!" says Alicia. "I just didn't know."

When they're almost finished taking everything upstairs, Cassie looks at one of the last boxes in the truck. "Fuck. I wasn't supposed to bring that. That was my stuff to give away." It was one of the heavier boxes Alicia carried, and Cassie asks Alicia *please please* not to be mad at her. "I just forgot! Anything you want in there you should take. Everything else I'm putting in the street."

The box contains very little of interest: several heavy textbooks and the pieces of a broken humidifier. The only thing that catches her attention is Cassie's discarded copy of *The Apple Bush*.

"Oh my God! I think this is a sign!" says Alicia, picking up the book. She says this in Jen's voice. The presence of Jen has no effect on Cassie, which Alicia finds difficult to believe. Jen is her only magic, and she's loath to go away without first affirming its power. Alicia-as-Jen holds the book to her chest. "It's an inside joke," she says to Cassie, who still doesn't care.

Cassie scans the inside of the U-Haul for anything she might have left behind. "You can take the van back, right?"

Alicia explains that she can't—that Cassie has to pay for the time. Alicia would prefer for her to come back to the dispatch location with her, but after some strategizing, Cassie figures out how to avoid this.

They take the last box upstairs. "I guess I'm just going to catch up with these guys for a while," Cassie says. She motions at the roommates. She makes no move to invite Alicia to come back afterwards. She yawns and says God she's so tired it makes her not want to see *anyone* or do *anything.* She puts money for the U-Haul in Alicia's hands, and then twenties for her time.

Alicia says no, really, that's not necessary.

"I insist," says Cassie.

Alicia experiences automatic, complicated joy when she sees the money in her hand.

"I'll see you at work," says Cassie.

When Remy gets home from his shift, he asks Alicia if Jake is home.

"No."

"Thank God."

He goes into the kitchen for a snack and complains that he's going to murder Jake for all the jam prints he left on the fridge handle.

Jake puts his head out of the door. "What's up?"

Remy looks at Alicia. She's smiling as if what amuses her is the movie she's watching on Remy's laptop.

"Dude, you're making a mess," says Remy, pointing to the jam prints.

"Haha, sorry!" says Jake. He gets a paper towel and dabs ineffectively at the refrigerator handle.

"Sorry, man!" he says, and then, "I just got carried away. You have *got* to try this jam."

"Just, like, use a spray-cleaner or something. It's not going to automatically come off. It's been there awhile."

From the bedroom, Alicia says, "Jake, you're inspiring very violent feelings in my boyfriend right now."

"Oh no!" says Jake. "Please don't hurt me. Haha." Jake puts up his hands and bends at the knees, in order to not seem significantly taller than Remy.

Alicia steps into the kitchen in a nightshirt, her arms crossed, her face greasy with Pond's. "I'm serious," she says. "You keep leaving fingerprints, and one of these days you're going to wake up with no fingers."

"You look ridiculous," says Remy to Alicia.

Jake says, "Dang, you're scaring me. I'd better behave!"

Alicia steps closer to him. "Just be careful, because we know where you live."

"Very true," says Jake. "Yikes!"

"If you're trying to be intimidating, it's not working," says Remy to Alicia.

Jake smiles as he sprays a paper towel with cleaner. He concentrates very hard on wiping the refrigerator handle, looking up periodically to see if his good humor has had a softening effect on Alicia's expression.

The air is pierced by the violent scream of an infant.

Jake drops the paper towel and runs into the bedroom. "Hello, this is Jake," says Jake.

While Remy's at work, Alicia applies a moisturizing facial masque and draws a bath. She's distracted by the ticking of blood in her temples. It's still too hot. The masque oozes down her face if she sits up too much.

Jake opens the bathroom door. "Oops, sorry!" he says. He closes the door with utmost respect. "It's fine! I can use the bathroom at the coffee shop next door."

"Jake?"

"Actually, I'm sort of on my way out anyways."

"You can open the door. You can't see anything through the bubbles."

Jake opens the door wide enough to look at her with a single eye.

She says, "I'm sorry for being an asshole about the jam."

Jake, kindly, pretends not to know what she's talking about.

Alicia says, "Sometimes I have these...aggressive urges that I normally have other ways of containing." When he doesn't respond, she says she's sorry again. "I'm really trying to be a better person."

Jake puts his chin on the doorknob, looking as wise as a Jim Henson puppet. He says, "For what it's worth, Alicia, I don't think of you as an aggressive person, but maybe keeping that aggression bottled up inside isn't the best way to handle it."

"You have no idea. It's much better this way. I can be really cruel." Without modifying her voice, she says, "The other day I called this girl a *goblin*."

"But it's good that you're taking time to yourself and relaxing. That's probably nice, right?"

"This actually isn't relaxing at all. It's way too hot. Jake—" Alicia splashes the water. "I don't even know how to relax. I don't know how to just *be*. I feel like I *could* be a relaxed person. How do people do it? You seem like a tranquil guy."

Jake waits to see if she's being serious, and then when he sees that it's not a rhetorical question, ticks things off on his fingers with increasing joy. "My dad used to deal with stress by doing Krav Maga. Maybe there's an activity you could do that would help you. You could take up a sport, or do something with your hands." He lists other ideas. He talks about something his "friends" do...whoever those people are, if they even exist.

"It's very sweet of you to try and help me," says Alicia. She tells him *she* actually has a friend who makes jewelry, and she seems to really like it. "Maybe I *should* do something with my hands. I've had this idea for an art project. Maybe I should just go for it. I've always felt like I might secretly be an artist."

"Totally! I can't wait, Alicia. That sounds rad."

"You don't even know what it is."

Jake grins at her silently. Then he says he'll let her get back to her spa day. "I really like your mask," he says. "Okay, have a great time!"

Jake shuts the door and stands behind it for a few seconds, then leaves. He's always out of the house on Thursday evenings, but neither Alicia nor Remy has ever asked why.

After draining the bath, Alicia's pulse is so fast from the hot water that it frightens her.

She lies on the bed trying to relax, but has no success. She imagines someone coming into the bedroom with a gun. *Bang.*

He shoots her and she counts each bullet going into her body, the way you're supposed to count sheep. In her imagination, the noise makes all other noises quieter. *Bang!* Each additional bullet makes it harder to move, and soon she's very still and relaxed as the imaginary blood leaves her body and a profound coldness settles in.

It helps, but not as much as it used to. She discovered this relaxation technique when she was fourteen. Her whole life might have been different had she been one of those silent "ninja" vomiters she met in treatment—she'd probably *still* be bulimic. But once she was caught and her bedroom was moved next to her parents' bedroom (humiliating, to no longer have a door with a lock), it was impossible for her to get away with it. She had to lie in bed, wide awake, trapped within a body that felt bloated and excessive. In order to relax, she had to imagine *something* leaving her body, so she imagined blood.

Alicia often wishes that her life retained some of the magic and discovery of her earlier years, even and especially during what her mom called her "illness." She remembers taking scientific interest in the transformed contents of her stomach, in the same way that she now imagines boys first take interest in their ejaculate. Sometimes, after exorcising several waves of some beige meal, she'd see a piece of half-digested candy glinting in the manger of fried food—something she thought had long gone—and feel amazed at her own alien immensity.

At the time, it felt like she was clearing away a mess in order to reveal a more perfect self. This idea persists, even if she doesn't vomit anymore, since it reminds her so viscerally of childhood. She still believes in reaching an essential part of herself through discipline: If she does everything right, she'll find her way to some mystical nugget...a form in which her beauty is self-evident, her destiny clear, her neuroses shriveled and fallen away. Often that version has seemed as concrete as a person sitting in the next room.

It makes sense that eventually, that person might knock on the door.

* * *

Alicia reads *The Apple Bush* until Remy comes home. In the introduction, the author outlines her qualifications as a "healer, lifestyle expert, and spiritual counselor."

> Whether you want to achieve your potential in a Fortune 500 company, found a small business, or break through the obstacles in an unsatisfying marriage, my guidelines for self-fulfillment can help you identify Signifiers of Flow, extinguish Toxic Antagonists, and zero in on your Consummate Result. *The Apple Bush* isn't just about saying yes to life, it's about recognizing Yes Opportunities!

Remy comes home and Alicia gets up and stands in the doorway, in the dark. The earrings hang from her ears.

"I totally forgot dish soap. Did you pick some up?" says Remy.

"You shouldn't have come here," says Alicia-as-Jen. "Horus is going to be home any second. We can't keep doing this."

Remy puts down the six-pack in his hand. "Do you want me to go?"

"I'm not kidding. I'll call the police."

"So call the police."

Alicia-as-Jen picks up her phone and Remy strides over to the door and knocks it out of her hand.

"You're pathetic," she says. "Go hassle your lame-ass girlfriend."

"Do you think you're too good for me?"

"I *am* too good for you."

They hear the sudden blare of a YouTube ad about *savings at Macy's,* and this reminder of Jake's presence makes them go into the bedroom and shut the door. There's a brief silence.

"You look so tense," says Remy. "Let me get those knots out of your shoulders."

Alicia laughs, and the careful, sexy spell they'd cast disappears.

"I've probably just been surfing *too damn hard,*" says Alicia. She waits for Remy to laugh, but he doesn't. They both feel ridiculous. She loosens her halter-top. "God! This is *so* embarrassing! My boob fell out of my bikini!"

Remy says, mainly to himself, "Why is she wearing a bikini at home?"

"It's not inconceivable."

"You thought you were rid of me, didn't you?" says Remy, trying to get the fantasy back on track.

There's a silence, in which Remy's poor acting sits in the air between them. In order to punish her for his own embarrassment, Remy tells Alicia that if she really wanted to look like Jen she could at least use an acne wash or something.

"I'm sorry," says Alicia, as if it's her fault that their sex game has devolved into a weird skit.

Remy touches the cardigan she's wearing. "Are you kidding me?" he says.

"It's not like I stole it. She let me borrow it." When Remy sits on the bed, Alicia reminds him that Jen deserved to have her shit stolen. "You weren't mad when I stole that wine."

Remy is silent for a while, and then says, "I feel like we established parameters. And what you've been doing lately exceeds those parameters. It makes me nervous."

"You mean back when you knew more about her than I did."

"I still know more about her."

"I can't explain anything to you." Alicia holds the cardigan tighter around her and says that at the time, it felt like the right thing to do. "I think it makes it easier to channel her. Things are different now. I have a relationship with her too."

While Alicia is at the register at the Hungry Goat the next day, a dirty-looking guy wanders in and stands by the door, having a phone conversation through his earbuds and chewing on the mic while speaking into it. "I dunno. I'm in some kind of weird place," he says. Alicia is confused at first about why she can't take her eyes off him, and then realizes that it's Jake Gyllenhaal. Cassie, unable to scream, squeezes Alicia's arm, painfully, as a substitute. She says in Alicia's ear, "You have *got* to let me ring him up."

"I don't think he's even buying anything."

"Move over."

Jorge asks Cassie to take out the trash, and Cassie says that Alicia just volunteered. "No I didn't," says Alicia, loudly.

"You're not even a fan," says Cassie in a whisper, and Alicia says, "You don't know that."

Jake Gyllenhaal looks around the shop with lowered lids, kicking the molding near the entrance with his shoe. His eyes pass over Alicia without registering her, in the same dismissive manner as Cassie's roommates. The hems of his boot-cut jeans are muddy. "Which ocean is the one with sharks in it, because that's the one I don't go in," says Jake Gyllenhaal into his shoulder. He's carrying a metal water bottle and walks around the shop as if it's a movie set, as if no one here is a real customer and this isn't a real business. There are currently no tourists in the Hungry Goat, so no one bothers him.

He sets the metal water bottle on the counter next to the coffee creamer, in a way that suggests there's an implicit command for her to fill it. It's unclear. Alicia hates it when people put their shit on the counter.

"I don't know where I am, but can you meet me?" he says into the mic.

Jorge says *Alicia, the trash* and Cassie says, "Yeah Alicia, the trash."

Alicia despises Jake Gyllenhaal, someone she normally sees on a screen, and therefore someone she normally has the power to *turn off*—to disappear. Jen would never be in this situation. Jen would never be completely ignored by Jake Gyllenhaal and then forced to take the trash out in front of him. And if she were, she'd probably have the guts to be a bitch about it. Jake Gyllenhaal meanders around the entrance area, partially blocking the door.

"Cassie, *you* get the stupid trash," says Alicia-as-Jen. She reaches under the counter, pumps Cassie's special hand lotion into her palm, and smears the lotion all over Jake Gyllenhaal's water bottle while he's looking away. Cassie reacts to this in an enraged whisper, and Alicia ignores her. She takes the next customer's order.

Jake picks up the water bottle and it slips from his hands, making a tremendous noise when it falls on the tile. Everyone waiting for their sandwich order looks at him and immediately looks away. "Jesus, shit," he says. He tells the person on the phone, "I dunno. Something freaky happened." He briefly makes eye contact with Alicia-as-Jen, looking frightened and confused.

"Solve *that,* Zodiac," says Alicia, under her breath, once he's looked away.

On her day off, Alicia goes to a skincare store to buy a serum and a cleanser. She's seen the serum in the background of Jen's photos before, and even, once, in Jen's hand in Montauk, while she was standing in the door of the master bedroom and smearing it on her face. Jen has certainly been to this store. She might even be there today.

The store is filled with attentive associates who have been trained to give compliments before engaging the customer in a granular conversation about their skin type. "I love your top!" says a store associate. Alicia is used to store associates pretending that she's fascinating, but this time she really is.

She names the serum Jen was holding, and says, "I'm also looking for something that's going to keep me moisturized while I'm on the water. I'm a surfer."

The store associate agrees that salt water will *really* strip moisture from her skin. "You want to avoid rinsing with water too, so make sure you're using an oil cleanser."

Alicia-as-Jen is persuaded to buy two more items besides the serum. Her posture doesn't change when she sees the final price. She observes the other customers in the store with languid interest. Alicia is often frightened of this genre of makeup-less shopgirl, but it occurs to Alicia-as-Jen that she could work here.

The store associate, for some reason, is smiling violently when she takes Alicia's debit card. She thrusts a sample at her. The movement is passionate, as if it were a dagger she'd like used on her. "Here! Have some free squalene!" she says.

Alicia fills out an application to work at the skincare store. Then she goes to Home Depot and takes pleasure in picking out interestingly shaped pieces of wood. She keeps herself open, throwing items in the cart on instinct. She buys several small towel racks, their placement appearing in her mind with sudden perfection. She stops a man in an orange vest and points at the package of screws she put in her cart. "What do you think? Are these all the screws I need?"

"It depends. What do you need them for?"

"I mean screws that I might need, like, in *general.* Just generally."

The man looks at her. Alicia-as-Jen stands up straighter, as if she's un-kinking to allow circulation of a brilliant substance that flows throughout her body.

"I'm actually an artist, you know? So I want to keep myself open. I want to know that if an idea strikes me, I'll have enough screws."

"What type of wood are you working with?"

"All types, I believe."

The man touches his face. Alicia-as-Jen says, "Perfection isn't really the goal here. I'm just making a prototype, initially. Later I'll make the real thing."

"Is this going to be a load-bearing object? Or are you making something decorative?" She asks him what load-bearing means.

The man says that his wife often makes little bears playing drums around Christmastime, to hand out to neighbors and family. "They're sort of her trademark. But that's an excellent example of something that doesn't have a load, because the bear just sits there on the mantelpiece."

The idea of these unburdened bears charms Alicia, and activates a deep affection for the man. She asks him where he's from, sure they have that in common.

"I'm from here," he says. He's confused.

"I've never heard of anyone here having a mantelpiece."

"Well." The man touches his face again.

"I don't mean to sound enigmatic," says Alicia, "but my object will be both decorative and functional. At least in its final iteration."

"Is it...a rocking horse?"

"Building it imperfectly will allow me to visualize it, do you understand? Only with imperfect steps can I shuffle my way towards perfection."

The man tells her that for any load-bearing part, she needs to make sure to drill a pilot hole first. Alicia-as-Jen finds such details stupid. She can learn the particulars later. They won't matter until the real thing.

Remy sees the pile of wood in the alcove when he gets home, and asks Alicia what the deal is.

"I think you know what it's for."

Remy vaguely recalls some mention she made of an art project. She's brought it up several times, but he thought that, like all of her projects towards self-actualization, it would never really materialize.

"Can you afford to spend money on this?"

"Maybe I'm refusing to allow money to hold a tyrannizing position in my life."

"Can I speak to Alicia please? For a second?" Remy opens his laptop and asks her what she wants to watch. He asks her if she's seen the photo Jen uploaded today, of her and Horus in a rock-climbing studio.

"It's too late to watch something," says Alicia.

"She posted another picture!" Remy shows Alicia the picture, of Jen at her workplace, and points out everyone he knows. "These aren't just *her* friends. I know these people too. I'm still in touch with some of them…kind of. If she thinks she's socially free of me, she's *wrong.*" Remy says Jen's picture is a clear example of a decoy post.

"What's that?"

"She posted a picture at midnight last night to act like she doesn't care about peak engagement times, but she knows that a picture with several tagged people will do well regardless. It's an *illusion* of indifference."

"Have *you* done that before?"

"I can't believe her. She's not chill. She's just as fraudulent as everybody else."

The picture is of Jen, her arms interlocked with two other girls in the low light of the cocktail-slash-tapas bar where she's currently employed. "We recommend the Riesling!" says the caption.

Alicia looks at the picture again in the morning, while smoking on the fire escape. Remy tells her that he doesn't like this new habit.

"Horus doesn't mind," says Alicia-as-Jen. Remy flips her off in a less playful way than usual. "Are you hungover?" says Alicia. When he refuses to interact meaningfully, she reenters the kitchen through the window. She points out that part of the background in the picture is suspiciously curved.

"So?"

"So she might be Photoshopping or Facetuning some of her posts." With her pinkie nail, Alicia traces a liquor bottle that doesn't have its customary shape.

"Jesus Christ. No wonder she didn't post any photos while we were there."

"Or maybe she was just having a nice time and *staying in the now.*"

Jake enters the kitchen and Remy hands the phone to him. "*You'd* know about this. Does it look like her waist has been Photoshopped to look smaller?"

"Oh yeah! Maybe. She could have just used an app." Jake looks up to see if this insight pleases them. "I think a lot of Instagram models do that to their photos—not that I'm an expert on Instagram models or anything."

"We don't know for a *fact* that she altered the photo," says Alicia. "It *feels* right, though."

Jake tells Alicia that he saw her pile of wood in the alcove. "I'm so excited to see your creation! I really liked the inspiration pictures you posted."

"Where did you post pictures?" says Remy.

"Jake and I follow each other on Pinterest. You're welcome to follow me too, Remy."

"Pinterest is the best," says Jake. "There are lots of great pages. You can follow anything you want! I have one for tattoo fails. They're hilarious!" He opens up his phone, swiping like mad to show Remy before his attention falters.

Later, Remy says to Alicia, "I didn't realize that you and Jake were such good friends."

"There's a lot that you don't know about me."

He asks Alicia if she wants to go to a movie, but she says that her horoscope told her she needs to concentrate on her work.

"So you don't want to let money be a tyrant in your life, but it's fine if astrology is?"

Remy has promised himself that he'll never be the type of smart-ass guy who trots out *that one NASA article,* but he tells Alicia that the planets have shifted so much that no one's sign is accurate anymore.

"Belief structures aren't about the beliefs *per se,* Remy."

Remy asks her if that's from the book she's reading. Alicia tells him he doesn't need to be so patronizing—the book is really insightful.

"And what are you learning?"

"That I should let go of that which 'occludes or contaminates my Essence.' And right now, with your negativity, I suspect that you are occluding or contaminating my Essence."

Remy laughs. "I feel like I hardly know you."

"I know. Isn't it exciting?"

"You were sleep-talking again last night. Did I tell you that? You should have seen yourself."

"Really?"

"It was pretty hilarious. You had your hand on my neck. I'm beginning to think you really did choke Jen."

Alicia smacks a bottle of wood glue against her hand. "Stop teasing me," she says.

"I'm serious. It really happened." Alicia focuses on the wood glue and Remy complains about the unexplained stains in the bathroom. "Do *they* signify anything to you? Do they give you any kind of feeling?"

"I think it's just a part of the sink rusting and bleeding onto the floor."

"Rust isn't black. It's probably mold." When she ignores him, Remy decides that his irritation mostly has to do with how dirty the bathroom is lately, since she's the one who normally cleans it.

Jake lends Alicia his drill and Alicia tries to watch a YouTube video about picking the right drill bit. It's nine minutes long. She does *not* have the time for that. She uses a hammer and nails to make a rickety square structure, bolstering the corners with packing tape. Jake puts his head in the alcove, observes the structure, and asks if she's considered taking a woodworking class. "Too expensive," says Alicia. "My style of learning is more autodidactic."

"It doesn't really look like anything I saw in your pictures."

Alicia's Pinterest board includes pictures of hot tubs, sensory deprivation chambers, expensive spas, retreats, swimming pools, beaches, Google image search results for "paradise," and tropical birds. "That was a mood board. It's more about my state of mind than what it's literally going to look like."

"But all of the objects were made of other materials. Like that plastic thing." Jake makes his hands into a clamshell to illustrate the sensory deprivation chamber on her Pinterest board.

Alicia tells him that working in plastic is unrealistic, and she needs to keep herself open to other options. She fits together two precut pieces of wood and says, "These fit together perfectly! I was imagining my windows as round, but maybe this is a sign that they're supposed to be square!"

"They're *supposed* to fit together. They're designed that way." Jake keeps observing her and eventually says, "I just can't help but think, Alicia, that maybe it would be a good idea to make it as good as you can the first time. If you give one hundred and ten percent the first time, then the next time, maybe you can give one hundred and fifty!"

"This is just a prototype. It's not supposed to look good. It's all a part of the process."

Jake says he didn't realize that it *wasn't* supposed to look good. "In which case, great job!"

From the bedroom, Alicia hears Remy laugh.

Alicia puts down the hammer and tells Jake that sure, she'd like to make it beautiful the first time. "Maybe, in an alternate universe somewhere, where I didn't acquire brain damage at a young age, there's an Alicia who makes it wonderful the first time. But I'm working with the limited capacities that I have."

Jake apologizes and says that she's the artist, and he doesn't always understand these things. "I always thought you were really smart."

Remy suggests that they go on a date over the weekend. "The way we used to, in the beginning."

"When did we ever go on dates?"

"We can get cocktails and shit. We could day drink."

Alicia says she has a job interview tomorrow. "We can't stay out too late."

They go to a bar in a different neighborhood than they're used to, spending money in a way that rejects its tyranny over their lives. It's surreal to drink with the sun still up. Remy talks about Jen's latest photos, and how, based on her social media presence, no one would suspect that her surf trip was anything less than stellar.

"Who's this kid?" says Alicia, looking at a picture of Jen with a small child.

"He's gotten so big!" says Jen's caption. They both look at the child, silently. Alicia points at the picture. "His face looks rounder than the rest of his body. Do you think...?"

"He's, like, ten. That would be crazy."

"Maybe. All I'm saying is that the proportions look off."

They attract the attention of a barfly with an alcoholic's bagged eyes. His face is oddly alert, and he has an easy way with the bartender that makes him seem like a relative of the owner. In any other situation, they would ignore his questions. But unlike most drunks, he's interested in them instead of exclusively absorbed in himself. When he asks them several leading questions, they tell this stranger about their weekend in the Hamptons, liberated by his ignorance of the situation and the distance of this neighborhood from their own. He validates their concerns, and agrees that Jen seems like "a real cunt."

"She took advantage of him while he had a concussion," says Alicia. "She hooked up with him even though her boyfriend was staying in the same house."

"Horrible," says the man. "Awful."

Remy shows the guy his phone. "She may very well have Photoshopped this child to look thinner. That's the level she's at—where we suspect her of Photoshopping children!"

"I had a girl once throw a bulk-size bag of milk at me."

"A what?"

"I worked in a cafeteria and we had this milk that went in the machines. It came in bags. You had to feed the bags into the machines. This girl threw one at me."

Alicia and Remy wait for the man to give them more information.

"Did it break?" says Alicia.

"It didn't break. It sure hit me, though." Alicia and Remy stare at him, and he repeats, again, "She threw a bag of milk at me," and smacks his shoulder to indicate where. They continue to stare at the man, less comforted by his validation.

Remy goes to the bathroom, suddenly cognizant, as he stands up, that he's *turned the corner*—a term he and Alicia use for the precise point when the euphoria of the first few drinks has passed and the futility of continuing to drink is apparent, even as you're aware that you won't stop. He walks towards the bathroom and thinks about the scene he's leaving behind: Alicia talking to an old drunkard once hit by a milk bag about a girl who isn't even their real friend. How many more times is he going to find himself in this scenario? What happens next? Do they just keep talking about Jen forever, until she gets old? Then what? Do they move on to someone else?

The bathroom mirrors are clotted with stickers and graffiti, and while washing his hands he watches very small sections of his face—whatever's visible between the decals. Assisted by the alcohol, he can almost imagine that he's someone else. The light bulb in the bathroom flickers, blinking out and back on, revealing Remy's wet mouth next to a sticker that says FUR LOOKS BEST ON ITS ORIGINAL OWNER: WEAR YOUR OWN SKIN NOT THEIRS #COMPASSIONISFASHION. Then it blinks out again.

Remy feels around the small bathroom for the doorknob or the light switch. He smells something electrical, possibly the burnt-out bulb. The doorknob isn't where it's supposed to be, and he gropes above and below his waist.

He touches the wet trash can lid and draws back, at the same time feeling a small breeze, as if a moth just flew past his cheek. Only now does he think to use his phone light. *I'm an idiot,* he says aloud. He holds up his phone and turns on the flashlight, which hits the mirror and bounces back into his eyes, too bright. He sees nothing but white, and then, in the cracks between the stickers on the mirror, he sees the reflection of his face, and then the reflection of another face, behind him—the lower half lost in shadow, but the eyes globular, black, larger than any he's seen on a human before. "Fuck!" he says.

He swings the phone down towards the wall, finding the doorknob, his fingers slipping on the lock. The electrical smell intensifies and Remy works on the doorknob, ignoring movement near his eye. He unlocks the door, his sweaty hands slipping on the knob, and swings it open. He stumbles out into the dark bar, which now seems very bright, arms wheeling forward as he stabilizes himself. A man waiting outside the bathroom says, "All good?"

Remy's breathing is ragged. "The light's out in there," he manages to say.

The man looks confused. Remy turns around and sees that the bathroom bulb hasn't blown out at all. The light's on. Everything looks normal. "Forget it," says Remy. "I'm just drunk. Sorry, man. Actually, hang on." He keeps the door to the single-occupancy bathroom open and puts one foot inside, keeping his other foot safely on the outside of the threshold. The flashlight on his phone illuminates every corner and reveals nothing. He turns off the flashlight. "All good," says Remy, and thumps the doorframe as if it were the hood of a car. "Go ahead."

He experiences no trace of the fear he felt only seconds before, and this reassures him—he was just drunk, or possibly still experiencing side effects from his head injury. *Perhaps I should see a psychologist,* he thinks, amused, knowing that he won't. Upon leaving the bathroom, he feels both more and less awake, as if exiting a movie theater after three hours in the dark.

A few days later, Remy suggests that they go back to the thrift store where they found the halter-top. Alicia says she doesn't feel like it, but Remy says he needs a jacket, now that it's colder. It's not a lie. Alicia is busy on her phone and doesn't look through the racks for items that will make her look like Jen. It takes several interactions with her before he realizes that, as Jen, she's ignoring him—Alicia would never ignore him like this.

"How do you like this?" he says, holding up a black hoodie.

Alicia-as-Jen smiles at him and says, "There's nothing to say about it. It's boring."

Remy tells her he's buying the hoodie. "If Alicia has an opinion about this purchase, she should speak now."

"I don't know what you want from me. It's a black hoodie."

"I said *Alicia.*" Remy complains about how unpleasant Alicia-as-Jen is being.

"I'm an *asshole*—didn't you get the memo?"

They take the train home and Remy holds on to his purchase, wishing that it could magically turn him into someone else, the way the halter-top did for Alicia. Alicia-as-Jen looks at her phone.

They pass a construction site on the walk to the apartment and a man in a yellow hat raises a flag at a massive, uncategorizable machine. The man indicates they should pass over the sidewalk, and all the construction men smile or direct pleasant, polite expressions at them.

"I love construction," says Alicia. "Not development, obviously. But the whole process. It's so dramatic."

"What do you think they're building?" The noise is tremendous and the activities cryptic. It looks like a shallow hole. Earth lies in chocolaty heaps all around the borders of the property—a jagged laceration disrupting the sidewalk.

As the man lowers his flag, no longer keeping the crushing machine at bay, Alicia has the ecstatic sensation of having been pardoned—as if she were the only person they spared from the machine today, and as if the construction workers' pleasant expressions were specifically and only for her.

Without discussing it, they stop and watch the machines, from the safety of a chain-link fence. After a few minutes, Remy brings up his previous complaint, about "parameters," and exceeding them. He points out that Alicia was an asshole to Jake, and now she's being an asshole to him. "I don't understand the plan. You're pretending to be Jen, and then what? How is it a transformation to become a poor imitation of someone who already exists?"

"Obviously she's not the final goal, she's just—"

Remy says "A prototype" before she can.

"—sort of a way station. Like a model or a guide. I think she came into our lives for a reason. She's a Signifier of Flow, leading me towards my Consummate Result."

"Is this what you read in that book?" He doesn't understand what she's saying. "I still don't even understand why it's called *The Apple Bush*. This book makes no sense."

"A. B. Fisketjon says to follow your intuition, and this is what I'm *sensing*."

"I hope your final transformation isn't a sadist who I can't take anywhere."

"It's just something working itself out. When people go on juice cleanses, their body rebels. You feel awful and you have crazy shits because your body is *purging* itself of the bad matter. And then you become *clean*."

"I just hope our relationship lasts through this purge." He says this hoping that Alicia will recognize it as a veiled ultimatum.

She doesn't react. "Me too."

During her interview at the skincare store, she tells them that yes, her ID says her name is Alicia, "but everyone calls me Jen."

"Cool. So it's like a chosen name?"

"Sure." Alicia-as-Jen occupies the plastic chair in a louche new way, like a cold-blooded animal.

The girl interviewing her wears a long shirtdress and masculine perfume. Her eyes travel up and down Alicia-as-Jen's presentation. "For sure!" she says. "I love that. This is a place where you should feel free to be yourself. It *is* minimum wage, just so you know. But you'll learn *so much* about skincare. It's really so much more than you think. It's like chemistry!"

"Wow. They should pay a chemist's wage, then."

"That's so funny!" says the girl. "You're so funny!"

While Cassie is in the bathroom, Alicia takes a hundred-dollar bill from Cassie's till and slips it under her own drawer.

Cassie comes up short at the end of the day. She counts and recounts the money. She sweats beneath her mandatory bandana. "I hate sweating. I absolutely hate sweating," says Cassie, recounting.

"Gosh," says Alicia, because she doesn't trust herself to say more.

Cassie says she's going to clean out the espresso machines and hope the money "starts breeding or something. I think I just need fresh eyes." She returns several times during closing to recount the money. Finally, Alicia pretends to find the bill underneath Cassie's own drawer. "It must have just fallen *really far* back there," she says.

"I absolutely adore you," says Cassie, kissing the air around her face.

Cassie keeps saying nice things. She even asks her if she'd like to go somewhere and get a drink once they finish closing.

Alicia waits so long to answer that Cassie repeats herself. "I could use a beer, couldn't you? I thought I was going to get fired. Seriously. I love you right now. I *love* you."

"I'm sorry, I can't," says Alicia. Alicia observes that she and Cassie are similar after all. They're both responsive to the language of rejection, although in different ways. A short time ago, no matter how grateful, Cassie would never have asked Alicia to get a drink. Now, the more Alicia refuses, the more Cassie insists. It's an aggressive insistence, unlike Alicia's might be, but the fear is the same.

Alicia says, "There *is* something you could do for me."

"Anything, babe! Within reason, obviously. Nothing that involves physical exertion."

"I need something unusual. Not a samurai sword. But something like that."

Remy tells Inez about Alicia's behavior while they're doing side work. She's heard a lot of complaining about Alicia in the past few weeks, and ignored his stories about the trip.

Remy says that he's considering getting Alicia a parrot. "At least it might distract her from this Spod project. And keep her from pissing me off so much."

"I feel sorry for Alicia."

"You wouldn't if you were in my position. You're so empathetic, Inez."

"I'm an actress. It's my job."

Remy makes a sly comment about casting couches, attempting to give the conversation a sexual charge, but Inez doesn't respond to this.

"If I were in Alicia's position, I'd be like, 'I'm going through something important right now, and if Remy doesn't understand that, then maybe my time with him is finished—'"

"She pulls shit like this and I'm beginning to think the same thing."

"'—and a parrot isn't going to distract me from the fact that my boyfriend isn't allowing me to work *through* something.'" Inez's version of Alicia is tinged with her own severity.

"What else would she say?"

"I don't know."

"C'mon, keep going."

Inez says no. Remy asks why not. He says it's slow right now, and she's not busy. "What else do you think she'd say? Let's role-play this, as practice. I'll be me."

"I don't want to," she says. "You're irritating me."

Alicia meets Marvin at a warehouse in Gowanus. The entire time he speaks with her, he doesn't stop wiping his hands with a rag. He's a man difficult to picture in sunlight.

"I guess you're an artist?" he says.

Blood goes to her face. She holds out her envelope of cash as if it gives her permission to be here.

"Follow me. Watch your step. I just put out rat traps."

Alicia makes small talk about rat traps—how they used to use adhesive ones at the restaurant. Marvin gives her a long and graphic explanation of why he prefers snap traps, recounting some of his notable experiences killing rodents.

She tries to talk to him as Jen, but in this warehouse, discussing rat-killing, Jen is unavailable. It's as if Alicia's ability to inhabit Jen were inhibited by the metal walls and the remote location.

The warehouse is dark, and intermittently lit with unkind light bulbs. It's a single room, but the objects are stacked in a way that partitions it into discrete spaces. Marvin leads her along a path delineated by plastic bins, along shelves stacked with appliances, antique furniture, and framed paintings. They happen upon two crèche-like scenes: a man, illuminated by a clamp light and stretching a canvas, and then two girls moving light bulbs from one pile to the other as they test them. They lift their heads as Alicia passes, and then return to the light bulbs.

Marvin switches the rag to one hand and holds her elbow. "Watch out," he says, and points down at a hose that traverses the ground and ends, running, into a bucket. Alicia steps over the hose.

"Here it is," he says.

The hot tub has a pearlescent white plastic interior, each body-shaped indentation delineated by nozzles. The exterior is blue and decorated with Patriots logos. "I don't know if you're into sports. I thought if I told you about the logos, you might not be as interested," says Marvin.

"I love the inside! I can always cover up the exterior."

The rag goes around his hands and under his fingernails. "It's your basic plug-and-play. Hundred and ten volts. A friend of a friend wanted it for a Super Bowl party last year but it came too late, and then the Patriots lost. I think looking at it made him sad."

Alicia runs her hands along the interior curves. Marvin's face brightens then darkens as the girls test their light bulbs. He says, "There are some nicks from storage and moving, so it's not in perfect condition, but it works. I tested it out."

"You did?"

Marvin explains the hose's presence by pointing at it. He stares at her for several seconds. "I'm very clean," he says.

"I believe you! I just—" Alicia looks at Marvin. It's true that his body seems clean. The illusion of grime has been created by the shabbiness of his clothes, and the way they dangle from his massive frame. "How was it? Was it fun?"

"It's a hot tub," says Marvin. He tells her what it will cost to have his "boys" bring it over.

Alicia sets up the hot tub in the alcove, briefly crowding the living room with her janky wooden structure, and transposing the junk in the alcove to the living room floor. Remy trips over a gallon of black paint that Jake bought a long time ago in hopes that they'd let him paint the kitchen black.

"Can you imagine what a nightmare it would have been if that had spilled everywhere?" Remy tries to get a reaction from her, but she ignores him. She doesn't have the money left for a hose, and fills the tub by toting mop buckets of water from the bathtub.

"And how are you going to drain it, once it's full?" Remy says.

"There are ways. I'll worry about it later."

"How did this Marvin guy drain it?"

"I don't know! He did somehow, so it's not impossible." She tells him that the plan is to fill up the hot tub, then put her wooden structure on top, enclosing it.

"Did you check your measurements first? So you know that the two pieces will fit together?"

"It probably won't fit. But I'll figure it out. It's all a part of the process."

He tells her it's a fire hazard and a mold trap. He tells her that she'll get a yeast infection, or *E. coli.* "And then you'll give a yeast infection to me. *Then* how will you feel?"

"Just think about how much fun you'll have telling your next girlfriend how nuts I was."

"Very funny."

"*Jake* is supportive of my project," says Alicia.

"But I'm *honest* with you. Isn't that a nice attribute in a partner?"

Alicia stands back to look at the hot tub. She says she'll probably cover up the Patriots logos. "Maybe I'll paint it blue."

When Remy gets home later that day, Alicia's wooden structure is sitting on top of the hot tub. The Spod is complete, and it looks like shit.

The top structure has been broken apart and shoddily nailed together again, in order to fit the hot tub. The gaps, where Alicia ran out of two-by-fours, have been covered with ragged sections of tarp and duct tape.

"Alicia?"

Remy looks in the kitchen and doesn't find her. He looks in the bedroom, and then the bathroom. He goes to the alcove and pulls back a flap of the tarp.

The lights have been turned off in the alcove, and lifting the flap doesn't allow him to see far inside the Spod. It's as dark as a stomach. "Are you in there?"

"Shhh!" says Alicia, her voice deadened by the surrounding wood. Water splashes against the sides of the Spod.

"Is it everything you hoped it would be?"

Silence. Then sloshing. "Alicia isn't here right now."

"Okay then. Can I speak to Jen?"

She doesn't say anything.

He says, "I'm going to make burgers. If Jen or Alicia is interested, they'll be ready in about twenty minutes."

Alicia doesn't come out by the time dinner is ready, and Remy eats both burgers himself. He looks at a picture Alicia posted under her new Instagram handle, @touchofjen. It looks like she used a face filter. Her solitary post—and the absence of any other person in that post—makes her account seem fake.

Alicia goes in to work at the Hungry Goat knowing that it's her last day, but not having told anyone that she'll be leaving. Much like the secret of being Jen instead of herself, the knowledge that she's quitting feels intimate and powerful.

During a lull, Cassie gets Alicia's attention by snapping her fingers in her field of vision. Alicia turns her head, and then turns back around. Cassie grabs her arm.

"Alicia! Is there still Cafiza in the espresso machine?" Alicia pulls her arm back and says, "Just in general? You touch me too much. We do *not* have that kind of relationship."

"If I make a latte for myself am I going to be poisoned?"

"Honestly? I hope you are."

The line cooks pretend to concentrate on the paninis. Alicia tells Cassie in a tight voice that she has no idea what it's like to be snapped at. "I'm not a *dog*. I would *never* do that to you."

"I don't know if you got your asshole bleached or what, but you are *not* the hot ticket you think you are all of a sudden."

Alicia gets her bag and tells Cassie that she can handle the whole shift on her own.

"Jorge is going to be pissed!" says Cassie. "I cannot believe you're being such a bitch. I didn't *have* to hook you up with Marvin. I did you a huge favor!"

"Jorge is going to be pissed at *you* for being the only reason I'm quitting this dumbass job."

Alicia has had three cups of coffee this morning. "Just think—*think* about how insufferable you are that single-handedly, you are the reason I'm quitting."

"You didn't think I was so insufferable when you were *begging* me to be your friend, dipshit." Cassie calls her pathetic and "unhygienic."

"I'm tired of listening to you talk about how oppressed you are because you're a redhead. You don't look bad because you're a redhead—you look bad because you're ugly as shit. You look like an... Irish goblin."

"You're trying to say *leprechaun,* retard. You can't even insult me right."

"And your content is terrible. My high school friends from home aren't even as boring as you are."

Alicia doesn't wait to put on her jacket, leaving before Cassie has time to formulate a zinger about her own physical appearance or social media presentation.

Remy comes home from a brunch shift and asks Jake if Alicia has returned from work yet. This is what it's been like lately—he asks Jake where Alicia is. It used to be Alicia he talked to as soon as he got home.

Jake says no. Remy tells him that he's considering what he said about a tropical bird. "She spends all her time in her Spod now. I think it would be good for her to have something to take care of outside of it."

"That's a great idea! Maybe I can help you look. I could be your wingman." Jake puts his hand on his forehead. "Dang, *wingman!* That pun was a total accident!"

"It's okay, I can handle it on my own."

"I want to help!" Jake weighs the advantages and disadvantages of different tropical birds. He walks around the apartment, identifying safety hazards. "We may have to change light fixtures," he says. "I never noticed how sharp these are before! This must be what it's like to be a parent. Your whole perspective changes."

"They clip their wings, Jake." Remy tells him not to get too carried away. "I'm just going to see what I can get that's not too expensive. Maybe they have *sales* on birds. Maybe if the birds are depressed or something."

"They live for a really long time. Like eighty years sometimes. Maybe you could get a discount on a *middle-aged* parrot."

"Yeah. Maybe I'll get her a middle-aged, depressed parrot."

"If anyone could take care of a depressed parrot, it would be Alicia."

Remy tells Jake that he's just joking around, and Jake laughs as if he knew the whole time.

Due to staffing shortages at the skincare store, Alicia-as-Jen receives only a few days of training and is thrust onto the sales floor with a shaky understanding of the items she's selling. This doesn't bother her.

Alicia-as-Jen doesn't feel self-conscious when she arrives in the morning, sweaty from her bike ride. Her coworkers are clean-faced and wear threadbare Rachel Comey. They talk about "investing" in "pieces." They mistake her ragged sweaters for better quality than they are. After a brief assessment period, they recruit her in their various personal and work-related dramas.

Alicia-as-Jen enjoys the slow, purgatorial morning and the blankness of the room, which elides one hour into another. The showroom is a white cube, with white-tiled floors, ceilings, and walls. Her coworkers say, ominously, that "there should be a drain in the middle."

To customers, she projects knowledge that she doesn't possess about hyaluronic acid, resveratrol, and caffeine molecules. They allow her to examine their faces. "You see this dryness here?" they say. Their eyes make decoding movements. The customers want to understand how they look to her. They apologize for their oiliness or redness and wait.

Alicia's life attains a simplicity it's never had before. There's her life, as Jen, in the blank room of the skincare store, and then her life in the Spod, which is simple in a different way. Inside, her body isn't buoyant, as it would be in a sensory deprivation chamber—she can't erase the sensation of the curved seat beneath her—but it's dark. For whole minutes, she forgets that she has a body. What surprises her most about sitting inside the Spod, thinking of nothing, is the sensation of privacy. What's less and less clear is to whom the privacy belongs.

It doesn't bother her that the Spod isn't perfect—the whole point was that it was a prototype. She's already decided that Horus may have been onto something when he brought up salination levels, and she keeps a running list of potential improvements in a notebook. It's not clear when she'll be able to move on to the next iteration, but she tells Remy that when it's time, the universe will provide her with the resources. In the next version, she won't feel the seat at all.

On a Wednesday morning, Jen walks into the skincare store with Horus. Alicia isn't surprised. Everything she's done these past few weeks was driven by a sensitivity to forces larger than herself—forces that work in inscrutable ways. It seems natural that these forces would bring Jen to her.

Jen doesn't see Alicia at first. Unlike other customers, she doesn't hesitate or look around before opening the sample liquid foundations and dabbing them on her hand.

Horus sees Alicia, and his expression is neutral. Jen looks at Alicia too. Alicia-as-Jen is wearing the earrings she bought from Jen, and the sweater that she stole.

Alicia-as-Jen waves and says, "Wow, it's so good to see you guys!"

"Are those earrings from my store?" says Jen.

"I didn't know you worked here," says Horus.

"Why would you know that? Can I help you? Are you looking for anything in particular?" Her voice isn't Jen's voice—it's a permutation of a permutation of Jen's voice, but slow and mocking in the same way. She steps from behind the payment counter and Jen steps back. Alicia waits, irrationally, for Jen to present her face like the other customers.

"I don't know what *all this* is? But it's really freaking me out." Jen's bracelets clatter as she indicates "all this."

Jen turns to Horus and says, "Do you see? She bought earrings from my store!"

"I enjoy supporting the arts. Is that a crime?"

A manager calls out Jen's name. Jen and Alicia say "What?" at the same time. Jen looks at the manager. The manager laughs and says, "Are you a Jen too? I meant the one who works here." She asks Alicia if she can ring up a customer.

"Let's leave," says Horus. Jen looks at the manager and then at Alicia.

She says, in a low, fast voice, "What the fuck? Where am I supposed to get my retinoids now? Is this what I have to deal with?"

"You can order online," says Horus. "Let's go."

"I'm going to get a restraining order!" says Jen to Alicia.

"I *work* here. What would you even tell them?"

Horus, again, tells Jen to leave.

Jen says something angry that Alicia can't hear.

"What do you expect me to do, punch her?"

They move towards the door, and Alicia says, "Wait!" Her voice sounds unhinged in the small showroom. "Would you like some free squalene?"

Jen stops and turns around, freezing in place directly opposite Alicia—a doppelgänger. Her expression is haunted. Then she turns and leaves.

"Who was that?" says one of Alicia's coworkers.

"Just this weird girl who's obsessed with me," says Alicia-as-Jen, throwing her hair behind her shoulder. It's not a convincing explanation, but she isn't embarrassed. Something important has happened. Alicia-as-Jen smiles at herself in one of the display mirrors. What she sees is no longer a convincing imitation, but herself. To employ that metaphor of escape velocity—which her recovery counselors liked so much—it's as if she has been ejected from the burning rocket and spat into the cold peace of outer space.

Remy sees a missed call from Jake during his lunch shift, but when he texts Jake, he doesn't get a response.

When he comes into the apartment, Jake steps out of the kitchen and says, "Okay, don't be mad."

"What did you do? Did you paint the kitchen black?"

"I think you'll like it! I know maybe you wanted this to be a joint project, but—"

Remy walks into the kitchen and sees a cage sitting on the table. It contains a parrot. The parrot points one eye in his direction.

"I just happened to be in a pet store," says Jake, "and I talked to the guy there and he said he'd give me a discount...and threw in the cage!"

"Jake, man, that's where we eat." The bird lifts a whitish foot and scratches at its neck, the feathers rising like scales. Vile particles fall into the bottom of the cage. "It probably has a disease. That's probably why the guy wanted to get rid of it."

"That pet shop was pretty bleak, dude. I bet this little bird's heart is so warmed by getting out of there."

"I was thinking of getting her a *nice* parrot. You do realize that when I said a depressed, middle-aged parrot, I was joking, right?"

"I don't think you want a nice parrot, man. Do you know what they cost? Some of them are over a thousand dollars."

Remy looks at the bird. It hasn't reacted to their argument. "I think you need to take him back."

Jake nods. He says that he understands. "Maybe we do a trial period. We foster the parrot. We can all be foster parrots, haha. You know how it goes, though. Before you know it, you'll fall in love."

* * *

Alicia still hasn't come home a half hour later, although her shift ended in the afternoon. Remy texts her, saying something about a surprise, and claiming enough credit for it that if she likes the parrot, he can say it was mainly his idea.

She doesn't respond. He asks Jake if there's any chance that she's been hiding in her Spod this whole time.

"I hope not. That would ruin the surprise."

The bird hasn't said anything. Remy takes his phone out and googles *parrot won't talk.* He says to Jake, "Maybe this one is broken."

"He's probably just nervous."

"That's why you got it for so cheap—he can't talk."

"Or she! I've been thinking of calling her Sandy. But I don't want to be presumptuous. She's your bird! Just an idea that I had."

Remy persuades Jake to remove Sandy from the kitchen table.

"Great idea. It'll be a bigger surprise if she's in my room, and then I take her out."

"Apparently not all parrots learn to talk. He may be too old."

Jake says that he'll play some "ambient sounds that will get her in the mood" and takes the bird into his room, shutting the door.

From the other side of his closed door, over the ruckus of Amazonian frogs, Remy can hear Jake saying, slowly, "Hello, Alicia! I love you, Alicia! Hello, Alicia!"

Remy texts Alicia again. He calls her, and doesn't hear her phone buzzing anywhere in the apartment. A few minutes later, lying on the bed, Remy hears another noise:

Knock-knock-knock-knock.

Remy sits still, hoping the sound will go away. And then: *Knock-knock-knock-knock.*

Alicia got trapped in her Spod, he thinks, with relief. This amuses him. But when he goes into the living room, near the alcove, he realizes that the knocking is coming from the front door.

Remy opens the door.

Two police officers are standing there, one woman and one man. The man says, "Are you Reymond Brundle?"

The cops ask to come in. Remy stands back and lets them into the apartment without processing the situation. The woman cop would be tiny without the bulging pockets and boxy structure of her uniform. Both of the cops creak mysteriously when they move.

"I have some bad news," says the woman cop. She tells him that they have reason to believe he's the best person to confirm the identity of a "decedent" brought to Woodhull Hospital for injuries related to a bike accident. "Shortly after she arrived at the hospital, she expired from those injuries," says the woman cop. "You were listed as her emergency contact."

The male cop says, "Based on the identification she was carrying at the time, we know the decedent was Alicia Hall. But we still need an official identification."

"Alicia wasn't in a bike accident," says Remy. "If she were, I would know."

"Why? Have you heard from her?" says the male cop.

Remy goes to the Spod, lifts the tarp, and examines the water. He puts his hand in the water and feels around. He tells them again that they're mistaken.

"Her bicycle chain broke," says the woman cop. "It must have been rusted through and she...took a tumble."

"I don't understand," says Remy.

The police officers give him more details, but cautiously. They're unwilling to fill in the gaps in Remy's visualization of this scenario. It takes several questions before they reveal that she didn't collide with a car, but rather a stationary junk receptacle for a building that was being gutted.

"A dumpster," he says, not believing. He learns that it was a head injury. “I think there’s been a mistake,” says Remy. “You don’t even know her.”

Jake opens the door, the parrot on his finger. “What’s up? Is Alicia home yet?”

“Did you get the parrot to talk?” says Remy.

This question surprises Remy; the impulse to protect Jake is unfamiliar and informs him that the stakes may indeed be serious.

When Remy retrieves these memories in later weeks, he can’t locate them within a timeline. They’re as real to him as the activities of a character he saw on television. The cops say they’ll take him to the hospital in their squad car. “It’s not like the movies,” says the male cop. “They have a nice sitting room. They’re gonna have you look at a few photographs and help you fill out some paperwork. You won’t have to view the body.”

The woman opens the rear door of the cop car and Remy looks at the back seat, its fake leather polished to a high shine from countless butts scooting in. It’s repellently glossy, like the sole of a foot. “I think I’d rather go by myself,” he says.

“No you don’t. Not on a Monday evening.”

“I really, really don’t want to ride in the car with you.” He doesn’t know why he doesn’t want to. He has the superstitious feeling that this is the wrong way to go about the process; if he arrives at the hospital with these cops, their mistaken worldview will follow him in and contaminate the situation.

The woman cop explains that this is protocol. “Reymond, it’s tricky without a guide. You’re going to have a hard time finding your way around without us.”

“I’m the bereaved,” says Remy. “Don’t you have to be sensitive to my needs? Doesn’t what I want matter?”

The woman cop asks the male cop what he thinks. They talk about someone who might be their supervisor. “We could call ahead,” says the male cop.

"Okay, Reymond," says the woman cop, closing the back door and opening the passenger side. "You go on without us. We'll make sure they're expecting you." Remy sees a blanket folded up on her seat, and a McDonald's cup in the cupholder. This woman will continue with her day, ensconced in the familiar objects that comprise safety and routine. If Remy does everything right, he may have this privilege as well. He's glad he made the correct decision to go on his own.

Remy points at the folded-up blanket and says, "Is it because you're short?"

The woman says that the seats are uncomfortable. "I can see why you would think that, though. I'm a little vertically challenged." She laughs, then stops.

"I guess pigs and blankets go together."

The cop looks at her feet, looks at Remy, and then grasps his upper arm. "You're having a tough time. I understand that. I wish you the best."

He takes an Uber to the hospital, thinking of nothing, then tabulating the ways Carla's predictions were incorrect. He checked and confirmed with the cops that there was nothing blue involved in Alicia's accident. The industrial receptacle was green. If Alicia were to do such a thing, it would likely be on purpose. But she couldn't have predicted when her chain would break, and even if she rigged it to break, she couldn't have timed it to cause such a precise impact.

Any more substantial considerations of Alicia's accident, beyond flitting anxieties about the financial impact on Remy in terms of shared rent, cannot be considered at this time.

Remy has difficulty locating the emergency room, and when he does, it occurs to him that the emergency room might not be the correct place for him to go. He tells the receptionist Alicia's full name, and then remembers what he's seen in movies. They won't let him see her if he's not family. He lies and says that she's his wife. "She's supposed to be dead."

"Is she now?" says the woman. For some reason, she has an Irish accent, which he finds unnerving. What route of life would lead an Irish woman here, to this country, to work as a receptionist in this Brooklyn hospital?

"But I think it's a mistake," he tells her. "She's definitely alive." The woman asks him to spell Alicia's name and types into her computer. She chews on a fake nail. "She's not showing up in our system."

"Do you have a separate system for the . . . deceased?"

The woman noodles with the system, talking more to herself than to Remy. After many serene seconds of searching, she says, "Ah! I knew it."

She explains that often she has to search possible misspellings, since "People get in *such a rush* that they put names in wrong. There's an Alicia *Halls*—with an 's'—who seems to be deceased. Unless I'm much mistaken, your wife, Alicia, has been admitted to the hospital for further treatment, and her emergency contacts notified."

"Yes! I'm the emergency contact!"

"She's in room four twenty-six. Take those elevators to the fourth floor."

Remy stares at her. "I knew it. I knew there'd been some mistake!"

"You've had a fright then, haven't you?"

Remy wants to walk away, but it feels irresponsible. This situation strikes him as far-fetched. Is she fucking with him? Shouldn't he ask more questions? He says, "So isn't that a big deal? Don't you need to do anything?"

"Mistakes happen. Don't you worry, dear. Go ahead and see your wife." The woman is already looking at the person in line behind him.

* * *

The hospital is filled with people speaking different languages, like an airport. Remy asks directions several times, but the people who look like staff say things like "I'm actually just here for a consult so I can't help you." The brown tiles are so shiny that Remy notices his feet blearily reflected right before each step. When he finally finds room 426, he knocks, and when he hears two voices tell him to come in, he enters. The room contains two beds. One of the beds is occupied by a teenager, and Alicia's bed is empty, although the sheets are disturbed.

The teenager looks at him with one eye. The other eye has a patch over it, and she watches him in the immobilized way of someone whose neck hurts. On either side of her are two people he assumes are her parents, who must have been the people telling him to come in. "Hi there," says the father. They watch Remy as he walks in, looks around, and then illogically pulls back the unmade blankets on the other bed, in case Alicia's hiding under it.

He says, "Did you see where the other girl went?" The parents look at each other. "Is she in the bathroom?"

"She's more like a woman," says the girl's mom. Remy hates her, profoundly.

"This is really not the time for your feminist agenda," says Remy.

The dad tells him to *just calm down,* and then draws back as if Remy might hit him.

Remy hears a door open behind him, and he turns around to see an older woman standing at the entrance of a wheelchair-accessible bathroom, the threshold lipless for easy exit. She says, "Are you the new nurse? Where's Bartholomew?"

Remy points at the old woman. He doesn't want an answer to the question he has to ask.

"I *told* you she was more like a woman," says the mom, quietly.

"So *you're* actually Alicia Halls?" he says to the old woman.

"*I* am," says the girl with the eyepatch.

Remy looks between the older woman, the girl, and the bed with its mess of blankets. He lifts up the blankets and searches through them again, as if evidence of Alicia could be hidden there.

"What are you doing to my blankets?" says the old woman.

He already knows that there's no chance he'll find Alicia under the blankets, but he also knows that if he leaves this room without thoroughly investigating, it will bother him forever.

A doctor knocks on the doorframe, then walks in with a clipboard. He heads for the girl with the eyepatch, but Remy intercepts him. He says there's been a mix-up. "Alicia Hall is supposed to be in this room but she isn't."

The doctor clicks and unclicks his pen. Remy explains the situation to the doctor, to the older woman now edging her way towards the hospital bed, and to Alicia Halls and her parents, pivoting around the room to address each portion of the crowd. The teenager's parents keep interrupting, and the hallway outside, surprisingly, is too noisy for him to make himself easily heard. Remy keeps referring to Alicia as his "wife," which makes him feel like he's lying about everything else, too.

As he turns and turns, he's reminded of the day when Jen gave him the wrong address and he turned around in the middle of the road, watching the dot that was him, expecting to see Jen appear at any second.

He isn't crying, he notices—he doesn't even have the impulse to cry. The doctor's eyes keep flicking towards the hallway, and he motions someone in scrubs to enter. "So you were informed of your wife's death, and yet you're looking for her here?" He looks at Remy with the distaste with which one would regard a hallucination.

"Please," says Remy, although he doesn't know what he's asking.

"But then he was counterinformed," says the older woman, now in bed, the sheets pulled around her neck. "And he had to check. Wouldn't you?"

"It *is* possible she was briefly admitted to the hospital before expiring later," says the doctor. "Let's discuss this outside."

"So you mean it's possible she was alive earlier?"

The doctor clicks his pen. "I don't see why it matters if she was alive earlier if she's probably dead now." Click. The doctor touches his forehead fastidiously, pulls his glasses up, and apologizes for his tone: "Mondays are rough around here." He turns to the male nurse he motioned into the room. "See if you can get some insight into his situation."

Remy waits in the hallway and is eventually handed off to another nurse, who points him down a staircase. Although the nurse could have been a doctor—Remy is suddenly aware that he's making these assumptions based on their race. This compounds his anxiety, since it's important for him to do everything right. The floor is chaotic and several patients atop rolling stretchers are parked and appear forgotten in the hallway. Remy goes down many stairs, following the nurse's directions.

Outside a basement room that is definitely not room 426, he sees Alicia, abandoned on one of those gurneys just like the patients upstairs. He recognizes her, even though a sheet is pulled halfway over her face. Her eyes are open, in the innocent surprise of a cartoon character whacked on the head with a frying pan. He isn't certain what the sheet and the absence of machines indicate—is she still alive? One can't always expect beeping machines like in the movies. Surely a real hospital isn't cheesy enough for *beeping machines.*

Two guys in scrubs, both with body piercings, come out and consult a clipboard before grasping the gurney on either end. Remy points, mutely.

"Can I help you?"

Remy says that she's his wife, and the two guys in scrubs open their mouths and exchange glances.

"I'm sorry, sir," says the guy with a clipboard. "She's not supposed to be just hanging out here in the hallway like this..."

"...Mondays are crazy," says Remy.

"Yeah! Yeah, they really are."

"Could you...could you do me a weird favor?"

"Do you want a moment alone with her?" says the other guy.

Remy wishes they'd just take their hands off the gurney. "Maybe? What I meant was, could you make sure she's dead?" There's a pause and Remy says, "I mean, not like that. Not like 'make sure.'"

The guy with the clipboard says, "Did you kill her?"

"There have been a lot of mix-ups today. I'm just trying to make sure you're not...doing whatever you're gonna do to the wrong person."

"I'm sorry, that was insensitive. I don't know why I said that." The guy with the clipboard invades Remy's personal space, penitently.

The other guy says, "I promise we're not *doing* anything. It's more like a temporary storage situation."

The man with the clipboard keeps apologizing, moving the clipboard through the air to express himself. "That was really unacceptable. Please forgive me."

This is exactly the type of overwrought apologizing that Alicia would do if she were here—or at least what the old Alicia would have done, before she was pretending to be Jen so much.

One of the men pulls down the sheet and checks her pulse, glancing up at Remy to assess his satisfaction with this method. The other man hands him a stethoscope and he puts it on Alicia's chest.

Remy looks at Alicia's uncovered face from close quarters. The bottom of her face is normal, but halfway up, this normalcy is interrupted by a bloody, diagonal dent that contains small amounts of green pigmentation. All of this makes Alicia's features present differently, as if she had a new haircut. People keep passing through the hallway—it's not a private moment. He listens through the stethoscope and looks up at her face from that odd angle, noting the shape of her weak chin, her nose, her mouth, and retracing these things over and over—like a maze on the back of a cereal box that he's solved fifty times before.

Remy stands up and looks at the girl who used to be Alicia, confused about where the real Alicia has gone. He must have been in the wrong room 426. He ignores the apologies of the two men.

He sets off in search of the *real* room 426, but all the doctors and nurses who ignored him before are suddenly hyperaware of his presence. When he goes somewhere he shouldn't, he's questioned, then escorted, kindly, to the sitting room where he was supposed to go in the first place. They show him several photographs while he drinks from a plastic water cup. One is of Alicia's face, and one of her sun-and-moon tattoo. "I already saw the body," he says. But no one listens. "That's her," he says, but he's not sure it really is.

Part 4

The Consummate Result

Remy is watching *Kill Bill Volume I* when Alicia's mom texts him to say that she's landed. He complains to Jake that she wants to involve him too much in the funeral arrangements. "I think she's trying to make me feel guilty for not helping out more."

"I'm sure she doesn't expect that."

Uma Thurman bites off the lip of her would-be rapist, who thinks she's in a coma, and Remy asks Jake if they can fast-forward to the martial arts stuff. "I'm really only in the mood for stylized violence. This is grossing me out."

Remy has taken a week off work, as has Jake. Jake has spent a lot of time alone in his room with the parrot. Remy and Jake watch movies together, without talking about Alicia's death beyond its logistical challenges. Remy has the sense that this is what it's like to get married: You leave your house, something massive happens, but then you go home and nothing feels different. It's as if Alicia's still at work. The main difference is that he's been receiving more engagement on his social media posts, and Alicia's mom, Cynthia, keeps calling him to "coordinate."

When Uma Thurman learns to wiggle her toes again, Remy's phone lights up with another call from Cynthia, and he pauses the movie and steps into the kitchen. She asks him a lot of unnecessary questions. It's possible that she simply wants to talk. "Do you have any framed pictures of her? Or any physical photos?"

"No. Just on my phone."

"That sounds lovely, Remy, just lovely. Are you able to get them off your phone?"

"I guess we could print them at the CVS. I don't know if you'd like the pictures I have of her. They're pretty goofy."

"*My* big idea was that we have a table at the funeral. And we can arrange a *tableau,* with pictures of her...and anything else she liked." Cynthia stops talking and cries for several seconds. Remy doesn't say anything. She finishes, and says, "What do you think? The funeral home wouldn't mind a *little* table, would they? I don't know how they do things up in New York."

Remy says he doesn't know. He doesn't understand why Alicia's mom thinks that he can magically divine the answers to these questions, as if living in New York and being Alicia's boyfriend give him unquestionable authority.

"You poor thing. I know you loved her so much. It's hitting you the hardest."

"...I think it's hitting you pretty hard. She *is* your daughter. Technically we weren't even family. I mean—" Remy hears how this sounds. "Yes, I did—love her," he says. He never used the word "love" with Alicia, but who will ever find out? It's not like Alicia will tell.

"People tend to blame themselves, and it's important to remember that there was nothing you could have done."

"I know that."

Alicia's mom repeats that there's nothing he could have done. Remy looks at Uma Thurman's face frozen on the screen. "I guess I could have nagged her more to get her bike chain fixed."

"There's *no use* thinking like that! You'll drive yourself crazy."

"I just keep...going over the details in my head."

Once Remy has adequately conveyed profound guilt, Cynthia is satisfied. Mentally, he checks to see if he feels guilty, but Alicia's death is still too abstract to elicit any specific emotions other than irritation. Remy wishes Alicia were here so he could complain to her about her parents.

He and Jake watch *Kill Bill Volume II,* shortened by Remy's impatience with the expository scenes, and then *The Matrix.* Remy has several beers and an edible that a busboy at work gifted to him when he found out about his "loss." He profoundly enjoys watching Keanu Reeves dodge bullets in slow motion.

Jake pets the bird, who still hasn't said anything. It looks healthier, although Remy is unable to pinpoint why. Jake asks Remy if he'd like to hold the bird and Remy says, "Absolutely not."

"Some studies show that physical contact with an animal every day is very helpful. It extends your life."

"Not if you run into a dumpster."

Jake is silent, and then asks Sandy the parrot, in a baby voice, what she thinks will happen next in the movie. He tells Remy that he should really think about "talking to someone."

"The way that you talk to Sandy?"

"I'm just trying to help, dude."

Remy has a dream that he's directing a community production of *A Midsummer Night's Dream* and he's managed to convince Charlize Theron to play the fairy queen.

Alicia plays Bottom, the guy who gets turned into a donkey. Unfortunately, during rehearsals, Alicia really does get turned into a donkey. "I just want to be a real girl again," she says, crying dark tears that smear over her face. Remy smacks the rolled-up script against his leg, impatiently, explaining how Charlize Theron is waiting for rehearsal to continue. "You know how the play goes," he says. "You'll get turned back eventually." He pulls on her ears as if they're the handles of a scooter, asking if she's sure this isn't a mask.

Remy has a sudden creative epiphany. A stagehand in dark

clothing passes by, watching Alicia's tears to make sure they don't go near the electronics, and Remy says to him, "I've figured it out! This is a dream!" He turns to Alicia, and says, "I can fix you anytime I want, since this is my dream!" However, he has a rehearsal to run, a show to put on, a Charlize Theron to keep happy, and therefore he doesn't think about how exactly he will turn Alicia back into a real girl. These are things to be dealt with later. For now, the show must go on.

The memorial service is held in a windowless room attached to the funeral home. It smells of vacuum cleaner. Alicia would have hated this room. Aside from the crêpe on the back of the stackable chairs, it's the sort of room where a standardized test might be administered.

Whenever Alicia talked about where she was from, Remy imagined her living in a treeless development; perhaps on some hot, gray stretch of highway, completely still except for the histrionics of a car dealership's wind-sock man.

But Alicia's relatives couldn't be from somewhere gray. Remy is exhausted by the intensity of sharing a room with people who manage to *teem* even in small numbers. Many of them remind him of Alicia's worst personality traits, but warped, amplified, and cheerful. Everyone at the funeral is wearing bright colors, to remember "how joyful" Alicia was.

"Don't you think she was so joyful?" Cynthia keeps saying.

"She was a lot of things," says Remy.

"We hope you'll join us for the ash-scattering ceremony. I've had the most amazing idea. We spoke to the *nicest* man at our hotel and he had the *best* suggestion."

Cynthia tells him that "the Halls" have become "absolutely *set*" on scattering her ashes in the Hudson Valley.

"Don't you think it would be better to scatter her back home?"

"No, she'd hate that. She hated coming home, to be honest.

Wouldn't it be great for her to be put to rest somewhere beautiful? Somewhere you can visit, and feel her presence?"

Alicia's dad says that it's supposed to be gorgeous in the autumn. He's a massive man with a big red crybaby face, and a loose neck held at bay by a Tweedle-Dum collar. Remy feels classic boyfriend anxiety around him. Alicia's parents both credit the man at the hotel with singular expertise. "He seemed like a real local," says Alicia's dad.

Remy says, "She didn't *love* the Hudson Valley."

He tries, politely, to convey that the Hudson Valley is a scam, full of eerily solvent puzzle stores, bad restaurants, and far-too-clean hippies. The only time Remy and Alicia had been there together—wandering around an idyllic town square, the hills rising fakely around them and the church bells striking three—Alicia said she was afraid they'd happen upon a public stoning.

"We don't have to scatter the ashes immediately," says Remy. "Maybe you guys could think about it for a while."

Alicia's dad says, "Did you know you have to pay extra to have your loved one cremated on her own? Instead of getting mixed in with other people? Isn't that outrageous?"

"Remy, we'll find a beautiful spot. *All* of the Halls hike, so this is a real Hall family sendoff. I think it's what she would have wanted."

"She never expressed an interest in the outdoors to me." Remy doesn't say that she also never expressed interest in being a part of the Halls.

"You'll change your mind once we're out in nature. You'll see it was a good idea." Cynthia grips his arm and says, not for the first time, "It's okay to cry. You don't have to hold back for us."

The service itself is tedious and over quickly. Cynthia makes him stand in line to accept condolences afterwards, although the line is painfully short, which embarrasses him. He doesn't know what to say to people. Inez says, "Anything you need" in his ear. Her breath is hot and leaves a longer impression than the words themselves.

Relatives he's never met offer to do huge favors "during this difficult time." He excuses himself to go to the bathroom as soon as he has the chance. He has the sense that the longer they cooperate with the ritual of Alicia's death, the harder it will be to undo it.

Abstractly, he knows this is foolish, but some uncertainty still lingers. Remy feels as if a mistake has been made, and if only he'd been able to find the correct room 426, they wouldn't have to go to all this trouble.

It isn't until later, when he's standing outside, assessing whether or not he has permission from Alicia's family to leave, that he realizes Carla came to the service. She puts her vape away when she sees him, perhaps out of respect. "I hope you don't mind that I didn't wait in line."

"It's not a problem." Remy looks at the strange guy standing next to her, with his hair gelled flat, and Carla introduces him.

"You brought a date to a funeral?" says Remy.

The guy tells Carla *I told you it might be weird* and Carla tells him to shut up. He tries to apologize to Remy: "Your girlfriend seemed... really cool," he says.

"She definitely wasn't *cool,*" says Remy, "and I don't know how seeing a slideshow of pictures taken when she was eight years old would give you that impression." It excites him to be shitty without the usual consequences.

"This isn't about you and your embarrassment," says Carla to her date. She points at a potted plant near the entrance to the funeral home and tells her date to go over and examine it.

When he leaves them alone, Carla rolls her eyes and calls the date "unbelievably self-centered."

"I actually enjoyed being mean to him. I'm glad you brought him."

"It's the randomest thing that he texted me today. Maybe it was a Signifier, trying to show me how I could provide you with some small amount of joy."

Remy looks around, and Carla knows who he's looking for. "Jen's in the Philippines."

"It's okay. I don't know why she would have come anyways."

"I'm going to call you to hang out in a few weeks. I'll give you a little time."

"Don't hang out with me just because you feel sorry for me."

"You don't understand. We have important things to discuss."

That evening, Jake is out of the house. Remy tries to clean the bathroom now that Alicia's not around to do it, but it's gone too long without attention, and he gives up. He dislikes the silence in the apartment, and lately has movies playing all the time, even when he's not watching. Generally, these are movies he never watched with Alicia, though he rejects the idea that this is how he's selecting them. He ends up watching older releases that normally wouldn't interest him: *Altered States, The Thing.* He finds these movies oddly reassuring, although he doesn't know why, since they don't qualify as "stylized violence."

Remy starts and pauses several things that irritate him before finally settling on *Hollow Man.* Kevin Bacon is administered a serum and disappears bit by bit, muscle by muscle, until even his skeleton fades away and all that's left is the indentation of his body on the gurney. "Vitals returning to normal, pulse one ten," says a fellow scientist. Remy interrogates the sense of security he's experiencing and decides that what he's responding to is the presence of the scientists. He's always enjoyed plotlines mediated by on-screen experts, since even when things go horribly wrong, eventually there's an explanation. There's no ambiguity or confusion when science is involved. Maybe he'll watch *Jurassic Park* next.

He divides his attention between the movie and pictures of Alicia. Although his iPhone has sorted his photos according to "People," it pleases him that he can identify pictures of Alicia that the algorithm can't. Here's Alicia holding a drink in front of her mouth. Here she is in a Donnie Darko bunny mask for Halloween. His phone doesn't recognize her, but Remy can always recognize her. He could even when she had a sheet over her face.

It gets dark earlier and earlier now. The movie ends and he doesn't turn on the lights. Four beers in, he gets a notification that Jen posted a new picture. Interestingly, she still hasn't blocked him. The picture is geotagged in Siargao, an island in the Philippines he's never heard of. The caption says, "6am an still goig strong!!!"

She and the other unknown people in the photo are holding fruity cocktails. Their eyes look happy, but manic from the camera flash. A bit of island foliage has wandered into the background.

Remy googles the time difference between Siargao and New York, just to be sure. It's exactly twelve hours. This symmetry impresses and frustrates him. He and Jen are experiencing six o'clocks of vastly different qualities. She's ahead of him—already in the six o'clock of a different day. At this moment, Jen is getting drunk with her friends, her shoulders bare, the future already here.

Remy is sitting in his cold apartment, staring at the red light of his coffeemaker, still stuck in yesterday.

Remy opens another beer. He thinks about these twin realities. One exists at the same time as the other, but they're incompatible. In the hours after he came home from the hospital, he was unsettled by the discrepancy between the gravity of the events he was supposed to be experiencing and the normalcy of the world around him. If Alicia's death were real, it should alter everything else. After seeing his bloody and disfigured girlfriend on a stretcher, he should have taken a bloody and disfigured train home to a bloody and disfigured apartment. He should have entered their bedroom and discovered a pit spewing dark ash instead of Alicia's unmatched socks in the same place they'd been that morning.

He looks at Jen's picture again. What he'd like is to unify these six o'clocks, or at least make them touch. He visualizes a needle threading through opposite edges of a paper and then bringing them together, the way he once saw a wormhole illustrated in a YouTube video. Yes. He would like a wormhole. He would like pollution; some of his reality leaking into hers, and vice versa. He'd like some of that island foliage.

Remy texts Jen, telling her he really needs a friend right now. The text bubble turns green, since she's out of the country, and he has no idea if she will receive it.

Cynthia eventually guilts Remy into accompanying the family to Poughkeepsie, where she wants to scatter the ashes. She read about a hiking path in a brochure.

In one of several rented cars crowded with relatives, Remy is reminded of the surf trip. It feels like a long time ago now. Instead of discussing astrological charts, however, the people in the back are having a competitive conversation about whose digestive system is most adversely affected by cheese. Remy idly hopes the car crashes. Cynthia puts him in the front seat to "act as a navigator," but every time Remy tries to assist with directions, Alicia's dad interprets it as a criticism of his driving.

The hike itself, on a low slope crowded with other, more celebratory families, is cut short by the sudden exhaustion of Alicia's older relatives. Cynthia keeps maniacally saying to everyone, "But isn't it beautiful out here? Wasn't this a good idea?" She carries the ashes in a backpack worn on her chest.

Alicia's aunt says, "This trail was marked easy but this doesn't feel easy to me. I'm a veteran hiker and this doesn't feel easy." When they sit down at a rest area, several relatives complain that they can't walk anymore. Cynthia says they might as well just scatter her ashes in the rest area.

"I thought you wanted a beautiful spot," says Alicia's dad.

"This is lovely. Look at all these people!"

Several families are sitting around on picnic tables eating hot dogs you can buy from a truck.

"There are vending machines here," says Alicia's dad.

"And Porta Potties," says Remy.

"If you go further, you're going to have to leave me behind," says a relative.

"We're not going to leave you behind!" says Cynthia.

"I don't want to hold anyone back."

"Look, there are all these families here! And children. It will be like they're visiting her!"

"Except that they won't even know it," says Remy. Alicia's relatives argue. Remy stands at a distance and pretends to consult something important on his phone. Everyone invokes what Alicia would have wanted. "She was very cooperative. Very compassionate. She wouldn't have wanted you to hurt yourself."

"Do you even know the name of the place where Alicia works?" says Remy, inadvertently using the present tense.

"Pardon?" says Alicia's dad.

After a long discussion, the family gathers in the weeds to the side of the mown rest area. Remy and Alicia's dad, as the most able-bodied men, dig a shallow hole.

"I thought we were scattering the ashes," says Remy.

"It's a figure of speech," says Alicia's dad, transposing his frustration with his family onto Remy. Remy observes that they're attracting attention from other people in the rest area, and Cynthia says, "Don't worry about them. For all they know, we're burying a dog."

"Oh, Cynthia, you're so *bad!*" says one of the cheese-afflicted relatives, her laughter transitioning to tears. Everyone laughs and says they wish Alicia could be here, laughing along with them.

They finish digging the hole and Cynthia takes the ashes out of the little cardboard box. She lowers a plastic bag of gritty matter into the hole. Alicia's dad says something about how everyone was trying to sell them an urn. "Those things can be hundreds of dollars," he says.

"Maybe we should sing something," says Cynthia. An elderly aunt asks Remy if Alicia had "any favorite songs."

"I truly don't know," says Remy.

He looks at the baggy. It was this tiny package of material to which most of his text messages were addressed, to whom he complained about work, this package of material that used to wear all the makeup sitting at home in their apartment, who used to make him late to movies, who hogged the bathroom sink, who gave him blowjobs.

He can't believe it. Alicia, contained in the same sort of thick plastic bag that beads would come in if you ordered them online? No. He can believe in the moon landing, but not this.

A relative suggests a hymn, but Alicia's father says that she "wasn't so much into the religious stuff."

"I only know the words to hymns," says the elderly aunt.

"I know what we can sing!" says Cynthia. "We sang this song to her grandmother when she was dying. She used to love this song when she was a little girl!" She looks around the circle to see if anyone can guess, and then says, "How about 'I've Been Workin' on the Railroad'?"

"Excuse me?" says Remy.

"Grandma Mary loved that song!" says an elderly relative. "And that's something we'd all know the words to."

Cynthia says, "She couldn't even speak anymore, but we could *tell* she appreciated it."

Alicia's family sings "I've Been Workin' on the Railroad," some of the elderly relatives swaying in time, and even clapping when they get to *Dinah won't you blow your horn.* Cynthia makes eye contact with Remy and enunciates the words, the better to help him sing along. Remy is profoundly unnerved, especially once they get to *Someone's in the kitchen with Dinah.* The song is more involved than he remembers, and when they finish the first time, Cynthia shouts, "Again!"

The second time they get to "Fee, fie fiddly-eye-oh," Remy visualizes Grandma Mary, hooked up to feeding tubes and too weak to protest.

At dinner, in a predictably low-quality restaurant with Alicia's parents and a few lingering relatives, Remy calculates how much time is left before he's free of her family. He wants to watch *The Matrix Reloaded* in peace, with a beer.

He takes out his wallet to pay his share of the meal, making the gesture slowly, so that he can be interrupted. Cynthia mistakes this as an offer to pay the entire bill. She says, "Remy, that's so kind of you, since we took care of the funeral costs."

"Oh. I'm sorry. I can't actually. I just meant to pay for me." Remy changes color. "I literally, truly can't pay the bill. I only have about one hundred in my bank account right now."

An aunt laughs and says, "I don't think you mean *literally.*"

"One hundred and forty-nine dollars and, like, thirteen cents. I stayed home from work this week. Obviously."

Alicia's dad takes out his glasses and looks at the bill. "What's the bill? One hundred and twenty something?" Remy is amazed by this low estimate.

Cynthia says, "Of course, Remy, we'll get it. We shouldn't have presumed."

"I'm happy to pay my share!"

"Young people are so hard up these days. Don't even think about it."

"First of the month and everything... Normally things are better."

"You're not so young anymore, are you, Remy?" says Alicia's father.

Remy says no, he isn't. "Getting on up there," he says in the fake, jovial way one speaks to parents.

"It's clear that Alicia meant so much to you." He smiles and smacks the credit card in the pleather binder. "So glad we came out here. It's such a comfort to see how much you valued her." He angles it towards the server.

When the server returns with the credit card and Alicia's dad signs the slip, Remy lowers his eyes to see how much he tipped. It both horrifies and satisfies him to see that it's only ten percent. No wonder Alicia was so fucked up.

Cynthia visits the apartment the day before their plane leaves, to sort through Alicia's possessions. Remy is embarrassed by the beer cans tombstoning the floor, the stench of the parrot and the Spod. "You guys sure have an alternative lifestyle!" says Cynthia.

Jake gets her a glass of water and calls her "Mrs. Hall." Jake is a huge help.

Cynthia picks up Alicia's ribbed tank-tops from the bedroom floor and rubs the material between her fingers. "I always told her that she should invest in high-quality staples, but she liked those cheap clothes. She never wanted to go to Marshalls with me. She liked that Forever Twenty-One."

Cynthia tries on a few pairs of Alicia's shoes, cheering up slightly as she walks into the kitchen, staring at her feet in a pair of mules that Alicia was too self-conscious to wear out of the house. Remy hates seeing her in Alicia's clothes, but Jake says, "Looking good, Mrs. Hall!" Cynthia stops next to the fridge, newly tall. "Alicia's father wanted me to make sure to get some of the stuff we gave her for graduation. Would it bother you boys if I took some of the kitchenware? I don't want you to be left without any way to cook."

"What were you thinking of?" says Remy. But Jake has already offered to help, pulling a cardboard box into the kitchen and offering to wash anything that's dirty. To Remy's horror, Cynthia lines the box with almost all of their pots and pans, as well as the cast-iron skillet, which they use every day. She asks for Remy and Jake's continuous reassurance that it's all right for her to take them. "That's actually mine," lies Remy when Cynthia packs up the food processor. It's really Jake's, but Jake is too polite to say so.

"I could have sworn we got her one just like this."

"Jake uses it to make pesto," says Remy, sensing that Jake's needs will be more persuasive to Cynthia. "...on Tuesdays."

"That's just marvelous, Jake," she says. "Of course I won't deprive you of that." Jake is confused. "I'm so sorry about this. It's just that Alicia's father *especially* reminded me to get the kitchenware. They were investments, you know. To last her whole life. And now...her father's having such a hard time. He really didn't want to deal with this part of the process."

Remy pretends to clean in the bedroom, but shoves some of Alicia's possessions under the bed. He gathers up her many mismatched socks and puts them in a pile, concealing the partnered socks. "You don't want these, do you?" he says to Cynthia. He thinks that he'll let Alicia go through the mismatched socks later, once the rehearsal is over.

What rehearsal? He doesn't know why this phrase appeared in his head, except that lately he has difficulty believing that this is his life now and not some prank that will be called off soon.

Cynthia puts Alicia's stuffed animals in boxes, along with her diploma and winter coats, but seems at a loss about what else to take. She picks up and puts down a plastic cup full of pens, a sweat-stained bra, and a Centenary College letter opener. Her eyes are as big as a Labrador's when she looks at Alicia's books, all with bookmarks halfway through. A box of paints that she had always wanted to use once she learned to paint. Clothes she planned to get tailored once she was "less broke" or "less busy."

"Most of this is just junk. I don't even know what to do with it," says Cynthia. "Maybe her cousins will want those tank-tops, but I don't know."

Remy says, "If you want, Cynthia, I can go through this stuff and donate whatever you don't want to take with you."

"Would you? Remy, that would mean the world to me. I'm just tapped out on this stuff." She cries for several minutes. Remy comforts her, badly, but more kindly than he would have if she had taken all of Alicia's possessions.

After she leaves, Remy puts the pens and letter opener back on the nightstand. He throws Alicia's clothes back on the floor, the way they were. As little should be altered as possible.

He watches *The Bourne Ultimatum*. He watches *Rush Hour*. At one point, drunk, he stands up and tries to execute one of the roundhouse kicks he saw on screen. He falls on the couch and bangs his ankle on the coffee table.

Carla comes over a few weeks after the funeral. Remy opens the apartment door and she hands him a casserole.

"Why?" he says, holding it.

"It's what you do when someone dies. Are you telling me no one brought you food?"

"Alonso from work gave me an edible." Remy looks at the tinfoil. Carla tells him that he'd better return the dish, because *she's* supposed to return it to someone else. She wanders around in animal-print Spandex, critiquing the layout of his apartment. She smells like hand sanitizer mixed with perfume. "Are you a Patriots fan?"

"That was Alicia's thing. Her Spod."

Carla puts a hand against the Spod and draws back. "It's hot."

"No it's not."

"Feel it!"

Remy puts his palm against the side of the Spod. He puts down the casserole. "Jake probably took it for a spin and then forgot to turn it off. What an idiot." He unplugs it.

"Interesting," says Carla. Remy tells her not to start with her superstitions. Carla says, "The world is full of Signifiers. If you paid better attention, you'd see that."

"I'm not susceptible to that shit like Alicia is. Was."

Carla takes a wine bottle out of her bag and asks where she can find glasses. Remy doesn't even pretend that it's too early to drink.

It's a relief to sit in the kitchen and listen to Carla's boy problems. She tells him about a bartender she's been harassing. "If he really wants to ghost me, fine, he should ghost me. I literally don't care. But if I text you a bunch of times, then *commit* to ignoring me. Don't respond the sixteenth time. That's just teaching me to be persistent."

Carla puts down her glass of wine and sits up. She looks into Remy's eyes. "So obviously, I didn't come here without an agenda."

Remy laughs. He says it's good that he can always rely on her to be herself.

"I thought three weeks was enough time." She observes Remy's face. "It's not? Okay. I can shut up."

"Please go on."

"What guys need when they're grieving is some kind of goal. You need something to do." Carla looks around the apartment, at the mess in the narrow living room, the humid, mildewy bathroom with the door open and the fan droning. "The vibes in this apartment are just...phenomenal."

"Do you know that your prediction was wrong? About an upcoming transition in her life?"

"No it wasn't." Carla lifts her wineglass at him. "Death is the biggest transition of all."

"You said the color blue would be involved. The dumpster was green. Her bicycle was black. She wasn't wearing anything blue."

"Remy, it's like you've never heard of an *ongoing practice*. I was right about the main point."

Carla adjusts her tube-top and looks out the window. Her next words are uncharacteristically deliberate. "Clearly, you want to be with Jen. You may even believe that you and Jen belong together in some cosmic way. After much thought, I've come to the same conclusion. To put it in A. B. Fisketjon's terms, this tragedy may be a path to your Consummate Result."

"What great news," says Remy.

"Am I wrong?"

Remy doesn't say anything. Carla downs the rest of her wine. "You really fucked things up in the Hamptons."

"I had a head injury!"

"You need to *really* lean on that, because it's the only good excuse you have."

"What made you decide this? Did Jen say something?"

"You're the only person she's expressed consistent interest in, even if she is pissed at you. She thinks you're enigmatic. I don't know why. I think it blows her mind when people are mean to her. By that logic, all dickwads are mysterious."

"Carla, my girlfriend just died."

"This is the only chance you have to redeem yourself. The combination of your piteous situation, coinciding with the slow implosion of her relationship…means that the Universe could be trying to speak to you about the way forward."

"Why are you so invested?" says Remy. "Just out of the goodness of your heart?"

Carla crosses her legs in the kitchen chair. She picks at her feet unselfconsciously. "I *do* think that Horus and I would be good together. From the standpoint of harmony in the universe, it makes more sense."

Remy laughs. He accuses her of being driven by selfishness rather than any cosmic force.

"You're not understanding me," says Carla. "Generally I try not to get *too* invested in my personal goals. But you have a *really* strong destiny, Remy. I can feel it."

"And getting with Horus is just a bonus."

"Exactly!" says Carla, without sarcasm.

At this point, the wine is almost finished. He says he's hungry and tells her how all the food he buys goes missing as soon as he brings it home. "I think Jake's way of grieving is to eat all my groceries."

"We need to get out of this apartment," says Carla. "Like I said, the vibes are amazing. But it smells like an animal in here."

Remy offers to buy Carla a drink and she doesn't argue with him. She orders an expensive cocktail even though Remy only buys a beer with his burger. He points out this discrepancy and Carla tells him that he should ask for a discount. "Tell the bartender your girlfriend died."

"Fuck off."

Carla calls the bartender over and says that her dear, dear friend is suffering because his girlfriend died. "Did you hear about that girl who was in a bike accident on Harman? That was his girlfriend." Carla asks the bartender to "be nice to him tonight," and sometime later, they get free shots. Once the bartender is out of earshot, Carla says, "Do you see what I mean? Good things come to you in life if you're able to view them as opportunities."

"I'd rather Alicia were alive and just pay for the shots."

She tells him he's missing the point. Remy says, "Do you remember the last time we were here? Probably two years ago. You completely ignored me."

"I'm *sorry,*" says Carla.

"Don't you think that it's fucked that something bad has to happen before people are nice to me?"

"It's fucked, but not for the reasons you think. You're a jerk. Of course people aren't nice to you. That's exactly why this is your only chance to get with Jen."

"Why are you so sure that Horus would even be interested in you?"

"We've hooked up before."

Remy says that this doesn't surprise him, even though it does. He tries to picture the two of them in bed. "Was Jen pissed?"

"*Jen* was pissed, Horus was pissed at her, and a little at me. It was kind of funny. Jen wasn't supposed to be pissed, because being open was her idea in the first place. And she wanted to hook up with Horus's friend."

"What friend is this? Do I know him?"

"She had a really hard time trying be Zen about it when clearly she just wanted to slap me. Remind me never to be in an open relationship, because it's fucking boring. All they talk about is rules and respect and boundaries and policies. It's like frickin' Parliament."

"No offense, but you and Horus seem really different."

Carla disputes this. She tells him that Horus needs someone who can "handle" him.

Remy says, "This is very entertaining, but I'm not feeling very motivated right now. Seriously, Carla—I'm not ready to move on. Obviously."

"You don't really think that, Remy. You're just saying that because that's what you think you're *supposed* to say. Because that's what a character with a dead girlfriend would say in *Grey's Anatomy*. I think it could be beautiful. Jen helps you during this tragic time in your life, and you're bound together by the shared process of healing. What I need from you, Remy, is to stay open."

"Whatever."

"Say yes to every new experience, and be receptive to any signs of a higher logic."

"She didn't even respond to my text message! She didn't even send me condolences!"

"Stop *fixating* and be open to whatever happens."

Remy makes fun of Carla's advice, but after she leaves (or says that she's leaving, before getting waylaid at the door by a pair of friendly strangers, flirting by slinging the fringe of her bag at them), some of her certainty lingers, and stays with him even when he goes back to his dark apartment.

Remy wakes up the next day to Jake tapping on his door. He asks if Remy would like to go to brunch with a few friends of his. "I think you'll like them!"

"I'm hungover!"

Jake opens the door a crack and says, "Perfect! You'll be needing a little hair of the D."

"The what?"

"Hair of the dog, dude."

Remy looks at the mess around his bed. He puts a hand over his eyes. Cold autumn sunlight comes through the window and makes the mess look worse. "I actually don't have any food in the house." He doesn't say that this is because Jake ate it all. "I guess I should be open to new experiences."

"I love that attitude! This will be great!"

Jake takes him to one of those loud brunch establishments that advertises itself with exposed light bulbs in the signage. Remy associates it with the kind of button-down-wearing bro who has electric toothbrush heads delivered to him monthly. He introduces Remy to a table of his coworkers, saying, "I love him like a brother!" The solemn expression on everyone's face indicates that they have been apprised of his tragic situation. Remy sits next to a girl with yellowish foundation that cuts off, distinctly, below her chin. She pinches his hand instead of shaking it. She tells him that she can't imagine what he must be going through, and then switches topics without altering the dramatic cadence of her voice. "So you live with Jake? What do you do?"

"If it's all the same to you, I don't totally want to do the whole *What do you do?* conversation."

"Oh my God! I know what you mean. I'm just, like, a robot. Wow, sorry!" The girl makes a face that Remy can't interpret and tells him what *she* does. Some kind of marketing. She says how great the company is and describes all the free food available on Fridays.

After two minutes of this, Remy goes to the bathroom even though he doesn't need to. He checks his phone and sees that Jen still hasn't texted him back. He checks her Instagram and sees that she's posted photos since his text. So clearly she has access to Wi-Fi.

He texts Carla and tells her that Jen won't even text him back when his girlfriend is dead. *She* doesn't respond either.

He washes his hands and thinks that he'll make fun of these people later, with Alicia, and then remembers he won't. He thinks he'll make fun of them later with Jake, but then remembers that they're Jake's friends.

When he sits back down at the table, the girl makes a bland comment about how she should really "see more art. I just love art," and Jake tells everyone that Alicia was actually an artist. "Do you mind?" says Jake to Remy.

Remy indicates, nonverbally, that he doesn't care at all.

Jake describes the Spod, failing to get the point across, and a guy next to him says that it sounds cool, like a man cave. "I saw an article about this guy who builds man caves on commission. They're amazing." He finds the article on his phone and passes the phone around the table. There are pictures of men barbecuing, playing video games, or drinking beers in a space as small as a garden shed.

Remy says, "Don't you think it's weird for grown men to want a clubhouse?"

"The best part is that the same company also makes little houses for homeless vets. They have these little communities all over the country."

"So cute!" says the girl.

"All it needs is a sign that says No Girls Allowed," says Remy.

The guy takes his phone back, scrolls to the bottom, and shows them a row of tiny houses.

"That's fucked up," says Remy. "At least when they were sleeping on the street, they had some dignity."

"Excuse me, but I'm sure these veterans are happy having any home at all."

"How is it a great idea to take these guys who fought in literal *wars* and make them live in dollhouses?"

"They're man caves."

"If you're going to give them houses, just give them an actual house!"

Jake's eyes move between the two of them. He says, "I think we'd all like a house. I know I would!"

"Just imagine. You're finally off the streets, you meet a woman in a bar and you have to take her home to your garden shed, which is in a whole row of garden sheds. She's going to think you live in a community of gnomes! Like, why punish these veterans for being homeless by emasculating them too?"

"Maybe just keep your voice down."

"I'm not yelling!" says Remy. He sort of is, but only because the brunch place is loud. Everyone in here is yelling. Remy goes on a rant about how everything is infantilizing these days, and how one can't even expect a real house anymore, just a sad approximation of the real thing.

"Just so we're clear," says the guy, "you'd just take these man caves away from these homeless veterans. You'd just burn them down."

"Sure. Yes. That's exactly my point. Thanks for understanding my point so well."

"Why not destroy them with the veterans in them? Actually, why not just hang the veterans first, and then burn the houses after the hanging?"

Jake laughs loudly. "You guys are a trip!" he says.

Remy decides that in the future, he will be less open to new experiences. He checks his phone. No messages.

After brunch, Remy is unable to escape this group of people, since two of them live close enough to Remy and Jake that they all share an Uber home.

Remy gets stuck in the back seat with the foundation girl. Jake and his friend take turns reliving some office experience so loudly that his conversation with the girl is difficult. She says something reminds her of *Wonder Woman.* "Did you see it?"

"No."

"God, you must be having such a hard time. But Jake is really the best person to have around during a tough time, because he's been *through* it."

"What, like, because he had knee surgery in high school?"

Jake's friend tells the Uber driver to turn up the radio. "I love this song!" says Jake. Jake yells over the music to ask the driver what country he's from.

The girl puts her mouth closer to Remy's ear. "I mean because of his…mother." The girl whispers, as if instead of saying "mother" she'd said "motherfucker." "Because of her murder, you know?"

"No way."

The girl is confused. "How long have you known him?" Remy looks at Jake in the front seat. Jake gives him a thumbs-up.

Remy says, "I'm just trying to incorporate that information into what I know about him."

"It was a home invasion, I think." The girl puts her mouth on his ear again. "I don't think they raped her. Just killed."

Remy briefly pictures this girl's life. The sparrow tattoo on her foot, and the Facebook albums of bachelorette parties. She smells of straightened hair. Then again, Remy also had a lot of assumptions about Jake.

His phone vibrates. It's a text from Carla that says, I'm working on it.

That night, when Jake's making himself a quesadilla, Remy watches him cook. He waits for Jake to turn towards the stove before saying, "So. I didn't know that your mom died."

Jake turns around, holding a spatula in his mouth like a terrier with a stick. He raises and lowers his shoulders. He says, around the spatula, "Don't worry about it, man."

"You never said anything." Remy remains standing. Up to this point, anytime they've communicated in an emotional register, Remy has been the one receiving sympathy. He hadn't appreciated that this was more comfortable for him. "It's good that you seem to have... handled it."

Jake puts the quesadilla on a plate and burns his fingers trying to shove it into his mouth. He blows on his fingers and says, "Yeah, it was pretty crazy. I was at college and then I got a phone call, so I guess it didn't really sink in for a while. It's weird because it still feels like a mistake, you know? Like maybe the police got it wrong."

"I know exactly what you mean."

"But my dad made me go to some support groups. You should really do it, man. It's tight. People tell the craziest stories. There was this girl? Her brother committed suicide by duct-taping a Seven-Eleven bag around his neck. Isn't that gnarly?"

"Ah." Remy tries to imagine someone doing this, and simply doesn't believe that it happened.

"But also very sad!"

Jake spits some of the chewed quesadilla into his hand and feeds it to the parrot, who's perched on the back of a kitchen chair. Remy says, "I don't think you have to pre-chew her food for her. She's an adult bird."

"I think she likes it better this way. My saliva cools it down."

Remy says, "But does *Alicia's* death feel like a mistake to you? It seems like you've been able to wrap your head around it."

"Yeah! Weird!" says Jake. "Maybe I've become...wise or something." He looks into the distance and eats his quesadilla. "There was one thing that really helped with my grieving process, but it's probably not healthy. I wouldn't recommend it."

"Weed?"

"No."

"What?"

Jake smiles and says, "Forget it, man." He finishes his quesadilla but doesn't leave the kitchen. He takes a wad of steel wool and works at a dark grease mark on the oven. "Dang, this is tenacious!" says Jake. Everything is dirty without Alicia here.

"I'm not going to beg you," says Remy. "I *will* forget about it, if you want me to."

"What?" Jake looks at him in his pure way. He's already forgotten.

Jake persuades him to watch *Crouching Tiger, Hidden Dragon,* and Remy sits on the couch and tells Jake he would enjoy it a lot more if he were high.

"Just watch it, man. This is classic stuff!" Jake, based on Remy's insistence that he's only interested in "stylized violence," has made a list of martial arts movies, pitching it as a project for them to work their way down the list.

They watch the movie. Remy says, "It's fine drunk, but I just don't have the patience to watch artsy movies like this unless I'm high." The fighters on the screen move through space with total confidence, never even considering whether their movements are physically possible.

Remy stares at the screen and scratches himself. "I'm on the wrong plane of reality." His phone vibrates. It's from Jen.

> Hi Remy. I was so sorry to hear about your loss. I know we haven't been on the best of terms lately. That doesn't change the fact that I'm sorry about what you're going through. Horus told me not to reach out but I want you to know that if things get really bad, you always have a friend in me. I'm sending good thoughts your way <3

Remy types back immediately: For what it's worth, I had a head injury.

He waits, and then types, I'm still sorry for how I behaved. I just want you to know that's not the real me. He presses Send.

Jen doesn't respond.

A few minutes later, Remy types, I'm glad you're not just doing what Horus tells you to do.

She still doesn't respond.

Remy sends Carla a screenshot and texts her, See? Not feeling optimistic, tbh.

Carla texts him back and says, be patient. She asks him if he knows where she can get tacos in the West Village.

Remy relents and asks Jake about "the thing" that helped him.

"What thing?"

"The thing you were saying wasn't healthy. That helped you through the grieving process."

Jake says he doesn't think it's right for Remy. Remy says, "You clearly want to talk about it."

Jake is holding the parrot on one finger and stroking her back. Instead of looking at Remy when he talks, he looks at Sandy, who responds by pushing her head into his hand. "Basically my mom used to text me every Monday to tell me to have a good week at work. She was actually a big texter. But then when she died, obviously she wasn't texting me anymore."

Remy doesn't know what to say. Jake, despite the clumsy social skills that Remy expects from him, seems acutely aware of Remy's discomfort and stresses that it was "a while ago now." "I downloaded an app that would send me her old texts. As long as you have enough messages saved on your iCloud, it doesn't get repetitive."

"I don't understand. Is it the same as talking to them?"

"It uses very basic artificial intelligence to select a response from the total library of responses, but it feels really random."

He tells Jake it sounds pretty fucked up. "And this was therapeutic for you?"

"Up to a point. It helped me for a while, but then she started sending me the same messages over and over again—I mean the app sent the messages—and it just made me more sad."

"Is the app free?"

Jake laughs. "No."

The app itself only has three stars, likely because the bereaved are difficult to satisfy. The graphic is of a cartoon woman being hugged by a less substantial, silvery cartoon figure, while looking at her phone.

He downloads the app and grants it access to his text messages. In the app, he clicks *Generate Contact* and selects Alicia. Under the field for *Initiates Messages,* he selects "random/intermittent," and then under *Responds to Messages,* "immediate." He receives a text message from the App that instructs him to save this number as the "Primary Contact for the Loved One." He saves the number as *Alicia New.*

He opens a new messaging window and types, What are you up to? but then backspaces, realizing that any response he receives will seriously freak him out.

> God. Your parents are so annoying. How come you never told me?

As if he's just checked the status of a bus, he receives an immediate response:

> Alicia New: Imagine him with bangs?

Remy remembers the context of the message when it was sent, more than a year ago. They were talking about Nicolas Cage. Remy briefly does imagine Nicolas Cage with bangs. It is accurate that Alicia once sent this text, but it doesn't feel like a realistic answer to his question.

He decides to respond in good faith, as if he doesn't remember the circumstances of this original message, and as if Alicia New were in fact responding to his initial question.

Imagine who with bangs? Your dad?

Again, the instantaneous response.

Alicia New: I'm in line for concessions.

Remy doesn't respond. He experiences irritation at Alicia for refusing to replace her bike chain.

On one of the many days when Remy returns from work and immediately sinks into the couch, Jake looks at him from the kitchen table, looks away, and then stands up and hands him an envelope. "Sorry about the pink envelope. It's the only one I had." Jake tells Remy a long story about how his aunt gifted the stationery to him. "I call her my hot aunt, but obviously that doesn't mean I'm really attracted to her, although we did bond a lot after my mom died."

"I don't mind the pink envelope."

"Man, I'm worried about you. I think this is a better option than an app."

Remy opens the envelope. Inside is a card with a dour-looking flower on the front. "That's not part of the stationery. I picked that out myself," says Jake. The card reads: *Thinking of you during this difficult time.*

Remy initially mistakes the fatness of the envelope for money, but instead finds a glossy brochure inside. The brochure has a picture of an older woman on the front. The picture is captioned

"Dr. Jane K. Graefer," and the paragraph below is headed "Compassionate Bereavement Group Therapy." In ballpoint, inside the card, Jake wrote, *Enjoy, man!*

"I can't afford this right now," says Remy. "You know I'm going to have to move out at some point because of the rent increase."

"It's just an introductory session! You don't have to pay unless you want to take the whole course."

"I didn't realize you had to pay for these things at all."

"Listen. I talked to my dad and I'm going to cover Alicia's share of the rent too. I know it's tough for you right now and it would be my pleasure!"

"Geez, Jake. That's really not necessary." Remy had been dreading having this conversation with Jake, and Jake has now resolved this dread for him.

"This is as much about helping me as helping you, you know? When we support each other, it's good for both of us."

Remy pauses for a long time. Then he explains to Jake that pressuring him to go to therapy is the sort of thing his parents would do, so *no offense but I think I'll pass.*

"That sounds like exactly the kind of thing that Dr. Jane would want you to talk about. No one will force you to do anything you don't want to do. Dr. Jane is very sensitive. I used to go to her sessions myself."

The idea of sharing a grief therapist with Jake strikes Remy as oddly unclean, like sharing a toothbrush, or a girlfriend.

Remy continues to argue with Jake, but Jake tells Remy he has "an obligation to get well." He says, "I love you, man," and enfolds him in an embrace that stinks of his soap.

Carla calls Remy on a Friday night and tells him to meet her. She names a bar and tells him that Jen is on her way. "She doesn't know you're coming, though. So she may have a bad reaction. But I need you to *power through.*"

"What you're describing is harassment."

"Where did these *scruples* come from? Am I speaking to the same Remy who broke into her bedroom while she was naked?"

"I had a concussion!"

Carla praises him for sticking to this line of argument, and he tells her it's really not a lie. That he's beginning to think he really did have one, in fact that he might *still* have one. "All this weird stuff keeps happening," he says. He doesn't know what he means by this. It was strange that Alicia died and strange to find out that Jake's mom had been murdered, and it continues to be strange to live in his apartment, waiting for Alicia to come back. But he can't blame these things on a concussion, although he'd like to. And sometimes he forgets that the concussion was made up in the first place.

Carla says, "I'm going to hang up now. I really hate talking on the phone, don't you?"

"*You* called *me.*"

"Just hurry."

* * *

He gets to the bar late and Carla is pissed. "I had to shave," he says.

The bar is the type of place where Remy is not always comfortable as a customer, although as a server he's worked in places with elderflower in the cocktails. Succulents are trapped in the bar's lightless corners and the drink list is on a folded piece of cardstock, like a dessert menu. Carla has taken over a table and several chairs with her shopping bags.

Remy says hi, sits down, and asks a harmless question about Carla's day. She launches into an extended story about how she got in a fight with a guy she's dating because she found a receipt for Plan B in his trash. "And he got angry at *me* for going through his trash! In the process of throwing something out, maybe I rooted around. So what?"

Even if Carla alternately repels and attracts him sexually, Remy can appreciate the status conferred by sharing a table with someone who projects so much confidence. He pictures someone walking by and seeing the two of them illuminated, sparingly, by the candlelight of the darkened bar. This theoretical person might make many assumptions about their lifestyles based on the venue, the shopping bags, and the indifference with which Carla stirs her expensive cocktail, splashing its contents onto the table. He says, "Carla, what do your parents do?"

"None of your business."

"It seems like you do a lot of shopping."

"I live in the faith that prosperity will come my way. It's not that complicated." Carla's attention is divided between Remy and her phone. "By the way, I had a dream about Alicia." She puts her phone facedown on the table and meets his eyes. Remy says *Cool.* "Do you know what I said to her the last time I saw her? I said *keep in touch.*"

"So you think it's a message?"

"The shower was on in your apartment. In the dream. The whole place was flooded, and all the mess in your house—the beer bottles and trash and everything—was floating up around my knees. It was really gross. But the door was open, and the flood turned into a river as soon as it went into the hallway. Alicia was standing in the door, arguing with someone. I thought it was an old math teacher of mine but it turned out to be this *creature*."

"What kind of creature?"

"Hard to describe. It looked like a person at first but when I looked at it directly it got weirder."

"What color was it?" He's annoyed with himself as soon as he asks this question.

"I don't know what *color.* You know how dreams are—they're less about the visual information than they are about the *emotion.* Alicia was fighting with the creature, sort of wrestling, trying to hold it underwater. And she asked me to help her. She said, 'I'm trying to get to the ocean.' "

Remy asks some clarifying questions, but finds the conversation less interesting than the conversation someone walking by might imagine them having. "Don't you think that 'finding the ocean' could refer to Jen?" Carla says. "Since she's a surfer?"

"Finding the ocean seems like a fairly conventional metaphor for death and the dissolution of the self."

"Maybe it's a Signifier, Remy. Maybe it's a message trying to tell you how to find your way to Jen."

"But why would this dream-Alicia want me to be with Jen?" As soon as he asks this question out loud, he remembers that it wouldn't be the first time Alicia pushed him towards Jen.

"I have a *feeling* that's what Alicia's trying to say. It felt to me like Jen was involved. Like she was off screen somehow." Carla waves. "Jen's here!" She looks at Remy. "You see how Jen showed up right at this moment? I don't think it's a coincidence."

Carla gets up to say hi to Jen, and Remy waits several seconds before turning around.

Jen looks at him, smacking a pack of cigarettes against the palm of her hand. Over the music in the bar, he hears her say, "This is *not* what I need right now." She's wearing a large men's coat and the paint-spattered Danskos ubiquitous among art girls who can afford to ruin expensive shoes. She looks dirty, and her hair is oily. But even in a bar like this, she looks like she's exactly where she's supposed to be.

Carla tells Jen she was just recounting a dream to Remy, but doesn't say who it was about.

"I didn't realize I was going to see you here," says Jen to Remy.

Remy concentrates on making his face look relaxed and friendly. "I'm trying to reintegrate into society. Jake's even trying to make me go to group therapy. He got me some kind of bereavement therapy flyer."

"Remy, that's great!" says Carla. "You should definitely go."

"Yes, you should," says Jen, not smiling.

Carla confirms that the therapist is a woman. "You naturally gravitate towards women. I suspect women are the only people you're capable of being emotionally vulnerable with."

"I don't think that's true."

"Look who you're talking to now!"

"You have to talk to *someone,*" says Jen. "Shit, Remy. Otherwise you're going to get *really* twisted. I can already see what kind of alcoholic you're going to become."

Remy looks up. Jen is smiling. "Jesus," he says.

"I'm just trying to lighten the mood," she says, in her podcaster's drawl.

Jen and Carla have a long conversation about a tiff between two celebrities, and Remy doesn't participate except to make comments that imply he knows more about the situation than he does. Carla waits for Jen to order a new drink, and then announces she's leaving.

Jen says, "I can't believe you! I just got here!"

Carla threads her arms through all the handles of her shopping bags. She says that she has to work tomorrow.

"I doubt it," says Jen. "You're the worst."

Before Carla leaves, she tells Remy to remember to stay open. "I really think you should go to that grief therapy thing. You never know what could happen."

Jen wants to smoke, and the two of them go out together. "Don't run away," says Remy, before he can think about how it sounds. Jen puts a napkin over her drink and doesn't respond.

While they're outside, Remy texts Alicia New:

> I guess maybe I didn't fuck it up. She's acting pretty nice.
>
> Alicia New: remember what she said.
>
> Who's she?
>
> Alicia New: Just pay attention.
>
> attention to what?
>
> Alicia New: This is like the longest period of my life. I'm bleeding so much.

Before he can mentally block this image, he sees Alicia the way she looked when she died, with that line of blood that stopped as suddenly as a shore.

> Is that what it's like to be dead? You're just in a never-ending period?

Alicia New doesn't respond for a long time. Then she says: Boobs!

You're almost funnier dead than you were alive.

Alicia New: Randolph street.

Jen returns to the table with another cocktail and two shots, tells Remy that they're both for her, and then, when he laughs, says, "I'm not kidding." She takes one of the shots. She doesn't make eye contact. "I'm sorry for calling you a future alcoholic. I'm having a bad day."

Remy says, "Trouble in Paradise?" and then immediately apologizes not only for saying this phrase, but also for the sleazy way in which it was delivered. He also realizes it's not the first time he's said this to her. "I might *still* have a concussion."

"This is the excuse you're using? That's bullshit. Your vision wasn't even affected."

"I know I've already said this, but I'm sorry about what happened in Montauk. Alicia was going through some crazy shit."

"You're never stepping in *Monica's* precious beach house ever again." Jen says the name *Monica* with disdain exaggerated by alcohol.

"Who's that?"

"Horus's mom."

"You're not a big fan?"

"She drives me crazy, but it's not really her fault. I'm *endeavoring to locate compassion in myself for her contributions and gifts.*" Jen's voice is sarcastic, but she refuses to explain further.

Several minutes later, after Remy has asked again, inviting her to reciprocate by talking about how Alicia's parents drove *him* crazy at the funeral, she tells him that Horus "fetishizes" his parents' marriage.

"Whenever we get in a fight, he needs it to be a marathon. He tells me that whenever his parents have a big disagreement, they get in these hours-long discussions and they don't eat or drink because they're 'committed to resolving the issue,' and then he's like, 'That's the kind of dedication we owe each other.' "

"I thought you *liked* fighting with him."

"That's just something that sounds good to say when it's not happening. I don't feel that way when it's my *reality.*" Jen takes the other shot. "He's the only person I know who *wants* to become his parents! It's so weird. I thought that being in an open relationship meant *freedom.* I thought that being free and whatever was his whole deal! But instead it's all about *feedback* and *accountability.* I'm tired of hearing how I fumbled some kind of boundary. Is it too much to ask for unquestioning adulation?"

When Remy doesn't laugh, she says, "I'm joking."

"It doesn't sound like you're happy."

Jen looks at her empty shot glasses. "So are you moving on already? Is Carla your next girlfriend?"

"I think you know I'm not interested in Carla."

"You two are kind of perfect for each other." Jen swishes her paper straw in her cocktail. "Although, as I'm sure you're aware, she's pretty unstable. You know she slept with Horus?"

"She told me." Remy watches her straw. He has the sense that unlike anyone else in the bar, *her* paper straw won't disintegrate. He says, "She's trying to be some kind of grief doula. Mainly by getting me to use my tragedy for personal gain."

"And how's that going?"

Remy switches seats. He occupies the chair that Carla vacated, which is closer to Jen. He tries to lean back in it the same way Carla did. "I think if Carla were here she would tell me to make a bargain with you. You seem to think I really need help. How about... I'll go to the group therapy session, and in exchange you have to get another drink with me sometime. As friends." He holds his hands up when he says the word *friends.* Then he folds his hands behind his head.

Jen looks at him with the straw in her mouth.

"I really need friends right now," he says, again.

"This is a weird exchange you're proposing. I don't even get anything out of it."

"You get to do a good deed. Aren't you always trying to be the best version of yourself?" Jen laughs without joy. "Do we have a deal?"

"Maybe."

Remy waits an appropriate amount of time before texting Jen again. The night before the therapy session, he asks her if they're still on for their bargain. She doesn't respond. He looks at her Instagram. There's nothing he hasn't seen before. He texts Carla, and then Alicia New.

> What do you think? Should I go to the group therapy session? Should I be open to the universe?

Alicia New doesn't respond immediately, the way she did before. This time there's a pause, and then, eerily, the three little dots in a cloud that indicate her typing.

"Jake?" says Remy, standing up.

Jake steps out of the bathroom, half of his face shaved. Remy shows him the screen.

"It's typing. Did it ever do that when you were using it?"

"Neato!" he says. "That's probably new. I wish they'd had that when I was using it."

Alicia New stops typing. Then starts typing again.

> Alicia New: It's not squirrels.

"Fucking hell," he says aloud. Jake asks him if everything's all right, but Remy doesn't answer.

Do you mean in the walls? It's not squirrels in the walls?

Alicia New: Not anymore

It's not there anymore, or it's not squirrels anymore?

Alicia New: Tell me when you get there. I'll wait.

Remy rereads the messages several times. He types, Do you mean, tell you when I get to the therapy place? What are you saying? Alicia New doesn't respond.

Remy had envisioned these types of groups meeting in fluorescently lit basements, but this bereavement group meets in a yoga studio with orchids in the window. Dr. Jane Graefer tells them to make a circle and sit on the sour-smelling pillows stacked against the walls. She uses her hands very little as she talks. Instead, she lets them rest on her crossed knees—the better to prevent the noise of many Bakelite bangles.

"It's important to think of ways you can continue a relationship with your loved one. Just because your loved one is gone in a *physical* sense doesn't mean that you can't *keep them alive* in your life. What would your loved one want if they were still here? How can you honor their wishes in your life?"

She emphasizes "what we will achieve later," and Remy is unable to forget that the rest of the course costs money. Remy looks at a woman across the circle, and thinks of Alicia. The woman doesn't look like Alicia, but she has the overplucked, half-coffee-ring eyebrows that Alicia used to enjoy pointing out to him on the subway. She called women with eyebrows like these "victims of the nineties." He would never notice this type of thing if Alicia hadn't been obsessed with the flaws of other women.

The woman makes eye contact. She's just enough older than

him that when she was in college, he could have had her as a babysitter.

Dr. Jane Graefer tells Remy that he "looks thoughtful." She says, "Tell us a little about your loved one."

"…I thought sharing was optional."

Dr. Jane says that it is, technically. "If it's easier, start by telling us something about them that you miss."

"Uh." Remy says his name, and then Alicia's. "I guess I was just thinking now about what my girlfriend would say if she were here—although obviously I wouldn't be here if she weren't dead…" The eyebrow woman is looking at him. Dr. Jane waits. He asks if he's allowed to use the word "dead." "Am I supposed to say 'expired' or 'passed away' or something?"

"The important thing, *I* feel," says Dr. Jane to the room at large, "is to use language that's comfortable for you, and that *you* feel will express your loss." Dr. Jane tells him to continue. "What would she have said if she were here right now?"

Remy does not say what she would have said about the woman's eyebrows. "Alicia had this…way of viewing the world that I really feel I've lost," says Remy. He looks around. "She would have loved that orchid over there. And…" He doesn't receive feedback that lets him know how he should perform. "She was always pointing out things I never would have noticed otherwise. And now, there will be this whole aspect of the world that is forever invisible to me." Remy milks this line for a while.

The woman with the eyebrows has her hand on her heart. The collar of Dr. Jane's linen dress lowers with each deep nod. Remy is amazing at this. He looks around the circle, satisfied that no one else can follow that.

The woman with the eyebrows also lost a partner, although it's unclear how long ago. Her name is Andrea and she tells the group a story that she's obviously told many times, about how her husband died after years of struggling with a degenerative nerve disease. She's open about her sexual frustration during his illness, but also about the sense of purpose afforded by her role as a caretaker.

"When you have a problem as big as an illness, it means that you can ignore all the problems waiting for you once the illness is gone. When he was getting better, all the other issues in our marriage would start again. We argued all the time, because he got superstitious—which is apparently normal in people who feel that doctors can no longer help them. He threw out all of our cleaning products because of secret messages he thought he was getting from the TV."

Andrea smiles in self-awareness. The laughter in the room is cautious. "Laugh, *laugh,*" says Dr. Jane, gravely. She makes one hand into a fist and strikes at the air, as if ringing a handbell. "Death can take so much from us, but it can't take our sense of humor." The laughter stops, and several people agree seriously.

Remy watches Andrea express herself, noticing that she's more polished than he was, especially in the inclusion of evocative details. She tells the group how her husband accused her of "sucking the life" out of him, to Dr. Jane's consternation. "He used to tell me that he dreamed every night that a little demon sat on his chest, and that she looked just like me."

"Terrible," says Dr. Jane. "So many of us here know the anguish of taking on a loved one's pain."

Andrea ends her speech skillfully, with a gentle warning about not making the deceased's burden one's own. "Sometimes the only way we can feel close to someone we've lost is by taking on blame for their passing."

"Too true," says Dr. Jane, and several people in the circle say *Mmm* in agreement. Remy decides that his awkwardness likely made him more sympathetic than Andrea, and besides, she's had more practice.

* * *

The session doesn't end with a trust fall, the way that Remy expected. His plan had been to ask Andrea to be his partner. But as he's putting his shoes on, Andrea taps him on the shoulder. She reintroduces herself. "Your loss is so recent, and yet you spoke so clearly, and so movingly about Alicia." She mispronounces Alicia's name. Remy wonders if this is some kind of subtle feminine power move. It occurs to him that this thought, at this time, is psychotic.

She says, "I know it might seem forward, but would you want to get coffee? If your loss is fresh, it can help to talk to someone who's *been through it,* you know?" Remy expects her to laugh, nervously, after opening herself up to rejection like this. She doesn't.

"Sure," says Remy. "You mean like…right now?"

"Hell yeah, right now! Life is short, right? Don't we know it!" This time, she laughs.

The coffee shop that Andrea suggests is closed, and the next one she locates on Yelp doesn't have tables inside—just a bench and a counter. Remy doesn't mind, but Andrea does. She suggests they get a drink instead.

Outside of the context in which he encountered her, Andrea seems different. Her shoes, which she wasn't wearing in the yoga studio, have an old-lady vibe. Her laugh is unapologetic, like a theater kid's. He assumed that her eyebrows correlated with low self-esteem, but she has none of the shrinking qualities of an easy target.

She takes him to a bar and expresses a bad opinion about a painting of a cat wearing glasses. "So adorable! I love the decor in here."

Remy looks around to make sure that no one he knows is in the bar. After a few beers, her face softened by the light of a neon

Budweiser sign, he stops looking up every time the door opens. Unprompted, and easily, she shares information about her husband. "We were best friends, not just romantic partners. Towards the end we were very close, but it was complicated. I think he blamed me when he got sick again. And the truth was, a part of me *was* afraid of what would happen if he didn't need me anymore. It took me a long time to come to terms with that."

Remy says, "Do you have kids? You seem very... maternal."

"Sean and I were trying, before everything."

Remy apologizes, but he isn't sure why.

She says, "Isn't *trying* a funny euphemism? Did you just picture me having sex?" She laughs again. She says he shouldn't feel the need to tread carefully around her, or apologize. "We're in the same boat. Isn't it refreshing when people don't act like you're about to break into a million pieces? I'm still flesh and blood! Aren't you?"

Andrea asks him about his relationship with Alicia, and responds using familiar words with an emphasis that makes them feel like buzzwords. "It can be so hard to find someone who really feels like *Home*. And yet with whom *Surprise* is still possible. Did you have that kind of relationship?"

"Sure. You could say we were close."

"It felt like Sean was irreplaceable! I thought I'd never be able to even *think* about moving on. But I'm here to tell you, healing is possible! You can work through it!"

"I did sort of feel that way once, with someone else." Remy is surprised by his own confession. "Maybe it's worth pursuing her again? I've always felt like we were going to end up together."

Andrea waits for him to say more.

He says, "I'm starting to wonder if that's actually my *destiny* or something."

"I think that's a bad idea." She reaches out and grips his hand. "If there's one thing I've learned on my journey, it's..." Andrea looks at the Budweiser sign meditatively. "No romantic partner is ever going to understand you unless they've experienced a similar loss. People who have lost a partner can only be emotionally understood by other people who've experienced a loss on that scale. It's the most powerful force of attraction that exists, in my opinion."

Andrea doesn't let go of Remy's hand. "That would really limit my options," says Remy.

"The statistics support it too. Seventy-five percent of people who have experienced the loss of a romantic partner end up with someone else who has also experienced it."

Remy is skeptical of this statistic. "This other girl, I really think there was something there."

Andrea skims the back of his hand with her thumb. "You don't realize it now because you're a newbie to this process. But you're going to require someone who *Understands*."

A few drinks later, Remy complains to her about people he works with and, annoyingly, Andrea insists on seeing things from their point of view. He complains that Rocco has absolutely no facial expressions, and no personality.

"He can't help that," says Andrea.

"He's the only person I've ever met who actually could be a lizard person."

"A what?"

"He looks like a lizard in a human suit, I swear." Andrea still looks confused and Remy says, "He's not even human, is what it feels like." He laughs, encouraging her to laugh.

"I don't know what you want me to say when you start describing people as not even human."

Remy doesn't enjoy Andrea's judgment, which seems all the more insidious for its compassion towards Rocco. "Tell me something. How long ago did your husband die? It sounded like you've had a lot of practice with that story."

"Healing can be a lifelong process! And by sharing my experience, I'm hoping that I can help others to feel less alone."

"Clearly," says Remy. He had hoped to sound flirtatious, but it comes out sounding mean.

Andrea finishes her beer and tells him that it seems like he *has a lot of defense mechanisms in place.* "I look forward to the day when those emotional walls come down."

She leaves shortly after, saying that she hopes to see him in the next course. He lies and says that she definitely will. He doesn't understand why she, like Jen, seems to believe that whatever is behind Remy's "walls" is anything good.

That night, Remy wakes up when he hears a noise in the bathroom. "Alicia?" he says. Then he remembers it's not Alicia. The noises move closer to the bedroom. "Jake?"

The noises are like scratching, but heavier. Maybe like footsteps, if someone were wearing heels. He looks at his phone. It's 2:48 a.m.

No response. He calls out Jake's name, but more quietly. He's not sure why he lowers his voice. What's the point of saying Jake's name again if he's less likely to hear it?

After a long pause, he says, "Alicia?" He says her name at medium volume, to remind himself that he isn't frightened. The sounds are faint, but still there. He waits.

Silence.

He sends a text to Alicia New: Are you in the bathroom.

The typing bubbles appear.

Alicia New: You're not going to believe me.

Remy swings his feet off the bed and places them on the floor, quietly. The noise clarifies as it approaches the bedroom. The footsteps—or whatever they are—are hard and high-pitched, like fingernails on a counter. But more resonant. Heavier. They don't land quite like footsteps.

The sounds move to the kitchen. He hears eating, and thinks about all the groceries that have gone missing. Maybe this is when Jake eats? He stands up, remembers what happens in horror movies, and sits back on the bed. He considers calling the police. He remembers what happens in horror movies when people call the police. He sits there, listening.

He calls out Jake's name again, louder this time. The eating noises pause. Remy gets up and presses down the button on the doorknob lock. The *ting* of the button doesn't make him feel safer.

The pause is long. There's a complicated sound of movement. This movement is unmistakably much closer to his bedroom door.

Then, after a long, long silence:

Knock-knock-knock-knock.

Remy doesn't move.

Knock-knock-knock-knock.

He hears Jake open his bedroom door suddenly, and light floods in through the crack under Remy's door.

"Jake!" says Remy.

"What's up, my man?"

"Be careful, dude—there's something out there!"

Jake turns on the living room light, and more light comes in under the bedroom door. "Are you okay?"

"Jake, do you see anything out there? In front of my bedroom door?"

"Open up the door, man! I can't hear you!"

"I can't!"

Jake approaches Remy's door and shakes the knob. "It's locked!"

Remy sits in the dark.

"Did you have a nightmare?" Remy gets off the bed and opens the door. Jake looks at him, unconcerned.

Remy says, "I heard something! Something was knocking on my door!"

Jake says *Uhhhh* and swings his arms, looking back and forth between the door and the living room, cooperatively.

"You don't believe me," says Remy.

"I do believe you heard something." Jake says that he has to pee. "It's pretty urgent. So um, excuse me."

"I swear it was real."

"Maybe it's something you should talk about with Dr. Jane?"

"Fuck Dr. Jane!"

"You didn't like her? I think she's really nice."

Remy puts his face in his hands. He looks in the living room. It looks the same as ever. "Come with me into the kitchen," says Remy, dragging Jake by the elbow. He turns on the light. The kitchen is filthy. Dishes are piled up in the sink and the counter is covered in sauces and other food particles. "See?" says Remy, indicating the mess. "It wasn't like this before." He picks up one of the plates that's in the sink. "This plate had rice on it, and now it's all gone! *You* haven't been eating my food—it's something else!"

Jake reiterates that he needs to pee. "I hope we don't have raccoons. They have those in New York now."

"It's not *raccoons,* Jake."

"Exterminating those little guys would be a real bummer."

"Do me a favor," Remy says, and pulls Jake over to the Spod. The interior, partially blocked by the tarp covering the entrance, doesn't possess the reassuring ordinariness of the rest of the living room. The dark opening gives Remy the same ominous feeling he had before Jake turned on the hallway lights, when he was still sitting in the dark. "Will you lift the lid off for me?"

"If it will make you feel better, man." Jake approaches the Spod and Remy pulls back. He stands in front of the mouth and Remy believes, *maybe,* that he sees movement.

"Get back!" he says.

But Jake lifts the cover of the Spod and looks into the water. Nothing happens. He motions Remy over. Remy looks into the water. He doesn't see anything.

"Fuck, this stinks," says Jake. "We need to drain this thing. You were right about it being a mold trap."

Remy feels the side of the Spod. It's cold. He puts his hand in the water and moves it around. Nothing.

Jake says, "Do you want me to feel your forehead? You seem agitated."

"Whatever," he says. "Whatever."

In the morning he texts Alicia New, but she doesn't respond.

Remy tells Carla that he had "a crazy dream. More like a hallucination. I'm beginning to think something's genuinely wrong with me."

He's sitting on the shag carpet in the living room of her apartment, ostensibly to return the casserole dish, but really to tell her what happened. Carla's apartment is extremely tidy, which surprises him—mostly unfurnished, but filled with crystals and antique figurines. These are organized on shelves, free of dust, and arrayed in tight rows, as if fortifying the apartment against the rest of the world. One of her roommates has a pet rabbit that roams the living room and sits in Carla's lap like a cat. Carla, unnervingly, doesn't use a baby voice when talking to the rabbit. "Do you want another blueberry?" she says to the rabbit, sounding pissed off.

Remy says, "What did the creature look like, in your dream? Are you sure that Alicia was different from the creature?"

"Why? Does that seem significant to you?"

He tells her about the footsteps, and the sounds of eating. The knocking. He says that Alicia used to wander into the kitchen at night and make those sounds. "It's almost as if Alicia were back again," he says, giving Carla the opportunity to laugh at this suggestion—or confirm it. He's annoyed with himself as soon as he says this out loud. "And wearing heels, maybe."

"Did you check the kitchen?"

"It *can't* have been real."

"Okay."

He tells her that he's disappointed by her noncommittal response. "You're the only person I know who I can talk to. You heard the knocking that one night, right?"

"I'll be honest, Remy. I didn't actually hear it."

"You said you did!"

"Just because I didn't hear it myself doesn't mean it's not your *personal* reality. I said I heard it because it was important for *you* to feel that *your* experience was valid. Otherwise, you would have dismissed it."

"That's fucked up! Why would you say that? *You* were probably the one making those knocking sounds!"

Carla points at the rabbit and indicates that she doesn't like Remy's yelling.

"I can't believe I'm saying this stuff to you," says Remy. "Do you just get off on hearing me sound like an idiot?" He's glad he didn't tell her about the other times—with the face, and those eyes looking at him.

Carla says, "Listen to me. Jen and Horus had a huge fight. It doesn't matter what it's about. Probably the same shit. The relationship is hanging on by a thread. Do you know what Jen does whenever she and Horus fight? She *acts out.*" Carla leans forward, causing the bunny to jump from her lap. "This is the very *definition* of a Yes Opportunity!"

"Of what?"

"Basically, this could be a way towards your Consummate Result. Remy, these things that are happening to you, that you're seeing everywhere—these aren't coincidences. They're Signifiers trying to communicate with you."

The bunny jumps on Remy's lap, and he draws back. "I still don't know what you mean when you say 'Signifiers.'"

Carla retrieves the bunny, lifting it up with both hands. "Imagine that Greta is us, and our reality."

"Greta is my ex-girlfriend's name."

"Yes. I actually turned her into a rabbit."

Remy is in a suggestible state of mind and dislikes this joke. "What do you mean, 'our reality'?"

"The technical term is that we live within our own particular Stream of Reality. But just think of it as, like, our *dimension*."

Carla turns and looks at her roommate's door, as if afraid of being overheard.

Remy says, "This doesn't sound like something you'd read in a self-help book."

"My knowledge is highly specialized," says Carla. She doesn't explain. She makes Greta float through the air, as if down a river. "We're going along in our Stream, but all around us there are all these other parallel Streams. All these other Remys and Carlas and everyone else, living different versions of themselves, but sometimes, *sometimes,* doing the same thing as each other."

Carla puts the rabbit down and uses both arms to show these streams flowing into each other. "Maybe, in many of these Streams, Remy succeeds in being with Jen. If it's meant to be often enough, then all these parallel Streams swell into a wave that's powerful enough to inundate our own reality! And details that might seem like trivial parts of your ordinary life are actually signs—Signifiers of Flow helping you to achieve that Consummate Result."

Remy thinks, involuntarily, about the text messages. Instead of telling Carla about them, he asks if she has something to drink besides green tea. He tells her that he's not sure she's the right person to ask after all. "I should just get myself committed. This is the practical advice I really need."

"Isn't it beautiful, though? Just because Alicia's dead in this reality doesn't mean she's dead in others. The chorus of all the other Alicias continues to speak, and maybe Alicias from other realities are showing you the way towards being with Jen. First through my dream, and then through your vision."

"Carla! Jesus. I don't care about my 'Consummate Result.' I'm—What was it that I heard that night? What was that *thing?*"

"Probably only you can say. Does it Signify anything to you?"

Remy looks for his coat. "I very much doubt that the universe gives a shit about my love life. This is ridiculous."

"It's not the universe that has these desires, it's other versions of you, and maybe other versions of Alicia! If you were paying attention, you'd realize that it's very romantic."

"I bet Jen would be pissed if she found out that you were using me to ruin her relationship."

"Don't you dare tell her!" says Carla. "These are the kinds of strong signals you don't get every day! Don't you dare waste them." Remy stops putting on his coat, surprised. Carla looks like she's about to cry. "Right now you're exactly where you're supposed to be. You get to take part in something larger. If you ruin things, then you lose your chance. You *have* to follow the Signifiers."

Remy thinks about putting his hand on Carla's back, but he's afraid of how she'd react. "I'll keep an eye out," he says, reverting to cruel sarcasm before he can stop himself. He leaves Carla sitting on her shag carpet amid the bric-a-brac, thinking that he's probably going to read about her someday, when she really goes off the rails. He's embarrassed that he bought into her bullshit enough to confide in her. "I used to know that girl," he'll say. "Doesn't come as a surprise."

When Remy gets home, Jake is scrubbing at another grease mark in the kitchen.

"Look at this!" he says. Jake has cleaned enough of the grease away from the counter to reveal a portion below. "Dang!" he says. There's an indentation in the counter that passes through the cheap laminate and into the wood. "Did you do this? Not that I'm blaming you! Accidents happen."

"Of course not."

"We are NOT getting our security deposit back."

"Jake. Think about what you're saying. Alicia was the one on the lease. There is no security deposit as far as we're concerned."

Remy blinks several times, hoping that the indentation will look different. It's eight inches long and deeper on one end than the other, as if a giant claw scraped the counter. He can't think of any reasonable explanation for the mark. His phone vibrates with a text from Carla:

Have you texted Jen yet? I don't want to hear any more excuses.

Remy watches *Terminator,* distracted by thoughts about Carla's unhinged theories. She has no theory about what he heard the other night, which was probably just a drunken hallucination anyways. What could it even Signify? If this thing visiting him at night is supposed to communicate some message, it's opaque. He remembers Alicia talking in her sleep, singing "I've Been Working on the Railroad," and how her family sang that song when they buried her ashes. If Remy had understood what that meant at the time, had recognized it as a Signifier of Alicia's imminent death, could he have prevented it? He thinks about what Dr. Jane Graefer would say if he told her about his visions, and laughs out loud.

What was it she said? "Just because your loved one is gone in a *physical* sense doesn't mean that you can't *keep them alive* in your life. What would your loved one want if they were still here?" Probably, Alicia would still be imitating Jen—"channeling her," or whatever she called it.

Why *would* Alicia want him to end up with Jen? Considering that Alicia was constantly trying to be Jen when she was alive, wouldn't it make sense that she'd want him to be with Jen once she was dead? Isn't Jen his closest link to Alicia? Wouldn't this be the best way to *keep his loved one alive in his own life?*

He's tempted to text Jen, just to see what would happen, but he's also not in a hurry. If it's *meant to be,* as Carla believes, it won't matter how long he waits before texting—the Signifiers will make it easy. He's still not sure he understands Carla's theories correctly.

At the end of *Terminator,* Remy calls out to Jake. "This movie makes no sense. Have you seen this?" Jake doesn't answer, because it's Thursday night. Remy pretends not to know this, and continues yelling at Jake's closed bedroom door. "How could a guy send someone back in time to become his own father? He wouldn't even exist in the first place." If Remy wrote a movie, the least it would do is make sense. There's no response, not even from the parrot. As Remy is thinking of something for Jake to say, something infuriating like *I don't know dude as long as it's a fun ride does it really matter?* he's struck by the sadness of having this imaginary dialogue.

He unlocks his phone and texts Jen—not because Carla told him to, but because he wants to.

Where are you. What are you up to, he says, carefully punctuating it badly. He says he had a particularly rough day, even though he didn't.

A few minutes later, Jen texts him back with a single phrase: Left Hand Path.

What is that?

Jen: A bar dummy.

Do you mind if I join you?

Jen: It's a free country

* * *

The bar has a wood interior, with a strip of mirrors running along a wall lined with stools. Remy sees Jen's face reflected before he even connects her to the person sitting in front of the mirror.

He sits on a stool next to Jen. She raises her hand in a wave but doesn't take her eyes off her phone. The seating arrangement puts him close to her, and he can smell her unwashed hair and expensive, sandalwood-infused eau-de-something. There's a chapstick imprint on her glass.

He says hi and makes some kind of judgmental comment about how "bratty" it is that she always gets cocktails.

"Why are you being a dick?" Jen's face is illuminated by her phone screen, and the corners of her mouth are wet.

"I guess cocktails are kind of your *thing*." Remy tries to think of something to say that isn't inane. He says he likes her perfume.

"Yeah. I took an Italian shower."

Remy laughs, but Jen doesn't. "I feel like I should catch up to you." He looks at her glass to specify that he means alcohol-wise.

"Yeah, you should. Go get a drink. You should get something *really* strong, because in order to talk to you, I'm gonna need you to get on my level." Jen indicates herself with a sloppy gesture. "Tell me when you get there. I'll wait."

"What did you say?"

"Tell me when you get there. I'll *wait*."

It takes a long time to get a drink. He keeps glancing over at her stool, to make sure she doesn't get up and leave. While he's standing at the bar, he realizes why this phrase sounds familiar—Alicia New said it.

These aren't coincidences. They're Signifiers trying to communicate with you, said Carla. He's exactly where he's supposed to be. Yes. Something special is happening to him. He sits back down and asks her if she's having trouble with Horus.

"Let me show you something," says Jen.

"Don't you want to take off your coat? It's pretty warm in here."

Jen takes a little piece of paper out of her coat pocket. She hands it to him. Remy looks at the piece of paper. It reads *Pad See Ew, Chicken Satay, Gaeng Panang.*

"You got Thai food?"

Jen nods, theatrically, like a trained dolphin. She watches herself nod in the mirror. "Do you see how bad it is?"

"Honestly, no."

"Sometimes Horus will ask me what we got to eat the other night. And I'll be like, *I don't remember, something with chicken.*"

"You were vegan when you worked at Belasco's."

"And suddenly because I can't remember that we got Chicken Satay it's like, 'You're never really present when you're with me' and 'Isn't it a little racist how you can't remember the names of ethnic foods?' and 'You might even have memory problems. You should go to a doctor.'"

"Seriously?"

"I might be exaggerating *slightly*. But now I can't even enjoy my meal! I have to fucking *record* this shit so I can be ready when he quizzes me later."

"Did he see you writing all this down?"

"He thought I was being dramatic."

"You should break up. Seriously."

Jen says, "No, I can't." She says to her reflection, "I need another drink."

"I'll get you one."

"No, I'll get *you* one. With Horus's money." She stands up and puts a hand on his shoulder. She shakes her head as if having a brief moment of sobriety. "I don't want to create the wrong impression. I *do* love the shit out of him. Horus is a really, really good guy. I think I might just be an angry person." She lingers with her hand on his shoulder, seeming to forget what she's doing.

"I don't even know what it would be like to just *give in* to all that negative energy. Like you do. No offense. I'm sure you would agree that you're a very negative person."

"There's nothing inherently wrong with being angry. You have legitimate reasons to be pissed at Horus."

"Yeah but—" Jen flips her hand at him. "The thing is, there sort of *is* something wrong with it." She remembers what she's doing, and turns towards the bar.

Later, he suggests moving to another bar. She agrees, but then they never manage to leave. She forces him to drink a cocktail by buying two of them. She tells him he would actually like cocktails if he could afford them. "Not to be a bitch, Remy, but what even is *your* thing? I have surfing, I have cocktails, I have giving easy targets like you a hard time. What the fuck is your deal? What do you *have?*"

Remy laughs. He doesn't know what other reaction he's supposed to have. He's never thought of the phrase "easy target" applying to him. "I *had* Alicia."

"And what about now?"

Jen is very close to him, the alcohol having erased her usual sense of personal space. Remy is struck by the hypersaturated quality of her Jen-ness. When she turns her head, she occasionally catches an angle much covered on her Instagram, animating those holy photos that have become part of Remy's private experience. It feels indecent to look at Jen in this bar, in front of everyone, when he's used to looking at her in private.

"Apparently, part of grieving is learning how to keep that person in your life, in a new way. It might sound weird, but—"

Jen holds up her hand. "Don't prime me for what you're about to say. Couching it in weirdness ahead of time is a stupid, fake way to make me try to reassure you that you're not a freak. If you're a freak, I'm going to tell you."

Remy laughs. He feels like he's laughing too much. Jen's eyes are dim.

He says, "I'm sure it's not a surprise, but Alicia kind of had a crush on you. Maybe a friend crush. Maybe more. I didn't realize how bad it was until that weekend in Montauk."

"And this crush is *all* Alicia. Nothing to do with you."

Remy says something noncommittal about how he's always thought she's an *attractive woman.* "But now when I talk to you, in some ways...it feels like I'm accessing a part of her. And it was this very sweet part of her that only I saw. And it's gone forever."

Jen doesn't say anything. Remy asks her if that's weird. He's so overwhelmed by the sensation of disclosing something true that he forgets that what he's saying is a distortion of the truth.

Jen turns away from the mirror and faces the rest of the bar. "I don't really believe you. Clearly *you're* obsessed with me. But I was a real bitch in Montauk. Which is not to say that I'm saying anything right now. I'm not saying anything."

"But if you were saying something, what would that be?"

"Just that—I'm tired and I can't even think..."

"What do you have to be tired about? You spend all your time doing yoga!"

"I'm not talking about yoga, and even if I were, yoga is very tiring. You've clearly never done yoga before."

"I'm sorry!"

"I do actually work *too,* you know."

Remy apologizes. He says that he ruined the moment and tells her to go ahead.

"I'm talking about— I just feel like there's a version of the life that I should be living that's just out of reach, and it doesn't make me as exhausted as this one does."

"You mean like...an ideal version of life? In some other version of reality?"

"Things should just be as easy as surfing. Technically, I can do what I want, but it doesn't really feel like freedom. I keep thinking, if I were really free I'd travel around the country in an RV or I'd go volunteer at an orphanage in Romania. These are bad examples but obviously I *could* do that stuff if I wanted. It would just be a huge hassle."

"You use that word a lot. *Freedom*."

"What does it even mean? I don't know."

"Jen. The world is your oyster. My girlfriend had to die before Carla would even bring me a casserole."

Jen laughs. It's the first time she's laughed all evening. Remy looks at the reflection of the back of Jen's head in the mirror. There's something off about it. It doesn't look like her hair.

And then, although Jen doesn't move, the reflected head in the mirror *turns around*. And it's not Jen, it's Alicia—except an Alicia that's subtly different from the one Remy remembers. Her skin is paler, and she changes even as he looks at her. Now it's another version of Alicia, now a version with short hair, now she's skeletally thin. She meets his eyes and speaks, but he can't hear what she's saying.

His phone illuminates. Remy looks down. It's a message from Alicia New:

Ask her to go home with you, now.

In bed, despite the number of cocktails she's had, Jen gives detailed, well-enunciated instructions. He assumes these are a by-product of her extra-communicative relationship with Horus. She says "Now from the back" and "Put your hand here" and "I have weak wrists. I need to change positions." She gives him perfunctory head at such high speed that she seems aggrieved, a line of concentration between her eyebrows as Remy watches.

When she's straddling him and looking down at him from above, she says, "You've been waiting for this for a long time, haven't you?"

He says, "Are you scared of me?" He hopes that this is sexy.

"You're an absolute creep."

He tells her to be quiet for a second, because he's concentrating. This makes Jen laugh. "You *freak,*" she says.

He tries to absorb the details of this experience, but it's difficult because Jen keeps talking and breaking his concentration. She asks him to tell her how he feels, and how she looks. "Do I look good to you?"

"You look beautiful." He wants to follow this with *Now shut up.* Why is it that every time he's close to enjoying himself, she insists on ruining things? Why can't she just cooperate?

Jen spins her index finger in the air and says, "Keep saying that." Her stomach sloshes rhythmically with each thrust. "You're beautiful," he says, chanting it like a spell, or a reminder for himself.

Afterwards, Jen asks him for water. When she speaks again, her voice is ragged and strange. "It's nice to be seen," she says. "I know I can be a dick sometimes. It just feels like all Horus ever does is *tell* me what I'm like. How I act, how I don't remember things, how I'm grumpy when I don't have caffeine." She stops. "I'm sorry, I'm drunk." She asks him if he has Advil too. He looks through a mess of clothes on the floor for the Advil. Jen watches him look through the pile and asks if the clothes were Alicia's.

"Yeah."

"I have something to tell you."

"We've already had sex, so I probably don't want to know."

Jen says it's not like that. "I'm pretty sure I'm one of the last people who saw Alicia. Horus and I were."

Remy doesn't say anything.

She tells him that she and Horus were in the skincare store where Alicia worked. "She was acting weird. She was wearing earrings from my online store. She looked like me. The people who worked there were calling her Jen. It seemed really twisted."

Jen rolls over on the bed and faces the wall. She says that she knew about Alicia's whole "crush thing." She's quiet for a long time. She starts talking, stops, and starts again.

"Horus was kind of an asshole to her that day. I think he was feeling defensive. The things he said…weren't nice. The two of us, I should say, weren't nice to her together. I really wasn't trying to be mean, but I've been thinking so much about that day, because I hate to imagine that right before her accident, she was thinking about that interaction."

"I didn't know that."

"Of course you didn't. I'm telling you now." Jen is silent. Then she says, "But her bicycle chain broke, right? It was an accident. She didn't crash into that dumpster on purpose."

"It sounds like you know more about how she died than I realized."

She doesn't say anything.

"So Horus is basically ruining both of our lives at this point."

Jen disputes his use of the word *ruining*. "He was just trying to defend me. And like you said, it wasn't his fault. It's not like he made the accident happen." She apologizes, several times. She says she should have told him earlier. "I feel so bad. I feel like I owe you something."

"I'll keep that in mind."

"I'm really, *really* sorry."

Jen props herself up on his pillows, naked. Her face is wet. His wildest dreams are here. He has experienced both physical and emotional intimacy with Jen, and yet he has no real sense of having possessed her. He can't even fully absorb what she's telling him. No sublime moment of the Consummate Result has arrived, and he has to pee.

He says, "I feel guilty about a lot of stuff too. But you know what *The Apple Bush* says."

"I didn't realize you'd read it."

"Alicia was quoting from it a lot before she died. In case you couldn't tell, she was fucking insane."

"Which quote?"

"'Forgiveness is a powerful medicine, both for yourself, and for others.'"

"That's a really corny one."

"I'll forgive you. You forgive me."

Jen says sure, whatever. Her voice sounds weird because her nose is full of snot. Remy sits on the bed and holds her. He sits with her for a while, even though he still has to go to the bathroom.

He envisions them being filmed or photographed like this:

Alicia's clothes scattered on the floor, now mingled with Jen's clothes, Jen's freckled boobs in the red haze of Alicia's twinkle lights, he and Jen at peace with each other, harmony restored, a happy ending. The satisfaction of seeing this picture in his mind is almost as good as actually being inside it.

In the morning, he awakes to a sound of Jake laughing. Jake knocks on the door. "Guys, you have to see this!" And then he corrects himself. "I mean, Remy."

Remy opens the door. Jake sees Jen in the bed. His expression is bewildered. "Remy, you have to see this," he says again, staring at Jen.

"This is Jen," says Remy.

"The parrot spoke!"

"What?"

Jake brings the bird into the living room on his finger. Jen and Remy, half clothed, stand there as Jake says to the bird, "C'mon, Sandy! Say 'Sandy wants a cracker.'"

The bird doesn't say anything. "Say 'Suck my balls,' Sandy," says Jake. He turns red. He says he's sorry. "I forgot a lady was here."

"I *really* don't care," says Jen.

"Sort of a guy joke I guess," says Jake, still red.

Jake keeps trying but the bird doesn't say anything. Then the parrot turns its head and says, "Hello, Alicia!"

"See!" says Jake.

"Hello, Alicia! I love you, Alicia!"

"Doesn't she sound just like a human?"

The morning sun comes in through the kitchen window and catches the undertones of orange around Sandy's neck. The bird looks healthy and interested in its surroundings. The head moves, the eyes move, the throat pumps, and Remy is struck by the fact that there is a small *being* inside this green mass of feathers.

"It's magical," says Remy, without irony.

"It's going to drive you crazy in a few days," says Jen. Remy tries to share a glance with her, but even though she must feel his eyes, she doesn't look at him. She says she has work, and goes to the bedroom to get her coat.

Jake leans on the wall and then slides to the floor, sobbing. "I'm sorry, man," he says, indicating the tears. "I don't know what's gotten into me. Damn."

In the evening, Jen doesn't text him and Remy doesn't text her. He'll wait, at least for a few days. He'll play it cool. As Carla said, the way forward will be apparent.

Jake comes out of his room and asks to use Alicia's full-length mirror. He's wearing one of the same polos he always wears, but holding his body differently. "What do you think? Do you think it's weird to wear a polo in this weather?"

"It's pretty weird."

Jake moves back and forth in front of the mirror and Remy says, "Where are you going?"

"I have a date," says Jake, at the same time as he touches his hair—as if someone with hair like his doesn't deserve to have a date.

"That's great, Jake."

"I'm feeling good. I think it's gonna be good."

"I find it's generally best not to get your hopes up. Then you don't get disappointed later."

Jake doesn't laugh.

"It's a joke," says Remy.

"Hey, I know this is weird, but can I get your opinion on a few other shirts?" Remy follows Jake into his room, of which he normally sees only a slice through the open door.

Jake has one of those novelty license plates on the wall that says his name, and a beat-up particleboard dresser. His wall is covered in posters that he's probably had since high school: a poster for the Live Aid 1985 benefit concert, a map of the solar system.

"Maybe you should clean it up in here, in case you take her home."

"Man, don't stress me out! Look at this." Jake raises his arms and shows him his damp armpits. He holds up a button-down. "What about this one?"

Remy looks at Jake's shirt and says, "It doesn't matter what you wear to a date. The important thing is not to look like you care too much."

"This girl's really smart. She was on *Who Wants to Be a Millionaire* one time."

"Did she win? Is she a millionaire?"

Jake laughs for a long time. "No offense, man, but are you kidding me? When people win *Who Wants to Be a Millionaire* they're on the *news* and stuff." Jake laughs again and says, several times, "I think I would *know* if I were going on a date with a millionaire!" The parrot laughs too, which makes Jake laugh harder.

"I really hope it goes well for you," says Remy.

The bird's head chugs up and down as it duplicates Jake's laugh. It's an exact copy, but dead in the center.

An hour after Jake has left, Jen still hasn't texted him. The heat in the apartment is insufficient and Remy turns on the space heater. He watches *Total Recall* by himself.

He checks his phone. Maybe it won't work out. Maybe the Signifiers have done all they intended to accomplish, and his Consummate Result has already been realized. Perhaps the most Consummate Result for Remy was the night before—a single evening that felt deeply inadequate, an evening that Jen might already regret. He feels that something more must be possible. It could have been better, if only he hadn't had to pee, if Jen weren't so drunk, if Alicia's clothes hadn't been all over the floor. Although actually, now that he considers it, this is the only part of the situation that felt correct.

Just when he's about to fall asleep, he receives exactly the type of text he doesn't want to get from Jen—the kind so long that it doesn't fit into the message preview. It begins, Sry to be that girl who uses this line but last night was prob a mistake. She says that she was "deep in her id," and admits fault at the same time that she belittles him: I think I was probably using you to work through some personal shit that doesn't involve you. I'd say we should be friends?? But right now is probably the time to set boundaries for myself. She implies that she only slept with him out of low self-esteem, and then disguises this insult by claiming that her momentary slip-up wasn't "fair" to him. The text is smoothly offhand, and yet, to Remy's practiced eye, masterfully dishonest.

He puts the phone down and doesn't respond. If Jen really wanted to set boundaries, she'd just ignore him. Maybe she felt that their night together initiated something fatefully consequential. Otherwise, it wouldn't feel so urgent to put distance between them.

Remy wakes up in the middle of the night when he hears a noise in the bathroom. He calls out Jake's name, but this time it's more like delivering a line. He knows it isn't Jake. And he can't explain it, but he *senses* that Jake hasn't come home. *Good for him,* he thinks.

"Sandy?" he says. Maybe the parrot is able to escape her cage and wander around at night. He calls her name again. He hears Sandy's dim voice say, "Suck my balls!" She laughs her ersatz version of Jake's laughter. The noises don't stop.

It *does* sounds like eating. The noises are louder than they were the last time. He hears heavy movement.

Remy's whole body is tense. He sits up in bed and subdivides the noises into their constituent parts. There's the subtle clicking sound, which is like footsteps, and then another clicking sound that might be separate from the first, or maybe not.

The sounds move into the living room, and then to the hallway. Then he hears something else—something between a rattle and a hiss, like breathing.

Knock-knock-knock-knock. The sound isn't on his door. The knocking is coming from the hallway, where there *aren't even any doors.* Remy can't stand to be in the dark anymore, but he doesn't want to move and cause more noise.

The light nearest to him is the red string of Christmas lights next to the bed. He plugs these in and the room floods with red light, which doesn't comfort him or make him feel safer.

Whatever it is, it's noticed the light. The footsteps pause. After a moment, the sounds begin again, progressing, churningly, down the hall. As they come closer, the noises don't clarify, but only become more confusing. There's more knocking. It sounds less and less like a human hand.

For the first time, Remy notices an odor. It's a familiar odor that he's noticed in the bathroom and kitchen. Up to this point, he'd assumed that it was a new variety of mold. And yes—it's the same odor he smelled in the bar bathroom, when he saw the face in the mirror behind him. It's chaotic, like garbage, but metallic, too.

The noises stop outside Remy's bedroom.

He can't even get up to lock the door. He's paralyzed.

Knock-knock-knock-knock.

Remy sees himself as if from above. He's disconnected from his body as he stands up, stepping on Alicia's wrinkled tank-tops and his own cast-off clothing, empty DVD jewel cases, pens, receipts, extension cords, and moves to the door. He stands behind it, his hand on the doorknob. He expects to hear more knocking, but instead he hears the rattling sound of something breathing in and then hissing out.

Remy opens the door. He doesn't see anything. The reason he doesn't see anything is because he's looking in front of him instead of down.

Before he can understand what's happening, his legs are knocked from beneath him and he's on the floor, pinned down by something strong and slick. His eyes reflexively shut tight as he kicks and punches to protect his face and stomach. The sound in the room is high-pitched and accompanied by an odor like an exploded battery. He opens his eyes and looks up. He's expecting to see Alicia. But it's not Alicia—it's not even a distortion of Alicia. It's the creature he saw in the mirror, and by the pool in the Hamptons.

The face is unlike anything he's ever seen before—an insectile parody of a human face suspended on a tubelike throat, which sways as it observes him. The eyes are massive and without pupils, like the eyes of a giant ant. The humanoid lips are closed around what seems to be a cone-shaped tongue, but which now splits, like a beak, or mandibles, and now closes and retracts back down the throat, then emerges again. The retraction and emergence of the mandibles is nimble, vibratory, and obscene.

For a moment only, as the creature seems to be observing him, the face looks more human and evokes inchoate recognition... *Who is he reminded of?* The creature's exterior is blue and translucent, like a deep-sea crustacean's, and shines with a dark sap. The mandibles appear again, slowly, and open, revealing a throat that pulsates as if speaking, the muscles bluish red from the Christmas lights.

Remy flattens his hand and strikes the creature's throat. The pressure on his rib cage lessens and Remy employs a front elbow strike, popping the creature's head back. He grabs Alicia's Centenary College letter opener from the nightstand and aims for the creature's eyes, but a shell-like eyelid flicks down, protecting them, and the mandibles close on his forearm. The letter opener drops on the floor. For now, Remy doesn't feel anything.

He brings his knee up sharply, briefly dislodging the eyelid, and the heel of his hand meets the membrane of one of the creature's eyes, his fingers sinking in as if into jelly. The mouth releases his arm. He performs a kip-up from his back, and once standing, delivers a roundhouse kick to the head followed by a crescent kick.

Remy doesn't understand why his head hurts, but then realizes it's because of the volume and pitch of the creature's screams.

Remy sees—vaguely in the red light—that the creature propels itself around like a four-legged mantis, or a dining table enchanted into life. It's awkward but fast, and tremendously ugly: a horrible mash-up of familiar components, grown inexpertly in the dark.

The creature backs up and strikes out with its long neck, snapping its mandibles, which close into a single sharp spike and jackhammer next to his face. Remy blocks it with a cheap IKEA nightstand, old dishes crashing to the floor and shattering. The creature's mandibles spring open and close around the nightstand, and powdery chips of paint and particleboard fall to the floor. Remy twists the nightstand, pivoting the creature's neck into the wall. The mandibles close and vibrate against the wall: *Knock-knock-knock-knock. Knock-knock-knock-knock.*

An impact, and somehow Remy is on his back again. His fingers grasp for the letter opener, and he jabs it into the first part of the creature he encounters—its belly. A dark substance pours out and Remy stands up, supporting himself against the wall. The substance is tacky to the touch, and sticks to him in long bubblegum strands. Remy slams a black-smeared hand onto the light switch, turning on the overhead lights.

The creature continues making a sound like a jamming food processor, but is partially immobilized by the bright lights. It recoils, two nasal slits expanding blindly, and inhabits several parts of the room at once.

This is the worst part. The image of the creature glitches over every part of the room, and Remy flinches as it appears and disappears from every side, with diminishing physicality. He strikes out with the letter opener and encounters only a smoky puff of dark air. In the overhead light, Remy briefly sees the face with the lips open wide, in an expression that seems utterly human.

The sounds stop.

Remy turns on the lights in all the rooms. He hears someone banging on his front door. "Quiet down your goddamn bird!" says a neighbor's voice.

"Go the fuck away!" says Remy.

Remy finds his phone, unlocks it before realizing that the black substance is smearing all over the screen. He dries off his phone with a paper towel, washes his hands, and calls Carla.

"I need you to come to my house. Now," says Remy. The parrot's silence unnerves him, and he opens Jake's door to make sure it didn't die of fright.

The background is noisy. "I'm actually kind of pissed at you," says Carla.

"I believe you now." Sandy's head ticks from side to side, presenting one eye, then the other. Sandy seems unperturbed by the noise. Could Remy be crazy?

Carla says, "I'm trying to help you. Has it occurred to you that I'm invested in your happiness?"

Remy puts a dripping hand on his face, startled by the warmth of the substance. "Yes, Carla, you were right. Please come over. You're the only person who can help me."

Carla arrives nearly an hour later, mascara pilling at the corners of her eyes. She's barefoot. Her shoes are in her hands and she drinks from something in a paper bag. She asks if she can wash her feet. "I had to walk barefoot for the last few blocks. Whenever I walk barefoot it's kind of cool, though. I feel like I'm a celebrity, raising awareness."

"What are you even talking about?"

"Like raising awareness for the fact that some people don't even have shoes. Don't you remember how Keira Knightley went barefoot for charity? And it was so controversial?" Remy looks up at her from the couch, amazed that Carla still exists in a reality where Keira Knightley is a topic that might be discussed. "Have you even looked around? Do you see what happened here?"

Carla leans over a puddle of black goo on the hardwood. "Did you try to paint in here?"

Remy stands up and grabs Carla's jacket, shaking her. "Stop joking around, Carla—this is serious!" Carla yells and Remy lets go of her jacket, putting both hands in the air in apology. "I'm sorry. I'm sorry."

"I came all the way over here, *Reymond.*"

"I'm just not in the mood for you to make fun of me right now."

"Asshole," says Carla, picking her way around the puddles of black goo. She stops when she sees the bedroom.

"Do you see what happened to me?" Remy holds out his arm. He washed and disinfected the bite with rubbing alcohol, but blood is seeping through the bandage. "There was a *thing* here. It left this black stuff everywhere. You should have seen me, Carla, it was crazy. I was doing all these karate moves. It was like I was in a movie."

He shows her the bite marks on the IKEA nightstand, the shattered dishes, the bits of eyeball matter on the floor, the puddle of black goo. Carla holds her temples. "I'm too drunk for this."

"Do you think I'm crazy now?"

"I never said you were crazy, Remy. Don't make the mistake of projecting your own narrow-mindedness onto me. *I* believe you. *I'm* a good friend."

Remy apologizes, again, for his impatience earlier in the day. "What do you think, though? What does it Signify? I really thought—"

It sounds stupid, now, to say it. But he was sure that when he opened the door, he would see Alicia standing there, her fist raised to knock again. Perhaps she would look thinner, paler from imprisonment in some forgotten place these past few weeks, maybe a little bruised from her bike accident. He had felt so certain that she would be back again. This certainty still feels more definite than any of Carla's convoluted theories.

"Do you think maybe that creature is possessing her? The shower used to make all these crazy noises, but they stopped a few months ago. Alicia was taking a lot of showers around that time, and she started acting weird right after that. I think maybe the creature…infected her somehow. We heard all these strange noises in the walls. It could have gotten to her through the showerhead. Do you think maybe it's keeping her somewhere?"

Carla pulls a scrunchy out of her hair and reorganizes her ponytail. "Remy, I told you. The Alicia that you knew is gone. Really. *She's really gone.* But there are still Alicias from other Streams of

Reality that can communicate with you. And that's what you have to focus on. The best way for you to access Alicia again is to figure out a way to keep her, or a version of her, in your life."

"I've heard that before," he says.

Remy sits on the couch and Carla sits next to him, removing her jacket. "And in my opinion, the Signifiers are showing that the best way for you to do that is to be with Jen."

"If this creature is supposed to be a Signifier, why would it attack me? What is that supposed to tell me?"

"If that *thing* was what I think it was…that means your Consummate Result is very close. It means you're headed in the right direction. The better you follow the Signifiers, the stronger it will be."

"Of course."

"But there may be something to your theory about the bathroom."

Remy's laugh is as dead as Sandy's. "What am I talking about? There's no way that creature could have been in a wall or a showerhead. I'm insane. Ignore me."

"You have to stop thinking in terms of physical space."

Carla asks him to make them a pot of coffee, and Remy is relieved to have a simple task based in the known reality. He inspects the coffee machine for possible contamination by the creature, and when he doesn't see any of the black substance, he prepares enough coffee for two—something he hasn't done in many weeks. Carla stands in the door of the bathroom. "Do you have pliers?" she says. "I'll also need a rag and an adjustable wrench."

Carla stands on the rim of the tub, holding the shower arm steady with pliers over a rag, and unscrewing the showerhead with the wrench. It comes off as suddenly as a zit popping. An explosion of black mucus sprays the shower doors and bathtub. Carla says *Ew ew ew* but doesn't flinch. She keeps her eye on the fluid. "I'm going to need you to get some paper towels," she says.

"What is it?"

"I think it might be waste products."

"You mean like shit? Like monster shit?"

"Or it could be some other bodily fluid. It could even be poisonous. Is it affecting the hardwood?" She doesn't seem concerned.

"I guess I'll check?" Remy wipes the fluid off Carla's hands and top while she looks away, breathing through her mouth. He looks at the puddles of black on the ground, and begins to sop them up with a wad of paper towels. He doesn't even know what he's looking for, and feels stupid. "It seems to be staining the tiles black, but I can't tell if it's doing anything else."

"Clearly this is a problem area, but I don't know if there's anything you can do about it. Aside from not using the shower. Although that could also be fine."

"What is it, though?"

"Do you remember when I told you that there are Toxic Antagonists that are too specialized to discuss in a book for the general public? I think this is one of them."

"So then how do you know about them?" It's getting closer to dawn, and Remy feels progressively more ridiculous, the same way he felt when one of his scenarios with Alicia devolved into poor acting. He's speaking nonsense that he's not even sure he believes, and he doesn't know what he's supposed to do next, aside from making coffee and cleaning up the shower.

"We need to call an expert," says Carla. "You're lucky that I know someone. It's late, but she'll understand."

The expert knocks on his door in under twenty minutes. Remy opens the door. "Andrea? What the fuck?"

She looks different than before. Her hair is swept back and she's carrying an expensive briefcase. One black leather glove squeaks as she clenches and unclenches the fist that doesn't hold the briefcase. She doesn't appear surprised to see him. "This seems to be a very Significant coincidence," she says. "You haven't been going to Dr. Jane's course."

"No," says Remy. On impulse, he lies. "I've been really busy. Some work stuff came up."

"Can I come in or what?" Remy has been too surprised to stand back from the door. Carla says *Hi Andrea!* and they exchange small talk that reveals their relationship to each other is casual, but mediated by professional and slightly suspicious distance, as if Andrea were Carla's weed dealer. When Andrea uses the bathroom—unperturbed by the black fluid—she takes her briefcase in with her.

"How do you guys know each other?" says Remy, as Andrea examines the mess in his bedroom.

"You know. The interested community," says Andrea, but she doesn't elaborate. Remy wonders if this question was inappropriate.

Carla brings her a cup of coffee, which Andrea periodically sets on the ground while she takes pictures with her phone. She wears rubber shoes with individual toes that Remy is used to seeing on dads. Her yoga pants are the expensive kind that remain opaque even when she's bending over. She stands up and says, without turning all the way around, "Okay, Remy. Tell me about this encounter."

Remy tells her what happened, and when Carla prompts him, explains everything suspicious he observed before and after Alicia's death, including the missing food. He unwraps the bandage so that she can inspect his bite wound. "Does this thing have a poisonous bite? Am I going to turn into one?" This is intended to be a joke, and he's hoping Andrea will reassure him that it is in fact a ludicrous idea.

"Probably not, but I honestly don't know if the bite will have effects."

Remy looks between Carla and Andrea. "Aren't you an expert?"

Andrea doesn't answer. She opens her briefcase and removes a leather bundle like a dental kit. She selects a syringe and a small bottle and fills the syringe by puncturing the bottle's top. After disinfecting Remy's arm with a cotton swab, she inserts a needle, and then places the needle in a clear plastic bag. "This is the issue, Remy." Andrea packs everything back into the leather bundle. "You may not understand what's going on right now, but one thing you should know is that despite the fact that I'm considered an 'expert'"—her gloves squeak again as she makes air quotes—"I basically know jack shit. You can thank the US government and its overzealous classification of research in the public interest for that sorry state of affairs."

"Suck my balls!" says Sandy from the next room.

Andrea looks at Jake's door. "You have another roommate?"

"That's Sandy, his parrot."

"Both of you will need to stay somewhere else. If *you* encountered this FMTA—"

"This *what?*"

"—then your roommate is just as likely to." Andrea stands up and removes a hatchet from her briefcase. She swings it around several times before sinking it into the wall.

"Hey!" says Remy.

"You said you weren't getting your security deposit back anyway!" says Carla.

Andrea works her way around the apartment, honeycombing the walls with the hatchet. She explains that the pattern is to "deter its movement through physical space, although at this point it's likely too strong for this to be a significant obstacle." More than once, a neighbor knocks on the door to complain about the noise. Each time, Andrea answers the door, speaks to the neighbor in a low voice, and removes something from her briefcase. The neighbors go away.

After an hour, during which Andrea ignores Remy's questions and occasionally stops to pick something out of the wall and place it in a plastic bag, she sets down her hatchet and sits on the couch, empty coffee cup in one hand and a pile of Ziplocs on the coffee table. “I have a weird question,” says Remy. It’s getting light outside, and Andrea seems nearly finished. “Is this going to cost me anything?”

“Are you *serious* right now?” says Carla. “Even if it did! You might want to think about rejecting the tyranny of money over your life, Remy.”

Andrea observes him, clinically, from an exhausted posture on the couch. “Isn’t it interesting? How we spoke that day and I just completely ignored the signs of a phenomenon I’ve studied for almost a decade?” She exhales loudly. It feels as if some of her disgust with herself is also directed at Remy.

“I guess you couldn’t know,” says Remy.

“But you used the word *destiny.* You said you felt drawn to this other woman, right? This is a textbook opportunity for a Paranormalagus to manifest. But what was I doing? I was thinking with my clit, not my brain.”

Carla asks Andrea if she told Remy *who she really is.*

“I don’t think that’s relevant,” says Andrea.

“She wrote *The Apple Bush.* She’s A. B. Fisketjon.”

“No way,” says Remy, briefly thrown by this coincidence. It’s unnerving, and possibly means something, but he’s incapable of processing this knowledge right now amid all the other new information.

“What are you, a fan?” says Andrea. “Somehow I doubt it.”

“Alicia was,” he says.

“Ah.” Andrea observes him, rubbing her lower lip with her thumb unattractively. “Some of this you may have already guessed. My husband, Sean, was killed by one of these creatures nearly ten years ago. You were right about my story being polished. I’ve been telling it in grief workshops ever since, hoping to locate others with similar experiences.”

Andrea takes some of the plastic-baggied items and places them between two metal prongs on a small, taserlike machine. The machine bites through the plastic bags and beeps. She notes the results on her phone.

"I told you how my husband got superstitious—noting down slogans he heard on the television, or fixating on certain phrases our friends mentioned, or opening books at random. Neither of us knew then that he was guided by Signifiers. He didn't even know what he was doing—he was just out of options and following his intuition. I thought it was luck that got him into a clinical trial, but he knew that he'd followed the signs to the right doctor, at the right time."

"I'm guessing that didn't work out," says Remy. He smiles, inappropriately, then stops. "This is all very surreal."

"The self-help stuff isn't bullshit—it's a good way to sneak really valuable knowledge into the public consciousness. If you pay attention to the signs around you, Remy, it might literally save your life."

"I still don't understand what you and Carla think I'm supposed to pay attention to. I don't even know what *happened.* Why did this thing show up? What is it?"

Andrea puts down the machine. "A Fully Manifested Toxic Antagonist, or FMTA, subset *Paranormalagus,* often shows up when Signifiers towards a Consummate Result are inundating our reality." Andrea is severe. "It's just like you said: It's like a destiny. When a Consummate Result is that strong, countervailing forces from other Streams of Reality sometimes interfere. In Sean's case, he really wanted to get better, or at least be free of pain. And in other realities, he may have succeeded. But just when he was getting close, that's when the Paranormalagus showed up." Andrea continues to explain the mechanics of Paranormalagus phenomena, making use of more acronyms.

Remy interrupts her. "So what's my destiny? To be with Jen? Like Carla keeps saying? And we know that for sure?"

"I can't comment on the specific result indicated by the

Signifiers. That's impossible for me to know. If anyone can answer that question, it's you."

Remy says to Carla, "This is ridiculous. I already slept with her a few days ago."

"Oh my God, that's great!" says Carla.

"So that's done. And that thing is still out there. If I'm understanding correctly, if just sleeping with her was my Consummate Result, then this creature wouldn't still be around."

Andrea doesn't look up from her iPad. "Correct."

"Isn't there some way for me to defend myself?" says Remy. "Like if it comes back? It seems sensitive to light, but does it hate garlic or something?" Carla and Andrea exchange frustrated expressions.

Andrea says, "Keep all the lights on, obviously, although it may not be vulnerable to light for much longer. Especially if it's corporealized to the point where it can consistently ingest food." She puts the iPad down. "Carla, you've been a big help, but would you step into the other room? I need to talk to Remy privately."

Carla doesn't move. "As Remy's friend, I think he would appreciate my support."

Andrea waits, until finally Carla goes to Jake's bedroom and shuts the door. Remy hears her delighted surprise at seeing the parrot.

Andrea lowers her voice. "Answer this, Remy, and it's very important: Have you seen this creature anywhere else?"

"I think I did, a couple of times. One time in this bar. And before that, when I was in the Hamptons."

"Did it leave marks of any kind? Was there physical contact? Did it attack you?"

"It just disappeared, before. It only attacked me tonight."

Andrea gathers up her equipment. "This is bad news. If it can *appear* other places, all it needs is a surge of energy for it to corporealize outside the apartment. If it gains access to human prey, then it can attack anywhere, anytime. You're probably safe once it gets light, but you and your roommate will need to leave soon."

"Human prey?" says Remy.

"I have one more question I wanted to ask, just between the two of us. Did you recognize the Paranormalagus?"

Remy is surprised by one of the first questions that makes him feel like Andrea really knows what she's talking about. "Yeah, it did look familiar. But I'm not sure *who* it looked like." Andrea's relief, and the softening of her face as she says *Good*, reminds Remy of what a gentler version of Andrea once said, in Dr. Jane's circle.

Before she can give him more instructions, he says, "The creature that was sucking the life out of your husband—that thing he saw was a Paranormalagus, right? And didn't it... look like you?"

"Yes," says Andrea. She pulls the belt of her coat around her but stays seated. "Yes. Although that Paranormalagus was very different from yours—it wasn't near as large or aggressive. Sean didn't have the tools to know what that creature was, but he must have known what it meant." Andrea seems tired, and Remy has difficulty imagining a version of Andrea that could look like the hideous creature he saw—she seems so benign.

"So what *did* it mean that the creature looked like you? Why does that matter?"

"Some people think that a Paranormalagus is a projection of someone who opposes your Consummate Result, warped and altered by travel through several realities. In Sean's case—as difficult as this was for me to admit—I suspect that some version of me was terrified of what would happen if Sean got better. Some version of me *wanted* him to stay sick."

"That's... Wow, fuck," says Remy.

"If you can figure out who the creature looks like, then it might tell you what your Consummate Result is."

"He could have *fought* the Paranormalagus though, right? If it was small, it might not have been so hard." He can't help saying, "I managed—I actually beat the crap out of it—and mine is pretty big."

Andrea says, "Being in pain is incredibly lonely. When you don't think you have the support of a partner, it becomes impossible. Sean stopped paying attention to the Signifiers, and the clinical trial didn't work out. He just"—Andrea has become even more severe—"he gave up. And he became prey."

Andrea doesn't look like she wants to be comforted, so Remy stays on his side of the couch.

Carla calls from Jake's room: "Can I come out now?"

"You can come out," says Andrea.

Andrea packs up her briefcase and Remy says, "So you're just leaving? What was the point of all these tests if you're not even going to help me?"

Andrea reaches out and squeezes his shoulder. There's nothing sexual about the touch. "Because the next time I see you, it's possible you'll be dead. And when I steal the autopsy results to do my own analysis, I'd like to have as much preliminary data as possible."

"It's probably going to be fine," says Carla. "I think this was helpful!"

Andrea shuts the briefcase and puts on sunglasses, which annoys Remy. Why does she need sunglasses? How is he supposed to take her seriously with affectations like these? "Even though I saw the monster and everything, I'm kind of struggling to take all of this stuff seriously."

Andrea opens the door. She says to him, in a low voice, "As you plan your next steps, I'll give you a word of advice. It's a cliché from my book, but a true one: Most of the time, we are our own worst enemies."

"Sure," says Remy, but he can't help but think that Andrea is talking more about her own experience than his.

Carla stays with Remy until morning, drinking the rest of the coffee. Theoretically, this is so they can brainstorm, but really it's because Remy can't stand the idea of being alone in the apartment, without Carla's confident, reassuring presence. He tells her what Andrea said to him. "The thing is, I don't think that the Paranormalagus looked like me. But I don't have any idea who else it could be."

"It'll come to you," says Carla.

"I still don't even know for sure what my Consummate Result is. Clearly just having sex with Jen didn't qualify."

"Aside from sleeping with her, don't you think there's some better way of being close to her? Something a little more substantive?"

Remy thinks of that grim thrusting scene. "Yeah. Something more satisfying is probably possible."

As Carla is searching through Remy's fridge for something to eat, Remy watches her proprietary way of navigating the apartment and the ease with which she takes liberties with his possessions. Carla's dress is tight enough to see where her underwear and bra bite into her skin. There are pimples on her shoulder blades, and her face is the same as it always is: snub-nosed, bossy, unremarkable. What must it be like to be one of Jen's closest friends, calibrating yourself to be appealing in every way and yet never succeeding as much as Jen does without even trying? To have to stand next to her and resign yourself to paling in comparison? Or does she not even notice?

Remy says, "Do you know what Jen said to me? She said that she thought you and I would be a good couple."

Carla stands up and looks at him over the fridge door. "Probably, in some universe, we *are* dating. Good for them."

"But if it's happening in a lot of universes, doesn't that mean we probably belong together?" He laughs so that she knows he's joking. What if the Paranormalagus looks familiar because it's actually a projection of Carla from another universe? Maybe a version of her who recognizes that what she really wants is to be with Remy, and who's therefore trying to prevent him from realizing his destiny with Jen?

"To tell you the truth," she says, "this whole cosmic matchmaking thing is really fun, but trying to follow the Signifiers to accomplish a goal… It's not the best way to approach Andrea's work."

"I don't understand. What's the point of it, besides that?"

"I think what's great about knowing one's place in the universe is the *experience* of it. How it feels." Carla sits on the couch next to Remy, eating Jake's ice cream. "It's just cool to walk around sensing the presence of all these souls and all their potential. Trying to maximize your own potential can be so isolating. I mean, I hope to *God*, Remy, that getting with Jen will make you less lonely, but real enlightenment would probably be union with everyone else, too. Don't you think?" She stares into the ice cream. "Maybe that's what death is."

"It's interesting," says Remy. "Jen loves to talk about living in the now, but you're probably doing it better than she is."

"Damn," says Carla. "Maybe that's why it pissed her off so much when I slept with Horus." Carla smiles, and it's clear to Remy that this is something she's known about herself for a long time. "I feel bad for her, in a way. I think it's a waste of time to try to achieve perfection, because if you look at all the versions of the world everywhere, overlaid one over the other, then that is perfection. It's nice to keep in mind that if something doesn't work out for me in this life, it does in another." Carla waves the ice cream spoon around, indicating that this moment, eating ice cream, is appreciated.

"I wish I felt that."

"Some version of you probably does."

Carla finishes the ice cream, complaining about the freezer burn in a cheerful way, oddly galvanized by the events that have so drained Remy. She leaves once she has to go to work, not at all stressed by the idea of showing up in last night's clothes.

Jake comes home around nine and Remy watches the door open, feeling as if he's emerged from a trance. "Oh man," says Jake, looking around the apartment, "I didn't even know we had an axe."

"It's a hatchet," says Remy, noticing for the first time that Andrea left it behind. "The date went well?"

"I think we're in love," says Jake. "She's really cool—but hang on, Remy. What did you do to the walls?" Remy sees the scene through Jake's eyes. His bedroom with the door wide open, the lights on in every room, the empty beer cans strewn about the couch, the mangled nightstand and the broken dishes, the black substance on the hatcheted walls. Remy has a headache. In some other world, somewhere, another version of Remy is waking up without a headache, Alicia is still alive, and *that* Remy doesn't have to deal with all of this crazy bullshit.

Jake examines the stains and says, "Man, I was saving that paint for the kitchen!"

"It's not paint. I have to talk to you."

"My dude," says Jake. "No judgment at all about whatever this is. But we're going to have to get a professional cleaner in here."

"No we won't." Remy stands up. "We have to leave the apartment. You do, at least. It's not safe here."

Remy explains everything that happened, preceding his statements with, "I know it sounds crazy." He shows Jake the bite on his arm. He describes the Paranormalagus. He tells him everything that Andrea and Carla told him.

Jake says, "And if I contact your friend Carla, she'll confirm she said all this stuff to you?"

"I basically have no chance of saving myself unless I make sense of these Signifiers." Remy sees that Jake is unpersuaded, and decides to use larger words in the hope that he will sound less crazy. "I can't really explain what little I know of the science, but essentially there's a symbolic order underlying seemingly random events. It requires interpretation."

"But why would anyone attack you?"

"You're not listening to me. I don't want you to die, Jake. This creature is dangerous."

"I'll be honest, Remy. I think you need help. I'd ask if there's someone I can call, except... I'm probably that person!"

"Look at these bite marks! What more evidence do you need?"

"Did you get a picture of this guy?"

Remy says he's not a *guy*. "I was too busy fighting for my life to take a picture."

"Do you want me to call in to work for you?"

"Shit." Remy has completely forgotten that he has a brunch shift. He says that he has to shower, and then remembers that the showerhead has been removed. He tells Jake not to go into the bathroom. "I'm not positive, but I think it might still be toxic."

"From what?"

"Paranormalagus waste products."

"How about you just stay home? I'm going to make some calls."

"I'm really fine, Jake. It's probably best for me to leave the house."

Outside, the world confronts him with pronounced normalcy—normalcy made bizarre in the same way that it felt strange to take a subway home from the hospital after seeing Alicia's body. Now that the evidence of the night before is no longer in front of him, he can hardly believe that it happened. He smells urine and McDonald's, as usual. Outside the subway entrance, a man asks for change, as usual. What seems strange is that he's wearing a child's unicorn hat, with a shiny plush horn on the front. Remy's eyes stay fixed on the man as he walks around him to enter through the turnstiles. Does it mean something? What could a unicorn signify? All he can think of is the Paranormalagus's vibrating mandibles.

On the aboveground platform, Remy texts Alicia New: Am I crazy? What the fuck do you want from me.

Alicia New's reply is instantaneous, not preceded by the typing indicator.

Any other type of Pringles is gross just get regular.

Remy says *fuck,* aloud on the platform. He types, I don't know wya right now, or which version of you is talking but it would really help if u could get to the phone.

Alicia New: look for the one with the bow on it.

Remy brings out the entrées for two older women in his section, and less than a minute later one of them waves him over. She dissects her side salad with her fork and draws back from it. "I must ask you," says the woman, "is this a soybean?"

"The salad is dressed with a soybean and fennel pâté. Is there an issue?"

"I told you that I have a deathly, *deathly* allergy to legumes." The woman presses her eyelids. She breathes in and out quickly.

"You said you had an allergy to peanuts."

"I said I had an allergy to peanuts and, more broadly, legumes. I emphasized this. I *emphasized* it."

Remy is frozen in place. He looks at the plate as if there might be some helpful information there. "Are you sure that soybeans are a legume?"

The woman's gal pal companion says that Remy needs to *rectify this now.* "We might have to take her to the hospital! This isn't the time to split hairs!"

Remy thinks about the word *rectify.* How can *rectify* be applied in this situation? Rocco, with a floor manager's sixth sense, is at the table instantly. He kneels next to the woman and she tells him about the soybeans, her eyelids fluttering. "How much did you eat?" says Rocco.

"I can't be sure."

"I'm so, so deeply sorry," says Rocco, not acknowledging Remy. Rocco indicates to the hostess that she should retrieve their coats. Other diners look at the table, mildly excited by the drama. The hypnotic flow of service is disrupted. The diners are quiet, the better to hear Rocco apologizing to the woman and to see if the woman will die from her deathly allergy.

The woman hyperventilates. It looks like a reenactment of a medical emergency rather than the real thing. She holds her throat, but keeps saying, "I'm fine." Remy's uncertain about what he should do—should he attend to his other tables? The way she has her hands around her throat reminds him of the night Alicia went into Jen's bedroom, when Jen held her throat, insisting that Alicia had choked her. Does the resemblance Signify anything? In another dimension, is the woman really suffocating to death instead of just waiting to? And if she is, what does it mean? Is it a sign of things to come? Things that could come? Or is this simply another occurrence in the insignificant story of Remy's life, Remy's *only* life, in the *only* universe, which will go on and on in the same old way it has before—except now with his girlfriend dead? Perhaps he'll be fired, and then at least every day when he goes to work it will be a different restaurant.

The woman gets up. "Nothing's happening yet," she says. While standing, then putting on her coat, then leaving, she continues to rehearse the allergic reaction, as if that will stop it.

He isn't certain that he's going to be fired until they cram an extra manager into the office. It always takes two managers to fire someone; one to fire, and one to bear witness in case he freaks out.

"I can't believe you're firing me right after Alicia died," says Remy.

"It's automatic, Remy, in a situation like this. It's just the policy."

"Why don't you just *pretend* to fire me, so the lady's happy? No one will know! She's gone now anyways."

"She could have died!"

"She should have said if she's allergic to soybeans! I asked her about her allergies."

Rocco gives Remy an extended lecture on soybeans and peanuts. Remy says he didn't realize he needed a PhD in *beans* to work here.

"It's your responsibility! She specifically said *deadly.* You should have asked someone."

Remy perceives, vaguely, that Rocco may have a point. Rocco exchanges a glance with Tina, the other manager, inhales in preparation to say something else, and then says *Never mind.*

Likely, Rocco feels an obligation to tell Remy that he also shouldn't have come to work stinking of alcohol. Except that Rocco—like many managers Remy's had—also smells of alcohol, and without the excuse of a dead girlfriend.

He isn't used to leaving a shift this early on a Sunday. The bright winter light makes him feel the wrongness of his placement in the universe at this moment, when normally he would be following his preordained path within the restaurant.

He goes to a loud bar where he's unlikely to meet anyone he knows—a bar with television screens. He has a beer and a shot, a beer and a shot, a beer and a shot. The television goes to commercial and he watches the screen, mesmerized by the gyrations of the Mucinex Man. Could this be a Signifier? What does the Mucinex Man indicate?

His phone dings. Jen has posted a new photo. It's a picture of herself in a car with some girlfriends that Remy doesn't know but recognizes from her pictures. The caption says, "Annual Girls' retreat in Woodstock," followed by several emojis including trees. He looks at Jen's photos for several minutes, although he's seen them all before. He scrolls further back and looks at photos he and Alicia looked at together, remembering where they were when they saw this picture of her with the goat, or on the sailboat, or in Spain.

His phone vibrates. Jake is calling him. Remy picks up and says, "Why are you calling me, dude? Just text like a normal person." Jake doesn't say anything, and Remy says, "I'm just giving you a hard time. What's up?"

"Uh. I'm just checking in. I'm trying to go out again with that girl, but if you're not feeling so good I could always stay in with you."

"Whatever you do, just don't take her home to the apartment. Are you at the apartment now?"

"Why?"

"Just leave."

"Why is it so loud? Where are you?"

"I got fired. I'm in a bar." Jake is silent. Remy says, "Where did you meet this girl again?"

"In my grief counseling group."

"Like, a long time ago? After your mom died?"

"I go to grief counseling every Thursday night. I've been going since we've lived together."

"Why didn't you say anything?"

"I've told you like ten times."

Remy confirms that the person Jake's going on a date with isn't Andrea. He tells Jake about how some older woman tried to prey on him at Dr. Jane's course. He begins to talk about how she showed up at the apartment last night, but it's difficult to make himself heard, and he senses that Jake will only take this as another sign of his mental unwellness.

"The point is, I'm fine," says Remy. "Have a nice time. The beginning of a romance is the best part, so enjoy it while it lasts."

Someone sits on the stool next to Remy, and from his peripheral vision, he senses that the person is staring at him.

"I gotta go, man," says Remy. "Wear a condom."

Remy hangs up, and delays for a second before turning his head. What has he done now? Has he offended some stranger who wants to fight him? Has he committed some new soybean-related crime? He turns his head.

It's Alicia.

And then it's not quite Alicia, and then it's an Alicia he doesn't recognize. Alicia is glitching in and out, first right next to him and then back on the stool, her face and location changing subtly but definitely. At one point she's wearing the halter-top, and then she looks older, and then she looks sick.

Remy reaches out to touch her, but the sensation is momentary. When he finally speaks, his voice is a whisper. "Where the *fuck* have you been?"

One version of her smiles. Her lips move but no sound comes out. His phone dings.

Alicia New: Something momentous is about to happen. I can feel it.

Remy reaches out again, trying to grab her. Trying to get her to *stay still.* "This isn't helpful! Can you please just talk to me?"

A version of Alicia who looks skinny and unhappy holds her throat.

"You can't talk?"

Her lips move again. His phone dings.

Alicia New: What did Jake say?

"He was just..." Remy makes a gesture to indicate that Jake was just talking about bullshit as usual. He sees, briefly, a bloody version of Alicia with a bit of scalp tucked behind her ear like a flower. Each version keeps her eyes on Remy, focused and yet impersonal, as if he were a pinball machine. If he could grab her, maybe he could pin her down. "Just stay. *Stay.*" His hands still close on nothing. "What am I supposed to do, Alicia? What do you want? What do you *all* want?"

She's not the only thing changing. In the area directly around Alicia, the bar changes too. The barstool next to her is red, then gone. Now the bar is well lit, now dark. Alicia's mouth moves again. She looks at the phone. It's silent. She keeps talking—she even shouts—but there's no sound. Her appearance alters again. Her eyes move back and forth between his face and his phone. She squeezes her eyes shut.

Ding.

Alicia New: The obstacle is the occasion.

"How about this? Nod if I should go home. Shake your head no if I shouldn't go home first."

Alicia looks at him, confused. She watches his face. She doesn't nod or shake her head. She looks angry. She points at his phone.

"Jake was just talking about his love life. I don't know!"

Remy replays his conversation with Jake in his head, and then understands what Carla and Andrea have been trying to tell him for a long time about remaining open to Signifiers. About how there might be details that have been in front of him the entire time without registering.

He drinks from his beer and covers his eyes with his hands. "No fucking way." He turns to look at Alicia's reaction, but the stool next to him is empty. He spins around in his seat. No one else in the bar seems to have noticed anything unusual.

Remy concentrates on the stool next to him, thinking that maybe she'll reappear, but she doesn't. He looks back at his beer. "Thank you," he says under his breath. He knows what he has to do. The universe is a beautifully arranged place in which even details that seem ordinary are the key to a larger design. Even now, sitting in this bar, having been fired, Remy sees that this barstool is exactly where he's supposed to be. When he looks back on the past few weeks, it's just like Carla said. He can see the Signifiers sparkling amid the minutiae of his life.

Andrea was a conduit for one of these Signifiers when she was hitting on him, by saying that no one would understand him except someone who had "experienced a similar loss." As was Jake, just now, when he mentioned that this girl was someone he met in a bereavement group. It was a Signifier when Jen told him how Horus was driving her crazy but said she couldn't break up with him. And how she revealed that Horus was shitty to Alicia the day she died. It was a Signifier when Remy felt compelled to buy that black hoodie, and it was a Signifier when Andrea left her hatchet at Remy's apartment. And most of all, it was a Signifier when Horus told Remy that he had *personally* smashed all the security cameras around his house.

The obstacle is the occasion. Is this phrase, like one of the slogans coming out of Sean's television, the code to his destiny?

Horus is the obstacle to Jen, and also, through his death, the surest way to bind Jen to Remy.

Any uncertainty he might normally have is eradicated by the brilliance, the neatness, of these Signifiers, and the clarity of their message. He can see perfectly how Horus's death will create an opportunity for him to bond with Jen: He'll be the only person she can talk to when she's devastated. They'll go to groups together. He'll do all kinds of crazy therapy shit—stuff he'd never do otherwise. And his bond with Jen won't be the frustrating game it is now, in which all he wins is a single drunken night followed by silence. It will be something deeper. He won't have to try to snatch his happiness from the few moments Jen gives him when she's drunk—instead he'll have days, months, years of her. More than enough time to concentrate properly, to enact the perfection of being with Jen that he knows is possible, in the way that he and Alicia imagined it.

Despite the alcohol in his body, he's filled with energy. Relief has eradicated everything except the Signifiers. He knows what to do. Sure, Horus deserves to die for being a pain in the ass, and even more for being one of the last people Alicia saw—and for being shitty to her in the small amount of time she had left. But, crucially, even if Remy didn't think this, it's not up to him: The Signifiers have spoken, and Remy has a destiny. He requests an Uber and goes back to the house to get the hatchet.

The flawlessness of his movement through the city streets and the smooth progress of the car surpass anything Remy has ever experienced. He calls Carla and tells her, in the clipped, efficient tone of a secret agent, to meet him at his house immediately. "Jake doesn't think he's in danger. I suspect that the Paranormalagus is less likely to prey on two people. Keep the lights on."

Only once has he experienced anything like this giddy correctness of motion—once, for a few moments, when he succeeded at surfing. But this time, there's no fear of failure. This euphoria is strangely like pain in its urgency. Also like pain, it feels eternal; it's impossible to remember what his life was like before.

The Uber drops him off, and Remy notices a black mark on the steps to his building. The glass of the front door has been broken. Remy stops and bends down to examine the mark, which is wet. Maybe it's not what he thinks it is. If the Paranormalagus can leave marks, then that means it can corporealize outside the apartment. And Andrea said that it could only corporealize outside the apartment once it moved on to human prey.

He opens the broken front door and runs up the stairs. Jake *can't* be home already. Black marks streak the wall in the stairwell. A mom and child who live in the building talk about the marks, even touch them, but don't seem alarmed. "Looks like someone had an accident of some sort," says the mother as she helps her son toddle down the stairs. But what accident could she be imagining? Carla was right. The world is filled with signs, and no one is paying attention.

Remy gets to the top of the stairs and sees that the streaks are everywhere. The apartment door is open, and he turns on the light. His hand comes away sticky.

Jake lies on the kitchen floor, his neck opened and his eyes moving with animatronic slowness. The wound in his throat has discernible layers. A weak, toiletlike pumping of blood overflows the wound. A plastic scoop is next to his hand and bird feed is scattered around his body. Sandy squawks repetitively from Jake's bedroom.

"Jake, fuck!" says Remy. He sits on the ground, placing his hand over the wound even though he's clearly too late to stop the blood. He sees four or five of these clean cuts on Jake's body—what's left of it. Large portions of Jake's body simply *aren't there*.

Jake's eyes don't move for several seconds while Remy cusses. His eyes move once, looking at Remy, and then look away. He moves his hand, maybe to touch Remy's arm.

"Wow, Jake." Remy laughs, trying to pretend that everything is fine. "Man, you've really made a mess haven't you?"

The strangest thing about Jake in this moment is that Remy expects him to smile, apologetically, as he often does. But Jake looks past him, nothing recognizably Jake-like in his expression. For several long minutes, Remy sits next to Jake, putting his hands over one wound and then another. Jake stops moving entirely a few minutes later.

"Remy?" Carla stands in the doorway. Remy keeps his hands on Jake. The light in the apartment seems incredibly bright.

"You're wearing sneakers," says Remy. "I've never seen you wear sneakers."

"Who is that? Is that Jake?"

"I came home and I saw the black marks... and then I found this."

"Holy shit."

"It's too late. There's no point in you being here." Remy holds out his arms and displays Jake's body. Liquid is everywhere—blood and black slime. Carla steps into the apartment, her mouth very small. She walks around the mess and shuts the door, then leans against it. "I told him not to stay in the apartment. He thought I was crazy."

"I'm calling Andrea."

Andrea picks up immediately, and Carla puts her on speaker as Remy tells her what happened. He says, "Do you think it was looking for me?"

"Oh geez," says Andrea. Her sigh over the phone is crackling and long. "You remember what I said, right? If it's moved on to human prey, then you're really fucked." Carla asks her what they should do, and Andrea says, "What do you think, that I have a magical answer? Christ, Carla, why are you even talking to me? I'm not a soldier, I'm an analyst. I don't have the ability to stop a corporealized Paranormalagus. I'm out of my depth."

Remy takes the phone and yells into it. "I know what I have to do. I finally saw the Signifiers."

"You did?" says Carla.

Andrea is silent. Then she says, "Okay. Listen, Remy. It's really important for you to follow through here. I need you to be absolutely sure."

"I *am* sure," says Remy, although his plan suddenly makes less sense. After Horus's death, it will take time for Jen to bond with him. It's difficult to imagine this new expression of Alicia in his life as a quick enough solution for the problem of the Paranormalagus. How long will it take for the monster to weaken and die?

Now Remy understands: The reason that the Paranormalagus looks familiar is because it's a projection of *Horus*. It must be. Of course Horus would be the countervailing force from another universe—he's trying to prevent his own death! Remy experiences minuscule uncertainties about this interpretation. *Was it really Horus's face that he recognized?*

Andrea says, "It's only a matter of time before the feds detect the presence of an FMTA. You're going to be dealing with all kinds of attention, so your chances of success are significantly reduced."

None of these issues bother him. Even if he doesn't understand now, he knows that eventually he will—the Signifiers will make sure of it. Alicia, or some version of Alicia, will tell him what to do.

"I know what to do," says Remy. "I need to go to Jen's house, now."

"Great. I'm going with you," says Carla.

"That's not necessary."

"If the Paranormalagus is seeking you out, specifically, then you'll need backup."

If Carla comes, she might not cooperate with his plan to kill Horus. Especially considering that she wants to date him. Remy perceives this obstacle, but his reaction is different than it would normally be.

"Sure. That makes sense," he says.

Carla says into the phone, "Andrea, do you want to meet us there?"

Andrea hangs up. "What a cunt," says Carla. "She spends her whole life studying this stuff, and now she's going to miss out?"

"It's better without her," says Remy. It feels good to have all the answers for once. He changes into a different coat—one not covered with Jake's blood—with the black hoodie on underneath. He washes the blood off his hands, or at least most of it, and puts on weatherproof gloves he hasn't used since he worked in delivery. Gloves aren't his style, even in cold weather, but his instincts tell him they are necessary. Carla asks if she should call an Uber and Remy says no. "We'll wait for a yellow cab. Do you have cash?"

"That's insane. How are we going to find a cab in this neighborhood?"

"That's what the Signifiers are telling me to do."

He asks again if she has cash and Carla takes out her wallet. She does. "See?" says Remy. "Have a little faith. You were meant to have cash. We were meant to take a cab."

He realizes, too late, that he forgot the hatchet upstairs. But that would give his plan away to Carla.

"What are you going to do?"

Remy remembers Horus's advice when they were out in the ocean together. "Right now my plan is to just...go with the flow."

They have no trouble finding a cab.

Five blocks from Jen's house, while Carla is having a self-righteous conversation with the cabdriver about how much he paid for his medallion, the cab is hit by a dark shape that tips the car over and makes everything go black.

When Remy's vision returns, he's upside down and Carla, also upside down, is touching him with strange intimacy, trying to get his seat belt unfastened.

"Shhh!" she says. She freezes. "It's *him*."

A figure is pressing against the front glass of the cab, leaving streaks behind. The cabdriver, his head bloody, opens his eyes and makes a pained noise. The shape whips through the front windshield, smashing it. The movement is so fast that Remy barely sees the creature's face, only the flash of a wet mandible, and then the individual platelets on its neck as it maneuvers inside the front seat, thwacking against the glass and spraying blood as the cabdriver screams and bits of flesh pepper the gearshift.

Carla and Remy look at each other, trying not to move, but it's impossible to remain completely motionless while dangling upside down. "What do we do?" says Carla in a voice barely above an exhale.

The creature releases the cabdriver and lunges towards the back seat, spraying them both with warm liquid, mandibles snapping. "Help!" says Remy. "Alicia, help me!"

The Paranormalagus lunges, but is stopped short by its shoulders, too large to fit through the hole in the windshield. The mandibles close into the single spike and vibrate uselessly, punching around the air to find them.

Remy says to Carla, "Undo my seat belt, now. Then we'll go out *your* side of the car. And run. Towards Jen's house."

The Paranormalagus keeps snapping at them, and then changes tactics and extracts its head from the car.

"Now!" says Remy.

Carla unbuckles his seat belt and Remy drops to the roof of the car. Carla opens the side door and Remy rolls over to exit after her, just as the Paranormalagus crashes through the passenger-side window where Remy was sitting a second before. It screams and tries to pull its head out.

Remy looks behind him and sees Carla running in the wrong direction. "Carla! Over here!" Carla goes the long way around the car, which gives the creature time to extract its head and shake the hazard glass from its face and shoulders. The glass skitters across the ground like fallen candy.

They run down one of the many dark industrial streets around Jen's apartment. Carla sprints to catch up to Remy and they both run together in the direction of Jen's house.

They can hear grunting, and the sound of wet galloping behind them. The stretch in front of them is dark—there are no streetlights at all. Remy hears the Paranormalagus exhale a horselike breath, and they both run faster.

They enter the dark section, the sounds zigzagging behind them. The Paranormalagus is gathering momentum. Remy smells something foul—less metallic now, and more animal. Remy reaches out for Carla's hand but touches something else, and the motion-detecting lights on a nearby warehouse blaze on, causing the creature to shrink away, screaming.

Carla and Remy stumble backwards, panting, and lean against

the wall directly beneath the lights. They don't say anything for what feels like a long time. Remy paces in front of the warehouse to keep the motion-detecting lights on. He sees a sign next to them that reads RANDOLPH STREET. He smiles. "Thank you," he says, quietly.

"What did you say?" says Carla. "What's so funny?"

"Nothing."

"Who were you talking to?"

Remy wipes his face with his hands. Blood and black stuff come off on his palms. "I just—the way that the Signifiers have been appearing to me sometimes…they communicate with me in the form of Alicia. Like, I actually *see* her again."

"Whoa," says Carla.

Remy removes one glove, spits into his hand, and wipes his face. "How do I look? A little more presentable?"

"That seems creepy."

"It's not. It's comforting."

Carla doesn't say anything. Her expression is solemn.

"What?" says Remy.

"Nothing," she says. "I just really hope that if we survive all this, you find what you're looking for."

Remy tells her to wipe the blood off her face. "You don't want to alarm anyone we see on the way. How far is Jen's apartment from here?" Carla points. At the other end of the block is her building. The exterior is dimly lit, and Remy can see several people smoking outside.

"Okay. Okay," says Remy. He looks around. Beer bottles are scattered on the ground around the warehouse, and Remy picks one up and breaks it against the side of the building. The entire bottle shatters inefficiently, and Remy breaks another bottle. This one is usable.

"Weapon?" says Carla. "Not sure how much help a bottle is going to be against that thing." Remy doesn't answer. He puts his glove back on. Carla says, "I just realized that Jen isn't going to be there. Probably just Horus. She left to go upstate today."

"What does the front door of their apartment building look like? I can't remember."

"It's one of those new doors that every building has now."

"Can you be more specific? Is it glass or metal?"

"It's panes of glass, but with a metal frame. It's like a metal grid. I think the Paranormalagus could break the glass, but the metal grid would be tough for it to get through." Carla watches as Remy swings the broken bottle in the air, and then says, "Remy, your plan isn't to hurt Horus, is it?"

"I don't know what I'm going to do."

"C'mon, fuck! That's bullshit! He didn't do anything wrong!"

Remy says that he might be the reason Alicia died in the first place. "He yelled at Alicia the day that she died! Maybe she ran into the dumpster on purpose!"

"You don't believe that! Is that what Jen told you?"

"I can't *argue* with the Signifiers."

"Her bike chain broke! Alicia couldn't make her chain break!"

While they argue, they both forget to move anything besides their mouths. The lights go out and they're in darkness again. "Run!" says Remy.

They both run towards Jen's building. As they get closer, the smokers open the front door, throwing their cigarettes on the ground.

"Wait!" says Remy. The smokers don't hear them. The door shuts just as Carla and Remy enter the dim, insufficient streetlight near Jen's building.

Remy presses every button on the keypad, hoping someone will buzz them in. If the buzzer even works.

"Remy."

He turns around. At the edge of the street, just outside the reach of the streetlights, is the patient shape of the Paranormalagus. The insectile legs are steepled next to the body, the sharp pincers at the end of each leg ticking forward so slowly that it barely seems to move. One eye is perfectly smooth, yellow as it reflects the light from Jen's building, and the other is disfigured by angry scratches from their first encounter. Both eyes are fixed on him.

Remy turns and presses button after button, but his movements aren't hurried. The sense of certainty has caught up to him again. He will allow his actions to be determined by the environment.

Carla says his name. She touches his arm, leaving a trace of cold sweat. "Oh my God. I don't want to say it, but doesn't it look kind of like—" The Paranormalagus moves towards them, accelerating, the mandibles sprouting from the human lips and opening wide, and once more, Remy experiences that vague flicker of familiarity. In one dexterous movement, the creature snatches Carla by her jacket. Carla twists around and brings a knee up into its lower jaw. It lets go of her and she lands on the ground, hard, just as the door buzzes open. Remy presses his shoulder into the door, steps inside, and Carla tries to stand up and follow him.

"I'm sorry, Carla," says Remy. He means it. But this is what the Signifiers require.

He shuts the door behind him, trapping Carla outside.

"No! Fuck!" Carla shouts his name.

The Paranormalagus flips Carla onto her back and bites into her chest. She screams. The creature lifts her into the air and shakes her, like a pelican killing a fish. It throws her against the door and the screaming stops. For a brief moment, Remy saw her face, stupid with fear and panic, pressed against the glass. Her lids were partially closed. Remy laughs. It's a laugh of surprise and fear, likely originating in the objective silliness of Carla's expression.

Her body is dragged away from the door and into the dark of the street. Once it finishes eating her, the creature will be very strong.

There's no sign of a struggle when Remy looks outside. The

night looks like any night that smokers might enter, spilling out of this very door. The only sign that something has happened is the pinkish, greasy streak on the upper portion of the door—Carla's lip gloss, dragged across the glass.

Remy readjusts his grip on the broken bottle and confirms that there's no visible blood on his black coat or black pants. There are two doors on this floor. Remy hasn't had the opportunity until now to think about the fact that he can't remember which one of these doors is Jen and Horus's apartment.

It's possible that it was actually one flight up. The door in front of him looks correct enough. But this door opens, revealing enough of the apartment to identify it as *not* Jen's. A young guy with red eyes and safety pins in his ears puts his head out the door and asks Remy what "all that noise" was.

Remy stretches his arms as if tired, and moves the hand holding the bottle out of the guy's line of sight, just behind the stairwell. "Just some kids," he says. "They're gone now."

"It sounded crazy!" He rubs his eyes with cigarette-yellowed fingers and tells Remy about something that happened sometime near the building—it's hard to tell what, since the guy keeps losing track of his thoughts. "It's wild around here, you know?"

Remy agrees for a socially acceptable amount of time, and even a little longer, and then ends the conversation and goes upstairs before the guy has even shut his door.

Once upstairs, he doesn't recognize the hallway, which means that Jen's apartment is definitely on the first floor—so it has to be the only other apartment downstairs. It's exquisite how this was made clear to him, how the guy downstairs opened his door on his own, as if guided by a divine force.

Remy goes back downstairs and knocks on the door that he now remembers as belonging to Jen and Horus. He holds the bottle in his coat pocket.

Remy knocks on the door for almost a full minute. When it finally opens, it's not Horus. It's Jen.

"Jen," says Remy, his face neutral.

"What are you doing here? What's on your face?" She's wearing a robe, and her eye makeup has migrated down to her lower lids, as if she were just taking a nap. Remy wipes his cheek with the hand not holding the bottle, and it comes away smeared with black slime.

"Were you sleeping?" he says.

"This *really* isn't a good time."

"Please, you have to let me come in. I wouldn't ask if it weren't serious." He tells her he just got mugged. "They threw me against the door to your building." This doesn't explain the slime, although it would explain the blood.

"Jesus Christ."

Remy expects her to stand back and let him into the apartment, but she doesn't. "Why were you even coming here in the first place?"

"Is Horus home?"

"He's taking a bath."

Jen looks at him, and Remy smiles, and then takes back the smile by looking at the floor. "I'm sorry, he's taking a bath? That's, like, the gayest thing I've ever heard." He finds this hilarious. "I just got fired, by the way. I've had a night." He laughs. He's unable to gauge how this laugh sounds.

Jen starts to say something and then stops. Remy looks up again, and some of his certainty drains away. He's exhausted. The apartment behind Jen is softly lamp-lit, instead of illuminated by a garish overhead bulb like his own. He can smell a recently cooked meal. Jen has a glass of wine in her hand, and he hears the expensive sound of music playing from an invisible speaker system. He remembered their apartment as an unclean hole, congruent with the grimy dude Remy saw next door, but now the apartment seems luxurious, warm, and wonderfully impossible, as if he were some fairy-tale huntsman stumbling upon a sorceress's hut in the woods.

He has a vision counter to his reason for coming here. In this vision, Jen brings him inside, and Horus and Jen don't ask questions, don't get angry, and don't judge him. They just take him into their home and relieve him of all his bloody clothes. They clean his face, and wrap him in a blanket, and hold him. They say, "It's okay." This picture, as corny as it is, feels real to him. Maybe *this* is what the Signifiers wanted for him, and why they led him here.

"Remember when you asked me if there was anything you could do for me? This is it. This is what you can do for me." Remy indicates the situation by pointing at the ground they're standing on. "Just take me inside for a second. I truly, seriously think I'm a danger to myself right now. And I don't know where else to go."

Jen looks at his face, which may still have black marks on it, and stands back. "Only for a second. Horus is *not* going to be crazy about this. Just be advised." When she uses the word "advised," her tone has an ironical intimacy.

The apartment is different than it was in daylight, when last he saw it. It's more alive. The bathroom door is slightly open and he can hear the bath running. "Nice gloves," says Jen. She goes to the bathroom, says something to Horus, and pulls the door shut. A powder-blue suitcase with a ribbon tied around the handle is open on the bed, and all of Jen's clothes are visible.

"I was supposed to drive up to Woodstock today but Gia had car trouble, so we didn't even make it out of Brooklyn. It was actually a huge inconvenience. Do you know Gia?"

Remy says no. Jen tells him about her annual trip to Woodstock and some inane story about Gia or a friend of Gia's. "Do you want some wine?"

"Do you have anything stronger?"

Jen goes to a cabinet and stands on a stool to reach a higher shelf, the robe swishing around her ankles. She turns around, suspended above the ground on the stepstool, and holds her arms out on either side of her, a bottle in each hand and a slight bend in each elbow. "Whiskey or tequila?"

"Whatever you'll drink with me."

Jen gives him a look, stepping down from the stool. She pours them each a tequila soda, and remains standing while Remy sits at the table. Remy makes fun of her for bringing such a large suitcase on her trip. Jen defends herself without investment, and Remy interrupts this argument to apologize. "I'm sorry for bothering you, seriously. I don't know what I'm thinking."

"Were you even really mugged?"

"It's hard for me to be vulnerable. I'm in a really bad place, Jen. It's just like you said before. I'm a nice guy, underneath. I just put up these walls, but they aren't the real me."

Both of them look at the closed bathroom door. Jen puts her face in her hands and then looks at him through her fingers. "I don't know what to do, Remy. I think you need Jesus or something."

"Would you do me a favor? Just tell me about your day. How you went to the farmer's market. How you waxed your board. How you got a wax." It's not funny, but Remy laughs.

"There's no farmer's market today, you dumb, sad idiot." Her voice has more pity in it than he's used to. She asks if he wants her to call Jake. "Aren't you going to take off your gloves?"

Remy's eyes go to the bathroom door and back again. He says,

"Maybe this will sound crazy. But I have this picture in my head. I think maybe, if I could make the picture real, or real enough, that I'll feel better. That something good will happen. I think maybe that's what the Signifiers are indicating."

"Is that a joke?"

"It's nothing creepy! It's just embarrassing. But I have this image in my head of you and...and even Horus holding me—I told you it was weird, it doesn't have to be him, it can just be you—saying that you care about me no matter who I am, or...where I've been or what I've done."

Jen flattens her hand in the air in front of her. "You *do* realize those are Backstreet Boys lyrics?"

Remy laughs. He bends over in his chair. Everything is incredibly funny.

"I'm *not* saying that to you," says Jen.

"So don't! Say something else. Whatever feels right. Maybe on the couch."

"Maybe let's not go to the couch." Jen puts down her drink, stares into space, and puts her arms around Remy, lightly. She says his name several times. She sounds frustrated. "You are valuable, Remy. You are accepted and cared for. Things are going to get better. The universe created you and the universe loves and accepts you." There's a long silence.

Remy opens his eyes. "This *isn't* it. This isn't the picture. I don't need this, this universe. Who's she? I don't know Universe, do you? I need you to say that *you* accept me."

"I'm worried about what sort of expectations that would create."

"Expectations? Don't you live in"—and here Remy makes savage air quotes—" 'the Now'?"

"You're making all these demands on me! What happens tomorrow?"

"No!" He points at her. "You aren't listening to me! It's actually a very easy thing I'm asking you to do for me."

Their voices are loud. Remy glances at the bathroom, surprised that Horus hasn't stepped out to see what's going on.

"Yeah. He likes privacy while taking a bath," says Jen, unprompted.

Remy notices a towel slung over a chair and realizes that Jen must have placed it there when she answered the door. "Were you about to get in the bath? Did I interrupt you?"

He looks at her, and then at the bathroom.

"Is Horus even here? You just started that bath for yourself, didn't you?"

Jen opens her mouth. She has a pimple on her cheek that makes her look younger and even more desirable.

"Are you scared of me? Did you lie about being alone?"

"He's out with friends. He's going to be back soon, though."

"No he won't. But that's fine! You're safe, Jen, Jesus. You don't have to lie to me." Remy puts his head on the table.

Jen sits next to him and puts her arms around him, in a different way than before, and apologizes. "I just don't think this is the best place for you. And you look like a fucking psychopath right now."

"I'm in pain!"

He says this in a voice that implies it's a joke, and this breaks the tension. They laugh together. They're both nervous.

Jen holds him, just like he wanted. "Tell me about your day," says Remy.

This is very close to the picture, although not quite there. Remy concentrates on every part of this sensation while Jen says boring stuff about Gia's car trouble—not at all the type of thing that Alicia would say when *she* was Jen.

The overall sense of satisfaction he ought to be feeling is divided between various sensory inputs: the proximity of her breath, the warmth of her arms, the scent of countless sprays of perfume in a sweater that likely hasn't been cleaned since she bought it, the synth music at low volume, a pile of bedsheets near the door as if on their way to the laundry and on which he can spot several intimate stains. Drunkenly, he concentrates on each of these details, but fails to integrate them into a holistic experience of pleasure.

He returns her embrace, as well as he can from this angle, increasing his grip on her hands, wishing to bury himself wrist-deep in her skin. He'd like to be dripping with her, to be so completely intermingled with Jen's total Jen-ness that there's no escape, and no separation between the two of them.

The other problem with his concentration is the steady banging sound that has started downstairs. He doesn't acknowledge this, but Jen lifts her head from his shoulder, and says, "What do you think that is?"

"Could be the people who mugged me."

"That doesn't make any sense. What, are they robbing homes now?" She gets up to check the locks, leaving the picture that she made with Remy—which she always does. *She never fucking cooperates.* "Just come back," says Remy. The banging gets louder, and then they hear the sound of breaking glass. Remy notices that water is leaking out from beneath the bathroom door.

"Maybe I should call the police," she says.

Remy's phone vibrates. Alicia New is calling.

He stares at the name. He picks up.

"Alicia?"

Jen turns away from the door to look at him.

"Alicia, is that you? Are you close?"

Jen's face changes. "Remy," she says. She looks at something behind him. Remy turns to see what she's looking at.

He isn't surprised to see Alicia standing there, or standing there in the inadequate, changeable way that he's become used to. She smiles, then doesn't. She's younger. The changing is choppier and more confused than it was in the bar.

There's a much larger smash, and then Remy hears the weird

gait of the Paranormalagus coming down the hallway. The door shudders as the Paranormalagus strikes it again and again.

"Did I follow the Signifiers wrong?" says Remy into the phone.

Something similar to Alicia's voice—which he hasn't heard in weeks—answers him through the phone:

"This is exactly where you're supposed to be."

Jen swipes her possessions off a dresser and tries to push it in front of the door. "Fuck!" she says, "Remy, help me! What the fuck!"

"The one with the bow on it," says Alicia New.

"Turn on all the lights!" says Remy to Jen, even though he knows that it's too strong now. "Turn on the overheads!"

Alicia smiles, and a coruscant light flits across this version of her. "It won't be long before we—" There's knocking on the door now, the vibrations of the Paranormalagus slamming its sharp spike against the wood. The hand holding his phone drops to his side. Alicia's gone, but he can still feel her presence in the room. She's with him now as the creature's head comes through the door, particles of wood silting down beneath the mandibular spike. Jen sees it for the first time, and Remy watches her see it. His own terror isn't the openmouthed sort now paralyzing Jen. His is tinged with delicious vindication—*she couldn't follow his simple instructions, and now look what happened.*

The creature tears a larger hole in the door, one insectile leg coming through the opening. Jen stumbles away from the leg. Remy hears the neighbor's door open, then cussing and the sound of the door slamming shut. Now another leg appears, the body compacting impressively and then unfolding on the other side, massive, and engorged by its recent meal. Its eyes are on Remy, ignoring Jen. "God what is that?" she screams. The mandibles retract down the throat, and then emerge again, slowly, in and out. Is it breathing? Remy doesn't know what to do—he simply watches the movement of the spike pulsing in and out of the human lips, wondering at this final image before his death. Then, as the spike splits into two mandibles, the face larger as it approaches him, the lips opening, he recognizes the creature.

Jen is screaming. She says *Fuck fuck fuck* and then, "What the fuck did you do to me? What is that?"

It was obvious, actually. Now that the creature is strong enough to withstand exposure to light, he can see how the mouth is Jen's, the cheekbones hers, how the sharp hairs at the front of the skull grow in the shape of Jen's hairline. It wasn't his destiny to recognize her before, because he wasn't yet prepared for his Consummate Result. Before, he wouldn't have understood, and he wouldn't have been strong enough.

The creature rears its long neck, exposing clavicular plates that resemble Jen's chest (not everyone would recognize her chest in this incarnation, but now Remy can see Jen's angles everywhere, even in its least human parts), and strikes at his face, hitting the wall behind him. Remy jumps to the side, knocking into Jen and pulling her down with him as he falls. Jen tries to get up but Remy pulls her down again, holding her against him to shield him from the Paranormalagus. They roll into something wet—the overflowing bathwater from the tub, still warm as it travels over the floor.

Remy turns his head and watches the Paranormalagus circle, crablike. With Jen on top of him, of course, it won't try to hurt him. The reason it's here is to prevent Remy from doing what he has to do—is *destined* to do.

Jen grabs onto the leg of the kitchen table and pries herself free. The Paranormalagus lunges for Remy, but Jen stands up too fast, and slips backwards, banging her head on the wet floor. The creature crumples, stunned in tandem with Jen.

He crawls towards Jen as she tries to get up. The creature tries to get up too, but Remy puts his knee on Jen's torso and closes his hands around her throat. The stream of bathwater catches her hair, which darkens and haloes around her ears, soaking her sweater.

The creature moves towards him, but Remy applies more pressure and it halts, neck crimping, legs spasming, unable to make a sound while his thumbs are pressing on Jen's windpipe.

Remy looks down at Jen and sees eternity, feels the simultaneity of all things. When Jen was so sure that Alicia was choking her that night, it might as well have been *his* hands that she was feeling, so inevitable was this moment.

But he doesn't like seeing her eyes bug out like this. She looks like Arnold Schwarzenegger in *Total Recall,* gasping for oxygen on Mars. Remy releases her throat and drags her towards the bathroom by both arms, grateful that the floor is slick. She can breathe now and he hears her, between coughing, say *Why?* He opens the bathroom door with one hand while Jen tries to plant her feet but slips, hitting the floor. He says *Please Jen come on Jen we're so close we're really almost there.*

The creature rises, drunkenly, then charges in slow motion, head maneuvering to reach him around Jen's twisting body. Her feet gain traction on the doorjamb, and she partially stands up, pulling against Remy's grip, just as the Paranormalagus dives over her at Remy. Remy dodges, but the mandibles snag his shoulder and Jen cries out in confusion, dodging too. The pain makes him release his grip on Jen's hands. He slips on the tile, grabbing the side of the tub to catch his fall. Bathwater splashes as Jen, unsteady, bleeding from the head, stumbles backwards, causing the creature to stumble back too. Jen turns to get away but screams, raggedly, when she sees the Paranormalagus. She spins back around but Remy is waiting, and punches her in the stomach, twice. Jen slumps over and the creature falls, making a keening sound that weakens at the end. One sharp leg extends and is still. Jen and the creature both labor to breathe, Jen coughing loudly, saying in a whisper, *Please Remy Stop Please*

Curled up on the bathroom floor is a stranger with bloody fingers whom he hardly recognizes, and yet it's also Jen, whom he knows more intimately than he's known almost anyone else—in his own way. He kneels in the water and touches her face. He'll just tell her, just explain. He kisses her bleeding hairline. *You want freedom, right? I'm just giving you freedom I'm setting you free come on let me have this one little thing, just one thing you have so much and I just want you, that's what it's about, really, I just want you.*

The whites of her eyes are red. Remy applies just enough pressure on her throat to prevent movement, and the bike grips on his gloves keep her from slipping free. He feels for the certainty that was present before. He thinks, *Signifiers, is this right?*

Jen's eyes widen, and Remy senses movement behind him. He turns around just as the Paranormalagus strikes out with its mandibles, and Jen is hit instead, deep in her arm. The Paranormalagus pulls back and squeals, having wounded itself. Remy grabs the first heavy thing he sees, some kind of artisanal brass towel container, dumps the towels onto the wet floor, and pitches it with all of his strength at the creature's head. The impact is satisfying, but Jen doesn't react to the creature's injury in the same way it does to hers, and now Jen is trying to get up again, scratching at Remy's face and arms with surprising strength. He hoists Jen into the tub sideways, sloshing in after her and straddling her. Jen twists but he holds her under the water, faceup. The Paranormalagus shrieks, immobilized, making the sound that Jen can't make underwater, and Jen manages to surface one more time. He slams her head into the faucet, denting the side of her skull above her ear, forcing her back underwater and watching the bubbles.

There's a new stupidity in Jen's movements, and it seems like she can't keep her mouth closed. Remy's vision is compromised—he keeps wiping his face. He even has to free one hand to wipe his face since his vision is so blurry. But it doesn't matter, because he only needs one hand now. It's fine. Not much longer.

When finally the tears have slowed down enough that he can see clearly again, he watches the Paranormalagus instead of Jen, waiting to see when it will stop moving. The creature is looking at him, whimpering, then silent, transfixing him with its great black eyes, its iridescent carapace turning a dull green, the skin of the lips split and bleeding. It doesn't have the strength to pull the mandibles back into its mouth, and so they remain half out, like one long snaggletooth. He keeps his hand in place even when the creature has been still for a full count of fifty.

He looks at Jen, her chin floating down towards her shoulder. He gets out of the tub, lifts her up from beneath the shoulders, stops to recover, wraps an arm around her torso, pulls, stops, pulls again, and eventually drags her over the side of the tub, breathing heavily. "Fuck," he says, to no one. He props her up against the toilet, adjusts her waterlogged sweater, and stands up. He adjusts her sweater again. His first ludicrous thought is how easily Horus fixed his arm when it was dislocated. Maybe it's not too late, and Horus will be able to fix this, no problem. He'll just leave Jen right here, like this, where Horus can easily find her.

Water flows out of the bathtub and fills the apartment. He steps over the carcass of the Paranormalagus, which bleeds, blackly, into the overflow. He kicks one foreleg. It's hard, like a tire.

He opens the door of the apartment. The water has made a river in the hallway, darkening the wood, purling around the baseboards, and agitating around the shattered front door of the building. Strands of congealed matter catch on the threshold and ribbon around a pipe next to the stairs. Where are the neighbors? Are they keeping their doors shut, terrified? Or have the Signifiers protected him yet again?

Remy opens the front door of the building and lets the water flow out into the night. His mental activity is concerned mainly with the sudden rush of cold air on his wet body. He hears the neighbor's door open, quietly, and turns around. The grimy neighbor's face appears in the crack of the apartment door. He sees Remy, covered in blood and black goo. "Whoa, man," he says, and slams the door shut.

Remy hears him putting on the chain lock. Is he going to call the police? Is he too high for that to occur to him? Maybe not. But the Signifiers want him to succeed, and the stream seems to indicate a direction. It's just as Carla said: The way is clear.

Remy goes back into Jen's apartment. He continues, oddly, not to hear sirens as he removes the damp gloves, washes his face, and puts on one of Horus's sweatshirts. It takes him a long time to leave.

As he's waiting outside for his Uber, a dark van pulls up. It parks, sloppily, with its ass against the curb and the driver's side jutting into the street. The back doors open. The figures that issue from the van wear full SWAT gear but are clean of insignia or badges. The last figure moves slower than the rest, but still efficiently. He's concentrating on a machine in his hand, and points, wordlessly, at the building, while the machine makes distressed *wowowowow* sounds.

"Leave the area!" says the man, his eyes briefly focusing on Remy.

"Are you FBI?"

"Leave the area, now!"

The figures file into the building against the current, water swashing around their boots with every step, like horses fording a river in a Western. Remy gets into his Uber and leaves. Who cares if an Uber isn't anonymous? If it will allow his location to be traced? This is a minor problem dwarfed by the inevitability of his Consummate Result.

It's snowing tentative flakes that dissolve upon contact with the street. As he watches the snow from the window of the car, he notices a total nothingness where his mind normally finds interest in the passing scenery. He'd never realized before that watching snow usually gives him childhood-inflected joy, but he's alert to the difference now. It's as if his brain is enclosed in Saran Wrap. He looks out the window, waiting for himself to react to the snow and finding instead a blankness of soothing perfection, as if the snow had already covered everything he saw in a flawless white expanse.

He checks his phone, more as a result of muscle memory than out of a desire to interact. There are no messages except some from Jake that he forgot to answer.

Remy hadn't realized that so much of his waking and dreaming life was characterized by a sense of urgency, but now that this urgency has drained away, he feels gratified by the empty thing that's replaced it; a delicious reprieve from the endless dramas and decisions that are sure to crowd in again if he lets down his guard. He watches two teenagers horse around on the sidewalk, on their way somewhere in the snow, giving each other friendly middle fingers. The optical information meets his brain but provokes no reaction.

* * *

Once in the apartment, he doesn't turn on the light. He has no desire to view Jake's body in greater detail. The only light comes from his phone, as he gives his driver, Basharat, five stars and a large tip for helping him with the wet suitcase—with a bow on it—that barely fit in the trunk. He even agreed to help Remy take it up the stairs, not realizing that it would turn into a long project with several pauses between landings. Basharat asked Remy if he was a student. "Are those all books in there?"

"My girlfriend is a student," he said. It wasn't a lie. In another Stream of Reality, Alicia might be.

Remy nudges Jake's body with his toe to allow passage of the suitcase into the apartment. He notices, at this moment, the parallels between his apartment and Jen's: the corpse on the floor, the tub of water at the far end. Remy rolls the suitcase next to the alcove and pulls back the tarp on the Spod. He unzips the suitcase—the metal freezing from sitting in the trunk while wet—and lifts Jen's body from its forcibly fetal position, shoving her into the Spod with uncoordinated movements. He drops her several times and flinches on her behalf when her shoulder hits the blunt edge of the Spod. Her body is much more cumbersome than it was when they were having sex, but the weight is still similarly exciting. Jen's fingers are pruned, which alerts him to the amount of time it took for her to drown. It doesn't surprise him that the Spod is turned on.

He succeeds, finally, by pitching Jen's body headfirst into the Spod, allowing the weight of her head to drag the rest of her body inside—splashing himself with hot water and sending a stagnant odor into his face. It's satisfying to toss the comparatively light weight of her feet in after her. Never before has he touched her feet, and their size surprises him. The word that flits across his mind to describe them is *adult.*

Remy turns a lamp on in his room, takes his clothes off, and puts on a terrycloth robe. He sits on the couch in his customary position, and considers texting Alicia New. But there's no rush, and he sets his phone on the table, resting his head on a couch cushion.

It's cold in the apartment, making him more sensitive to the heat emanating from the alcove, and he remembers a morning in early February—right before Valentine's Day—when he and Alicia woke up, hungover and exhausted. All the weather reports said that a major snowstorm was about to hit. Alicia was horny in an urgent way that prevented her from going on with her life until she orgasmed, but Remy had no interest in sex and felt ill. She went out into the snowstorm and got him a Gatorade. He drank the blue Gatorade with his eyes closed while she masturbated next to him, keeping enough physical contact with him to make him feel necessary. Her eyes were closed and he had a passing sense of wonder at her opacity; what was she imagining?

It's an oddly soothing memory even though it culminated in Alicia thrashing around as if having a medical emergency while Remy kept his eyes closed like someone ignoring her cries for help. But when she was finished, there was a beatific feeling in the room, and the snow brightened the light coming in through the window. Not only did they have nowhere to go, but even if they wanted to, the snow would have made it impossible. Unlike all the other limits on their lives, this one had been comforting.

He doesn't know how long he's been asleep when he wakes up. He hears knocking. *The police,* he thinks.

Knock-knock-knock-knock.

He lies on the couch, waiting for the knocking to turn into banging. It doesn't. It continues until he hears a grinding, wooden sound, and then the sound stops. The knocking wasn't on the front door, but from the Spod. Sandy, from Jake's room, laughs Jake's laugh.

He hears the top of the Spod dislodging from the hot tub, and then a crack as the entire top portion of the Spod falls.

"Hello, Alicia. Hello, Alicia. I love you, Alicia," says the parrot.

Her feet make light, sucking sounds on the wood floor. He doesn't look at her, but feels the couch cushion bloat with her weight when she sits down.

"Don't tell your girlfriend I'm here," says Alicia-as-Jen. "I know it's wrong, but I just couldn't help myself." She laughs. Remy looks at her, once.

There's no dent on her forehead, no blood on her clothes, and her eyes aren't bulging and bloodshot. They're like they always are. Green. She touches his hand. The slimy sensation of her fingers against his skin is as intimate as the taste of his own saliva. He closes his eyes again, the better to see everything perfectly.

This time, there's no gap between the picture and his experience, and no paranoia about *when it will end* intrudes. Her smell, voice, and touch are correct, and the moment has a purity unlike anything he's ever felt. He presses his face into her sweater, and she puts her chin on his head, enfolding him. What's there is really there. Everything has harmonized at last.

Acknowledgments

Thanks so much to my agent, Alexa Stark, as well as Jean Garnett, Ben Allen, and the team at Little, Brown. I'm also indebted to everyone who read partial and complete drafts, including David Miller and everyone in Tony Tulathimutte's CRIT Workshop: Alina Cohen, Concepción De León, Calvin Kasulke, Rax King, Lilit Markosian, Hannah Nash, Jon Schaff, and Elina Zhang. I am endlessly grateful to Tony Tulathimutte himself not only for reading and editing this manuscript at several stages, but also for his support and advocacy for the book.

Thanks to the kind people at Metafilter, a great resource for anyone who wishes to write what they don't know. Thank you, Elaine Thoma, for sharing a little of your life with me, and thank you, Kate Nichols, for your inspiring pranks. Thanks to Bobbie Reyes for being there in the moment of genesis, and for getting me to the Philippines in the first place. Thanks to Lee Clark for the wallet game.

Thanks to Joshua Henkin, the most attentive MFA fiction director there ever was, and to the Truman Capote Foundation for making it possible for me to finish my book while at Brooklyn College.

Thank you, David, for believing in *A Touch of Jen* from the very beginning, for your constant emotional support, and for your insightful, copious, and brutally honest feedback. This book wouldn't exist without you.

About the Author

Beth Morgan's fiction has been published in *The Baffler,* the *Iowa Review,* and the *Kenyon Review Online.*

Now in paperback

Acts of Desperation

A novel by Megan Nolan

"A psychosexual thriller about the ecstasy and embarrassment of being a woman who has sex with, and who falls in love with, men... Bodily and alive—hot as viscera, inward-looking, dark, and soft... As true-seeming a document of toxic and manipulative love as any published within memory."

—Philippa Snow, *New Republic*

Assembly

A novel by Natasha Brown

"An elegiac examination of a Black woman's life and an acerbic analysis of Britain's racial landscape... Brown's rhythmic, economic prose renders the narrator's experiences with breathless clarity."

—Lovia Gyarkye, *New York Times*

How to Pronounce Knife

Stories by Souvankham Thammavongsa

"An impressive debut... Thammavongsa's spare, rigorous stories are preoccupied with themes of alienation and dislocation, her characters burdened by the sense of existing unseen... It is when the characters' alienation follows them home, into the private space of the family, that Thammavongsa's stories most wrench the heart."

—Sarah Resnick, *New York Times Book Review*

Available wherever paperbacks are sold